# REGIME

Sophie reached in, picking up the most enormous wooden paddle, laughing as she skipped back to Annabelle and handed it to her.

'A good choice,' Annabelle said. 'Now, Penny, fill my glass, and Marcus's too. You shall be maid, but you may take some yourself if you wish.'

'Maid?'

'Don't question me, Penny.'

'No, Miss Annabelle.'

'That's Mistress Annabelle to you. Sophie, I think, had better call me Miss Yates for now, at least until after her punishment.'

'My punishment?' Sophie blurted out.

'Your punishment,' Annabelle said. 'Get up.'

'But I thought Penny . . .'

'You have just earned yourself an extra two cane strokes. Now do as you are told. Stand up and take off your panties.'

# REGIME

*Penny Birch*

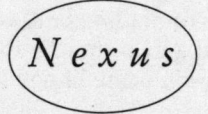

*Nexus*

This book is a work of fiction.
In real life, make sure you practise safe sex.

First published in 2002 by
Nexus
Thames Wharf Studios
Rainville Road
London W6 9HA

*www.nexus-books.co.uk*

Typeset by TW Typesetting, Plymouth, Devon

Printed and bound by
Clays Ltd, St Ives PLC

ISBN 0 352 33666 8

Why not pay Penny's website a visit at
*www.pennybirch.com*

# One

They had attended to my bottom, so it was only fair that I attend to their cocks.

I was glowing, my cheeks hot and bare behind me, tingling with that lovely fresh-spanked feeling. My little skirt was tucked up into its waistband, my panties rolled down, just to the top of my thighs. I could feel the heat in my pussy, along with a wet, tickling sensation around my bumhole. What I wanted to do was just spread my thighs, then and there on the grass, masturbating to orgasm in front of the men who'd punished me, the men who had given me a bare bottom spanking.

Both had their cocks out, and I do know my duty. It was nice to think they were both so excited, by having stripped my bottom, by having punished me, by me. I went to Anderson first, crawling, as a spanked girl should. He pushed his cock out towards my face and I took it in, sucking up that lovely male taste, mouthing on the firm, hot meat. Bart watched, stroking his own cock, his eyes flicking between my face and my bare bum.

I gave him a wiggle, inviting him in, up my pussy. He grinned, responding immediately, and a moment later he was on the grass behind me, taking my hips in his strong, smooth hands, his cock probing between my thighs. Up he went, deep inside me, filling my pussy with hard cock, just the way my mouth was filled. I let

1

them take control, fucking my head and rear end as I put my hand back to masturbate.

It was so good, just rocking to the motion of their cocks, my fingers busy with my pussy. I could feel everything, the prickling of my skin, my bare boobs swinging against the material of my top, the tight, expectant feeling in my tummy. All that was good, gorgeous in fact, but not so good as having a hot bottom, a hot, bare bottom, a hot, bare, spanked bottom.

Skirt up and panties down, that's the way to treat me. No warning, no elaborate ritual, no fancy clothes, just a good, firm spanking. It's what I deserve, what I need, what ought to be done to me, frequently and without a thought for when or where. My bum had come out of my panties, bare and pink in the summer sunlight, then pinker still, then red as I kicked and squirmed and wriggled my way through my punishment, squalling like the naughty little brat I am, my head full of pain and humiliation.

I came, feeling my pussy clamp on Bart's cock and hearing his answering groan. Anderson's cock jerked while I was still at orgasm, filling my mouth with hot, slimy spunk just at the right time. For a long moment I held it, one finger pressed to my clit, sperm dribbling out around my lips, sucking and swallowing in a frantic, instinctive rhythm. Then it was over and I was slumping down, my body going slowly limp. I stayed there, holding Anderson, while Bart finished off. He stayed inside until he was close, pulling out at the last moment to come all over my spanked cheeks and finish off by rubbing the head of his cock in the sweaty, sperm-soiled crease between them.

Ten minutes later we were sipping cold white wine on that same lawn, relaxed and happy. Both of them had that rare quality of being able to thoroughly abuse a girl when she wants it, yet to treat her as an equal when she

2

doesn't. It is rare, and much appreciated. My girlfriend Amber has it, and a handful of others, but not many.

It was especially satisfying because I'd only called in on Anderson on the off chance. Amber and I had been driving down to a show near Petersfield. Not really in the mood for a day of horses and horsey people, I'd asked if she could drop me at Anderson's. She'd gone one better and swapped me for Vicky, Anderson's girlfriend, leaving me to the tender mercies of the two boys. My panties had been down before the sound of the car had even faded.

'Sorry not to see you at Morris Rathwell's club last night, Penny,' Bart said, filling his glass.

'I didn't even know it was on,' I admitted. 'Any good?'

'Noisy, smoky and irritating,' Anderson cut in. 'Vicky was in just a pair of rubber knickers and high heels, and on a lead. Male subs still kept pestering her to dominate them. I let Melody Rathwell put her on a cross in the end and use a dog whip on her. It didn't stop them.'

'The cabaret was good,' Bart said. 'They had Sophie Cherwell dressed up in a traffic warden's uniform. They did this little scene with Melody as an angry driver.'

'Melody put a mince and onion pie with chips down Sophie's knickers and spanked her,' Anderson added. 'That was worth seeing.'

'I dare say,' I answered, thinking of little blonde Sophie with her panties full of mess. It made an appealing picture.

'We made a good bet as well,' Anderson went on. 'There was a new couple there. Well, I suppose they've been around about a year, but they think they know everything, the girl especially.'

'Annabelle Yates,' Bart added, 'little Miss Dominant herself. Good looking, yes, but so far up herself you wouldn't believe it. Marcus is as bad; fancies himself as Sir Stephen from *O*.'

'They're both dominant?'

'Old school naturals, no switching, nothing. Annabelle even thinks it's submissive to have her boobs out. Pity.'

'That's what they say,' Anderson cut in. 'I don't believe a word of it, especially with Annabelle. The trouble is, looking the way she does, she gets every male sub in the place expecting her to act the perfect mistress. I don't suppose she'd dare admit she wanted to be on the receiving end.'

'Wishful thinking, Anderson,' Bart answered him. 'You just want to spank her.'

'And you don't?'

Bart just laughed.

'So what did you bet them?' I asked.

'Oh they were going on about how people are either naturally dominant or submissive; the usual crap,' Bart answered. 'Annabelle believes everything the male subs feed her, about being her eternally devoted slave and so forth. I said it was all just flattery, to get her attention, and that they'd say the same to any pretty girl in head-to-toe black leather.'

'Sure.'

'She answered by saying that there was this guy who's not just devoted to her, but actually dependent on her. He claims that to him she is the centre of existence, not himself, apparently. I said it was just bullshit and she got pretty pissed off. In the end we agreed to admit she was right if they could get a girl to have herself tattooed as their property, on her own accord. They went for it.'

'You're a bastard, Bart Pelham. What if some poor girl ends up with "Property of Mistress Annabelle" tattooed on her tummy or wherever?'

'Don't call me a bastard, Penny Birch. It was Annabelle's idea, she was really hot on it. Anyway, it has to be on the girl's pussy mound. We went through all that in detail. To win, they have to find a girl who'll go to a tattooist, on her own, with her pussy shaved. The tattoo has to be an unequivocal declaration, including her own name, like "I, Penny, declare myself the property of Mistress Annabelle Yates and Master Marcus Sowerby".'

'She'll need a good tattooist.'

'Well, whatever. She has to sign a contract too, in front of Anderson and me.'

'Why does it have to be a girl?'

'Well mainly because Marcus insisted on it. Anyway, knowing Annabelle, she could probably find a man. She's strong and looks really impressive. Our bet is she can't find a woman to do it.'

'What counts as failure?'

'They get three chances, and they're one down already. There was a guy doing piercing and tatts at the club. Annabelle spent an hour tormenting some girl I don't know, on a cross, feeding her shots of vodka and Red Bull as well, then asked her if she'd do it. The girl just freaked.'

'Doesn't mess around, does she, this Annabelle?'

'It was far too fast; she never really stood a chance.'

'That's not what I meant. Is this for money?'

'Not cash, no, a case of La Tâche.'

'That's expensive, isn't it?'

'A few hundred a bottle. They can afford it. He was a floor manager for one of the big Japanese banks. She was a broker, in commodities I think. Both of them were on silly money salaries. They quit to set up an organic farm somewhere near Buckingham.'

'And if you lose?'

'We don't intend to lose.'


Those of my friends who go to kinky clubs every week or two can be pretty blasé about it. I don't, and I'm not. Walking through the London streets with my coat clutched tight over a diminutive school uniform felt

5

naughty, and slightly scary too. It was the right image, rude but not too knowing, and very English.

It was actually the real thing too, which I was pleased to be able to get into. All Amber had done was shorten the skirt so that my panties showed when I bent over. Other than that and the plain white blouse, I had the genuine tie, tight white panties, a plain sports bra, little white ankles socks and sensible shoes. Bunches in my hair and a lollipop completed the look.

People were looking at me and, however much I kept telling myself they'd just think I was going to a fancy dress party, it was hard to accept. Far easier was to imagine they knew exactly what I was doing: that I wasn't dressed to flirt, but to improve my chances of getting a spanking; that it wasn't just a bit of fun, but an image I'd chosen because it makes me feel sexy.

It was a lot easier inside the club, with everyone in rubber, leather, other uniforms, even stark naked. Morris Rathwell spotted me almost immediately, waving me past the queue and taking a leisurely grope of my bum in payment. I told him to pretend not to know me and to pass it on to Melody, Harmony and anyone else there who knew me. He nodded, grinning and I was sure he was going to demand his cock sucked for his compliance when Melody came over with some problem for him to sort out. I excused myself, moving on into the club.

It was typical – a big, gloomy cellar, with several rooms connected by low arches. The walls were painted black, with whipping stools and bondage equipment scattered around. The music was deafening, the air hazy with smoke and thick with the smells of rubber, leather and sweat. It was already packed, mainly with submissive men, in collars and black leather pants, little else. Two offered their leads to me as I crossed the floor. Unable to be heard, I declined by shaking my head.

Morris had bothered to get a licence for once, so I managed to get a glass of brandy rather than the normal bottle of warm beer. I took it to a corner table, watching for people I knew and also for Annabelle and Marcus. She was supposed to be easy to spot: above average height, very slim, with blonde hair cropped short. What really marked her out was a solid silver ring and cross, the female symbol, which she apparently like to wear in her tummy button piercing. He was less easy: marginally taller, or the same height against her in heels, dark haired, but fairly nondescript. Together, they couldn't be hard to find.

They weren't. I'd hardly settled myself into the dark corner I'd chosen to watch from when a man stepped through an arch. He was in black leather, boots, trousers, jacket, with a black riding crop and handcuffs at his belt, a typical male dominant image. I looked, automatically wondering what it would be like to be spanked by him, only to have my attention taken away and my breath too.

It was Annabelle, it had to be, and Bart hadn't been joking when he said she was impressive. Just to look at her made me want to crawl to her feet and beg to be punished. She was in skintight rubber, a two-piece, hugging every contour of her slender body, black and shiny, with the gentle curves of her hips and breasts cleverly picked out in textured panels. Her midriff was bare, the silver symbol plain to see, also her face, immaculately made up in black and silver, nothing more. Shiny black leather boots reached to her knees, buckled at the sides and with at least five inches of spiky heel. A hood covered her head, leaving her face exposed in an oval and with a tall platinum blonde ponytail sprouting from the top.

I saw that she was holding something and, as she stepped into the room, I realised that it was a cluster of leads. Each led back to a collar, and each collar was around the neck of a male slave, seven in all, crawling behind her with doglike servility. She had a whip hanging from one wrist and was holding a long black cigarette holder. As yet another man hastily positioned a chair for her without even having to be told, she drew on her cigarette, flicking the ash on to the back of one of her slaves with a casual motion. She certainly had the image, and with all the attention she was getting it was easy to imagine her falling for her own propaganda.

With her seated, the slaves formed a semicircle at her feet, kneeling with their heads bowed. This left their bottoms towards me, and I could see that they'd been whipped. Two others stood behind her, and at a click of her fingers one scurried away to the bar. I settled down to watch.

I felt sorry for Marcus. He was her boyfriend, and he'd been cut out completely. Nine men were paying court to her, eager for her slightest touch, and not one had the courtesy to ask him if he minded or even to address him. I suppose he was just irrelevant to them, with everything focused on the woman who had condescended to be their mistress. I know a lot of submissive men think of women as naturally dominant, so presumably to them he was just one more slave, despite his dress and attitude.

That attitude was very clear. He stayed close to Annabelle and her pack of slaves, but his eyes were elsewhere, glancing at those girls in cute outfits, submissive or otherwise. He was even watching Melody, who looked very good indeed, with her big, muscular bottom packed into torn leather trousers, her dark skin showing through the gaps. If her image wasn't intended as spankable, then that wasn't what Marcus's eyes were saying. There were several other pretty girls too, all with plenty of attention on them, and I could see that he was trying to work out how to get the best out of the situation. I didn't want him fixing on me, in case it made her jealous, so I stayed back in the shadows.

I was so focused on Annabelle and Marcus that I nearly jumped out of my skin when a hand closed on my bottom. I turned, ready with a hot answer, only to find Sophie Cherwell grinning at me. Like me, she was in school uniform, with her blonde hair in a ponytail. The main difference was that her blouse was open and she had no bra, leaving her boobs half on show with her tie hanging down between them. They're quite big, bigger than mine anyway, and I could see red marks on what was showing. She was aroused too, her nipples making little hard bumps under the thin cotton.

'Hi,' I greeted her. 'Been punished?'

'Harmony gave me a titty whipping,' she answered. 'What's this we're not supposed to talk to you?'

'Oh you can talk to me, just don't give away that I'm not a novice.'

'Right. What are you up to?'

'Something complicated. Do you know the girl with the dogs?'

'Mistress Dominique, or Annabelle to you and me. Yeah, she's cute. A bit old school, maybe. She won't go sub, not for anyone.'

'So I hear.'

'Mel tried. I was there. I thought Annabelle was going to wet herself, she was that scared.'

'Scared? Why?'

'Search me. Maybe she thought Mel was going to get her out of her precious little knickers whether she liked it or not.'

'Melody wouldn't do that.'

'No, but she could. I'm not sure Annabelle understands how Mel is.'

'More likely she wants it done.'

'Could be. Look, anyway, I've promised Morris I'll go in the cage. Come in with me, it'll be more fun with two.'

'I hate dancing like that.'

'Who said anything about dancing? Come on, Penny, we're dressed the same, it'll look good!'

All the time we'd been talking she had been fondling my bottom, first through my panties and then with her hand down the back of them. She was hard to resist at the best of times, always bubbling with enthusiasm and full of dirty ideas. Now, with her fingers gently tickling the turn of my bottom and the promise of much more if I complied, it was impossible to resist.

I'd seen the cage, a cylinder of thick wire mesh with a massive iron ring set at the top, like a giant birdcage. Girls danced in it, often nude, and usually suspended above the audience, so that everyone could get a good look but they couldn't be touched. With two schoolgirls trapped in it, it was going to be pretty popular, which I didn't mind at all, especially with Sophie to take the lead.

She led me over by the hand, to where the thing was standing on the floor of one of the smaller rooms. A heavy chain had been padlocked to the ring and led up to a massive iron hook in the shadows of the ceiling. I got dragged in, Sophie giggling in delight as Harmony locked the door on us. Sophie's arms were around me, and we were kissing even as the cage was hauled clear of the floor.

It wasn't hard to let go, and I'd quickly let her unbutton my blouse and flip my bra up over my boobs. The thing with showing off in school uniform, or any sexy costume really, is to keep it on but let everything show, eventually. They could all see up our skirts anyway, but Sophie and I had a long snog before our panties came down, and by then I was getting genuinely turned on.

We were sitting, cross-legged and face to face, skirts rucked up so our panty-clad bottoms pressed to the mesh of the cage floor. Both of us had our boobs out and we were kissing and stroking each other's chests, with perhaps fifty people watching us from below. The mesh was wide, which left squares of panty-covered

10

bottom sticking through, which people would occasionally pinch or flick at with whips and paddles.

I was hoping she'd take charge, but so was she, and it was me who eventually could hold back no longer. Our legs were locked together, with her thighs wide and the gusset of her panties stretched taut. She was wet, with the material clinging to the folds of her pussy. I could smell her, and I wanted to lick her, but there wasn't much room in the cage and there were just too many people watching.

Suddenly I just had to have the attention on her. I grabbed her around her bum, tugging at her panties. She squealed in mock protest, but lifted herself obligingly. Her panties came down in my hands, to cheers and claps as her bare pussy settled on the mesh. Someone smacked at her sex with a crop and she gave a squeal of pain, looking down. A man had done it, some muscle-bound oaf in a leather jacket, looking up and grinning at her, his shaved head directly beneath her pussy.

She had lifted up as he caught her, and he demanded that she sit back, ordering her so that he could continue with her whipping. In answer she gave a hangdog look, calling him master and promising to be good. He may not have heard, but he got the idea, grinning up and calling her a whore. She spread her pussy lips for him, an inch from the mesh, right over a hole, settling slowly, her belly tensing as he pulled back his crop to take another smack at her.

Her pee caught him full in the face, right up his nose, to leave him cursing and spluttering for an instant before ducking down. Not that it did him much good. The crowd were packed too tight, and she had emptied most of what was in her bladder on him, splashing on his bald dome and running down his neck before he managed to get away.

As he ran for it, Sophie was laughing so much that she couldn't keep herself steady, spraying her pee out over the men below us. One, a huge, tattooed man, came up close, his mouth wide, catching her stream as she steadied herself. He drank what he could, the rest trickling down around his face until she had finished, when she pressed her pussy to the mesh and let him kiss it as he strained up on tip-toe.

She was giggling crazily, and so was I. We went back to playing, Sophie rolling herself up with her panties around her knees to leave her pussy sticking out, right in front of me. She was shaved, her plump little mound quite bare, her lips puffy, the opening of her pussy glistening wet. I wanted to go down between her thighs, but it was so open, so exposed, with so many people watching us and egging us on. Their words were mainly drowned out by the music, but it was obvious what they wanted – us, with everything that mattered bare, two schoolgirls with their clothes disarranged, pleasuring each other.

I'm not sure I could have done it, but Sophie didn't leave me much option. She was tussling with me, trying to pull me down on top of her. With a sudden motion she had kicked her legs up, trapping my head under her panties. I was pulled down, my mouth open in surprise, then full of pussy flesh as she pulled me in.

Having another girl handle me like that is more than I can resist. Her lowered panties were pressing me down into her sex, and I just had to lick. It was a really awkward position too, with my own bum stuck up and pressed to the mesh, while the cage was swinging. I licked anyway, tasting her pussy, my inhibitions fading in my excitement. She held me there, licking, as somebody with a long whip began to smack my bottom through the wire.

It hurt, and I was soon squirming, but Sophie wouldn't let me go. She was going to come in my face, with everyone cheering and demanding ruder and ruder things. Somebody yelled at me to pull down my panties and I did it, reaching back and tugging them down, so that it was my bare flesh that was pressed to the wire. My pussy was showing, actually pressed to the wire, and I could just imagine the squares of plump, hairy flesh with the wet pink centre. My boobs were showing too, dangling under my chest, just touching the wire so that my nipples poked through.

Fortunately the cage was far too high for anyone to stick a cock up me, or I'm sure I'd have been fucked. There are always plenty of cocks out at Rathwell's club, and any girl who wants to show off the rear view of her pussy needs somebody to guard her or she'll get taken by surprise. As it was, I'm not sure I'd have minded, because Sophie was starting to come and I badly wanted the same.

I would have done as I was told, and masturbated, but Sophie was not in the mood to be selfish. No sooner had she come than she released my head and began to pull at me to get my body over hers. I obliged, swivelling around to let her get at my pussy. It was difficult and I had to get one leg out of my panties, which put me in some pretty ludicrous positions and drew laughter from the crowd. I didn't care, I was too high, and as soon as I was properly bare I sat down squarely in Sophie's face, wiggling my bottom.

She began to lick and I was in ecstasy straight away. Her tongue was on my clit and I could feel her nose pressed to my bumhole, wriggling in my slimy wet. I had her ankles, holding her legs up so that everyone could see her pussy while she licked me. Both of us were really enjoying showing off; two rude, dirty little schoolgirls, dishevelled and sweaty, wet with sweat and each other's juice. I could see the expressions on the faces below me; lust and envy, delight and shock. I was bare, showing it all to a crowd, rude, naked, stripped, with pretty, sweet Sophie licking at my pussy, taking me higher and higher still.

I called out when I came, not that anybody could have heard, but it was good, so very good. As it hit me my mind was focused on the crowd, dozens of people, all focused on me in their lust, all wanting to fill my body with hard cock or to make me lick them to their own ecstasy. For a moment it was pure pleasure, only for the shame and confusion of being so dirty to well up inside me as my climax started to subside. Only for a moment though, until I had climbed off Sophie and we had our arms around each other, kissing and cuddling as we giggled together over what we'd done.

It was only when I felt the lurch of the cage that I realised we were being let down. The big guy who had drunk Sophie's pee was on the chain, along with Melody, but we still came down with a bump. The crowd had given back, but not far, and I crawled out of the cage to find myself looking at a pair of perfectly polished five-inch heels. I kissed one – just an automatic response to the way I felt, and because I was pretty sure whose they were.

Sure enough, it was Annabelle, looking down on me with an amused expression on her face and her cigarette holder between two fingers. Marcus was beside her, also looking down at me, Sophie too as she squeezed out of the cage door.

I looked up, expecting some gesture of dominance, a booted foot on my neck, ash flicked on me, even spit in my hair. Instead she squatted down to stroke my cheek, then Sophie's, looking into our faces and smiling. She reached out, putting a finger under my chin to tilt it up. I met her eyes, which were violet, the most beautiful colour, and very bright, sparkling with mischief.

'So pretty,' she said, 'both of you; small and pretty and a bit impudent. Not broken yet, I judge.'

Sophie gave a nervous giggle. I shook my head, uncertain what to say.

'You will come and sit with us,' she went on. 'Somewhere a little quieter. Slave, drinks.'

One of her attendant men responded immediately, pushing through the crowd. Annabelle took hold of us by our ties, pulling us to our feet. We followed her through one arch and then another, to a small room with a few chairs, a bench and a barrel at the centre. It was a mess, cluttered with glasses and bottles and awash with beer.

'Clean this up; I wish to sit here,' Annabelle instructed, waving vaguely to the barrel.

I watched as they did it. One was really servile, a fat guy in a badly made PVC pouch, actually licking up the spilt beer from the barrel top. Most were less enthusiastic, but they obeyed. I could see how it worked. They wanted attention, and with so many submissive males for every dominant female in the club, there was a lot of competition. If they displeased her they would be dismissed, and that would be the end of their chances. So they cleaned up, only to have Annabelle attach their leads to a piece of equipment in the next room and just leave them there.

The one she'd sent to get drinks returned, and knelt by the barrel until she told him to join the others. He went, but I could sense his reluctance. Annabelle seemed not to notice, but perched herself on the highest of the stools, gesturing to us to sit on the much lower bench. We went, Sophie cuddling up to me and sipping her drink.

The slave had bought vodka and orange, which I hate. My mother always said it was a tart's drink, and I thought for a moment of saying this and of having him punished, but I noticed that Annabelle was drinking the same and held back. I wasn't really in the mood for a whipping and something told me she wasn't the sort to go easy with the crop.

'You have probably heard me called Mistress Dominique,' she said, addressing me, 'but that's for the slaves. You may call me Annabelle. This is Marcus.'

Marcus nodded, grinning and raising his beer bottle to us before taking a drink from it.

'Penny,' I answered.

'Very *Malory Towers*.'

'It's my real name.'

'Then is suits you. Is this your first club?'

'Yes,' I lied, before Sophie could forget what she was supposed to say, or rather not say. 'I'm a friend of Sophie's; we go way back.'

'A very good friend, I see.'

'Well, yes, I got a bit carried away there. It's just the atmosphere. It's so ... so charged, so easy too. I thought I'd be scared, with guys in masks and carrying whips, but I'm not. In fact I feel really free. I mean, it's hard to feel embarrassed or inhibited when everyone else is being so open about their sexuality. I feel I can do things I've only dared to think about in my fantasies!'

'Submissive fantasies?'

'I suppose so. I've always like the idea of being spanked, but it's not just a physical thing.'

'Do you feel the need to be under somebody's discipline?'

'In a way, yes. To be cared for, and punished when I'm bad, that sort of thing. Sophie's been trying to explain, but I can't claim to really understand. It's all been in my head and, like she said, you've got to experience it first hand.'

'Well, yes and no. This is a good club, as they go, but not everybody takes it seriously.'

'No?'

'Far from it. A lot of the men are just here to gape. Others have no real understanding of what dominance and submission means.'

'Me for one.'

'The first thing to know is that it's not just a role you choose to play. It's who you are.'

'It's a part of me, yes.'

'No, Penny, it's who you are, a submissive woman, which is a very special, very privileged thing to be, but only if you can come to terms with what you are.'

'I see.'

'Do you? I think you are genuine, but you've got a lot of learning to do. A true submissive would never have sat on another woman's face; it would be against her nature.'

'I would rather it had been the opposite way around, really.'

'Naturally.'

She took a sip of her drink, with great care, never risking her lipstick. Watching her brilliant red lips, her burning eyes and the fine, chiselled form of her face, I could feel the power in her, the air of strength she projected, real dominance.

'I . . . I'd like you to do that to me,' I managed.

Annabelle smiled, glanced at her watch and then at Marcus.

'Would you like to come back with us, both of you?' he asked. 'Don't worry, Penny, Sophie's been before.'

'I have,' Sophie answered, gulping down her drink.

We left the club immediately, Annabelle striding out with a trail of disappointed male subs in her wake. One had even asked to come, the man who'd been buying the drinks, almost begging, and promising to act as servant all night if he could only come with her. Annabelle ignored him completely but, as we got into our coats, Marcus turned to smile at him and gave her bottom a meaningful squeeze. I really thought the poor guy was going to burst into tears.

After that I understood why he put up with all the men. After all, not one of them had even been permitted to kiss her feet, and she made it quite plain that, to them, her body was out of bounds. Touching her bottom or breasts was out of the question, let alone her

17

pussy, despite her rubber trousers being so thin and tight that her sex lips showed in perfect detail. He, on the other hand, could not only have a good squeeze of her bum, but was going home with her, and two other women as well.

There was an odd incident as we left, with Melody, who had been taking some fresh air and talking to the bouncer on the door. She gave Sophie a hug, and me, then cracked a joke about what Annabelle ought to do with us. Annabelle answered really hastily and tried to hurry us along, quickly stepping away so that Mel couldn't hug her as well. I thought Mel would tell her to lighten up, but she just smiled.

It was a real 'cat that's got the cream' grin, and Annabelle almost ran, dragging me behind her by the hand. Having had my face pushed into a cowpat by Melody Rathwell before, and a lot of other things, I know she can be scary, but she would never break anybody's will, so I couldn't see what the problem was. Marcus didn't seem to either, and wanted to linger, but Annabelle hurried him on.

They had a Range Rover, which Marcus drove. Annabelle regained her composure once we were moving and began to explain her philosophy. It was hard to concentrate with Sophie trying to undress me in the back, but essentially she saw everybody as either dominant or submissive by nature and they were only held back from expressing it by their inhibitions and social conditioning. There was no room for compromise, but on the other hand there was no rubbish about women being inherently dominant and men inherently submissive, which you hear so often and which I hate because it denies me my own sexuality.

The flat was in Docklands, with a FOR SALE sign outside it. By then I had no panties and my bra was up and my blouse undone, with Sophie fastened on to one of my boobs. She was sucking really hard and wouldn't get off until Annabelle smacked her legs for her, telling us to tidy up and make sure we weren't seen.

Inside, it was a great open barn of a place, presumably one of the early eighties warehouse conversions. Beams crossed the main room, too high to touch, while the sleeping area was on a platform reached by a spiral staircase. It was all very neat and tidy, with no hint of anything kinky. I'd been expecting some sort of customised dungeon and was a bit disappointed until Marcus threw back the lid of the bench, which ran the length of the end wall.

It was packed with bondage gear, to the brim, thick, black leather fitted with heavy-duty buckles and clips. I'd seen the style before, in gay men's shops, one designed for the biggest, heftiest guy, never mind a woman of my size. There were canes too, and whips, and paddles, rope as well, hundreds of yards of the stuff. Even the lid had been used, with rows of nipple clamps and body jewellery, each carefully held in a clip. Marcus was grinning, and I suppose I must have had my mouth open pretty wide. I felt a gentle hand on my shoulder and turned to see Annabelle.

'Don't be scared,' Marcus said. 'After all, it's for your needs.'

I nodded.

'We're going to punish you,' Annabelle went on. 'I hope you understand that. Unless you want to leave.'

'No, you can punish me.'

'You may choose then, any five items from the chest.'

I nodded again, looking down at the frightening array of restraints and implements. It was cruel to make me choose. During the punishment I'd have only myself to blame. That always makes it worse because, whatever I choose, it always seems a really stupid decision when it's actually being used on me.

What I like best is a good, firm, panties-down spanking, and that is appropriate for a schoolgirl. So is the cane, but it stings so much. I did want to stay in role, though, as far as possible, so I chose one anyway, a beautiful dark brown dragon, like the one Amber keeps for my domestic discipline. Annabelle smiled back as I passed to it her, and she tapped it on her palm.

The cane really is the best way to punish a schoolgirl. Over a desk, skirt up, panties down and six of the best across her bare bottom, preferably with plenty of people to watch. That's it; it doesn't really take much in the way of fancy equipment. She'll generally do as she's told as well, and certainly she doesn't need heavy duty leather restraints. Some restraint might be needed, sometimes, so I took a hank of white rope for my second choice, something that wouldn't raise any eyebrows at a girls' school.

Sophie was watching, enjoying my fear and indecision immensely. She's an exhibitionist really, more than a masochist, but she does love to watch another girl punished. Who doesn't, after all?

So I was going to be tied and caned, which was enough to set the butterflies fluttering in my stomach. I needed three more things, and my resolve to keep in role was weakening. It would have been so easy to choose ankle and wrist cuffs, and being forced to stay in place is no worse for me than the shame of thrashing about as I'm beaten.

Schoolgirls don't get put in gay bondage restraints, not normally anyway. I was determined, but I didn't mind the idea of being fully restrained so much. Taking another piece of rope, I showed it to Annabelle. She shook her head.

Only very silly girls argue with somebody who is about to punish them. I went back to the chest, feeling more worried than ever. Marcus had brought a bottle of wine from the kitchen area and they sat down, Sophie snuggled up to Annabelle, drinking and watching me. My fingers were trembling and I was feeling very small and very pathetic.

I tried to think of what might be done to an errant schoolgirl. She could be stripped, obviously, but that didn't take special equipment. She could be whacked, and I had my cane. It might be necessary to tie her up, and I had my rope. If she was noisy she might be gagged, so that would be my next choice.

There were plenty of gags. Ball gags, strap gags, inflatable gags, even ones with dildos sticking out so that a dominant woman could fuck herself on her plaything's head. None were appropriate for schoolgirls, but I knew what was.

'May I be gagged with my own panties, please, Miss Annabelle?' I asked.

'Naturally,' she answered.

'Two more then,' I said.

'Three,' she stated firmly. 'Your panties are not in the chest.'

'But ...'

I almost did it, but I held myself back in time. Annabelle's mouth curved up into a slight smile, enjoying my frustration. Going back to the chest, I struggled to find something suitable and not too painful. There were vibrators and things, butt-plugs too, but then schoolgirls don't normally have things stuck up their bottoms during a caning. Well, not unless it's a man doing it and he gets a bit carried away.

It had to be done though, and I don't mind my bottom filled, as long as I'm well lubricated. I chose the smallest of the cock-shaped plugs, blushing as I passed it to Annabelle. Sophie giggled, her eyes bright with mischief.

For my next choice I took a vibrator, reasoning that if schoolgirls would hardly be expected to masturbate during a caning, they might well do so afterwards. With a hot bum and all those awful feelings of shame and exposure turning to sexual need, it's hard not to. I thought Annabelle would reject it, but she didn't, leaving me with a final choice.

So I was going to be tied up, caned, buggered and frigged off. What else could there be? The obvious answer was that I could be humiliated, or at least more than by having my bottom stripped, which is bad enough. With my fingers shaking harder than ever, I chose a razor. They could shave me first, or make me shave myself, then cane me with my pussy and bottom crease pink and spick, quite hairless, making a yet ruder picture of my rear view. To my surprise Annabelle frowned and shook her head when I offered it to her. I put it back, hesitating once more, only to hear Sophie from behind me.

'I'll choose the last one as she's being such a little girly about it,' she declared and bounced over to me, peering down into the chest.

Immediately she reached in, picking up the most enormous wooden paddle. It was a great thick thing, more like a chopping board than anything to be used across a woman's bottom. I opened my mouth to protest but thought better of it, realising that there was no better way to ensure that it was used on me, hard. Sophie was laughing as she skipped back to Annabelle and handed it to her. I followed, feeling scared and promising myself that I'd get my own back.

'A good choice,' Annabelle said. 'Now, Penny, fill my glass, and Marcus's too. You shall be maid, but you may take some yourself if you wish.'

'Maid?'

'Don't question me, Penny.'

'No, Miss Annabelle.'

'That's Mistress Annabelle to you. Sophie, I think, had better call me Miss Yates for now, at least until after her punishment.'

'My punishment?' Sophie blurted out.

'Your punishment,' Annabelle said. 'Get up.'

'But . . .'

'Get up, I said, and do not answer me back.'

'But I thought Penny . . .'

'You have just earned yourself an extra two cane strokes. Now do as you're told. Stand up and take off your panties.'

Sophie obeyed, reluctantly. As she stood to take her panties off under her skirt she had a look of absolute horror on her face. Her eyes kept going to the huge paddle she had chosen, thinking all the time that it was my bottom it was to be used on. It was impossible not to grin, and when her eyes met mine I stuck my tongue out at her. That earned me a slapped hand from Annabelle, but it was well worth it.

After struggling her panties off under her skirt, Sophie stood there looking forlorn, the little scrap of white cotton dangling from her hand. They made her wait, sipping their wine and watching her. She didn't dare speak, but kept licking her lips in nervous reaction to what was about to happen to her.

It was Marcus who got up, taking the hank of rope I'd chosen and ordering Sophie to hold her panties in her teeth and cross her wrists behind her back. She did it, standing there looking worried as Marcus lashed her wrists together, firmly, so that there was no possibility of her wriggling free. Taking hold of the rope, he led her into the middle of the room, an open space on polished floorboards. The rope he threw over a beam, pulling it to force Sophie to bend over with arms high up behind her back.

The pose left her in a wonderfully ridiculous position, with her bum sticking out and off balance, so that she had to plant her feet apart to keep still. He got it just right, so that she was helpless but could keep her weight on the floor, just. I laughed at the sight and she gave me a really dirty look, then hung her head in submission, her discarded panties still dangling from her mouth.

Marcus knew how to prepare a girl for beating. Showing her bum off is one thing, but then it's necessary. Any girl who's going to be beaten knows her panties are going to come down. After all, why leave them up? It's not as if her modesty matters, especially for a schoolgirl. What she doesn't expect is to have her boobs pulled out, but it's good to make a girl show them during a beating, any girl, and Marcus knew it.

So Sophie's boobs came out, with her blouse undone and knotted behind her back to leave them swinging from her chest. Her skirt came up, lifted and tucked high to leave her bare. She was showing everything, her fat little bottom spread wide with her pussy lips peeping out from between her thighs. It would have been so easy to fuck her and I wondered if Marcus would, or if their sex play didn't extend to that. What was certain was that the little butt-plug was going up her bottom. Her bumhole was showing, pink and glossy with sweat, the little rude hole that was about to be penetrated. She couldn't hide it either, because her arms were pulled up too high. I told her what was showing, to add to her humiliation and because I knew she'd have done the same to me.

With her boobs and bum showing, Marcus went to her head, took the panties and balled them in his fist. He held Sophie's nose to make her gape and stuffed them in her mouth, using her school tie to hold them in place, knotted around the back of her head. With that he stood back to admire his handiwork and I hurried to fill his glass and pass it to him.

Sophie really did look the part. With the bare floor and the white-painted beam it was easy to imagine her in a gym, while there was nothing in her appearance to suggest that she wasn't a real schoolgirl, tied and helpless, gagged and ready for the cane. At five foot nothing and just ever so slightly chubby where it counts, she could easily have been some puppy-fat seventeen-year-old up for a beating in the school gym. Her hair was right, the little blonde ponytail bobbing to her movements, and even her shoes, flat and sensible with no heels to ruin the effect.

It was lovely, and I wanted to see her caned so badly. I could feel the heat in my pussy and wondered again if Marcus was allowed to fuck the girls. I needed it, badly, and preferably after a good spanking, or even what Sophie was going to get and which I might very well have to endure myself.

They left her swinging there while they finished their wine, allowing the anticipation to rise in her head. I could feel for her, and if I felt ever so slightly resentful that she was the centre of attention, then there was a lot of relief as well. It really is awful waiting for a caning, no matter how much it turns you on, and nobody who hasn't experienced it for themselves can possibly understand.

I understand, because it's been done to me often enough. I've seen strong, confident women burst into tears because they know they're going to get their bottoms whacked – and that's when they've asked for it. Sophie didn't cry, but she was whimpering through her gag and the muscles of her bottom and thighs kept tensing.

Finally Annabelle stood up and took the cane, then the paddle, one in each hand. Sophie was looking back, her eyes round in fright, shivering so hard it made her boobs quiver. Annabelle nodded, hefting the paddle. Four quick steps took her behind Sophie, who gave a miserable little sob, deep in her throat, as the thick piece of polished wood was pressed to her cheeky bottom.

It came up, and down, landing across poor Sophie's bottom with a loud crack. Her bum cheeks bounced, flattening to the impact, which left a broad area of red as Annabelle once more lifted the paddle. Sophie was sobbing through her gag, and I could hear her breathing, while she was trembling with reaction. Again the paddle came down, and again her bottom jumped to the impact, and yet again as Annabelle set to work, spanking her victim's fleshy little bottom.

I think she was given about twenty smacks, and I felt every one of them. By the end she was crying, with big, oily tears running down her face. Her bottom was wet with sweat, the skin reddened and shiny, rough with goose-pimples. She had kept her legs apart but had also begun to make little treading motions with her feet, trying to dull the pain.

Whatever her reaction, the beating had worked. Sophie's pussy was absolutely gaping, and running with juice. It had smeared the insides of her thighs where she'd closed them during the beating, and I could smell her, musky and feminine, a really rich, aroused scent.

When she had started to cry Annabelle had asked if she'd had enough, but she'd shaken her head. As the paddle was put down the question was repeated, and once more Sophie refused the offer. Annabelle was smiling, a really pleased, sadistic grin, and for all her efforts at self-control I could see her fingers trembling as she lifted her wine glass. She was aroused, maybe as aroused as Sophie, with her lips slightly parted and her nipples poking up into little humps beneath her rubber top.

I was sent for a new bottle, and once more Sophie had to wait. They made me serve, bending at the waist to pour the wine. Not having bothered to put my panties back on, I was bare under my skirt, so every time I bent over my bum showed. As I filled Annabelle's glass I felt Marcus's hand on my thighs, then my bottom. I stayed still, letting him explore my bum and wondering if Annabelle would object. She gave no sign, merely watching as her boyfriend fondled me.

After a couple of sips she got up again, her poise fading quickly with her excitement. I was pulled down on to Marcus's lap as Annabelle took up the cane. He continued to grope me, and I stuck my bum out over his leg, letting him get at whatever he wanted. His response was to go between my thighs and slide a finger into the wet cavity of my pussy. He chuckled at the discovery of how wet I was and put his slimy finger to my mouth, making me suck up my own juices.

Sophie was looking back again, which is a really silly thing to do when you're being whacked, but not easy to resist. She'd been chewing on her panties in her distress, and little bits of soggy white material were showing, while the bit of her tie between her teeth was sodden. There was even spittle running down her chin, and her eyes were wide and wet with tears.

Annabelle set her feet apart, making the pert cheeks of her bottom quiver in their rubber casing. For some reason I immediately thought of how she'd look in the same shameful, rude position as Sophie, with her neat little bum about to get whacked and absolutely nothing she could do to stop it.

Then the cane lashed down and all I could think about was Sophie's pain. It really hit hard, making her jump and kick out. A white line sprang up across her bottom, cheek to cheek, turning quickly to angry red tramlines. She really writhed, wriggling her bottom and jumping up and down on her feet, all the while making little grunting, sobbing sounds deep in her throat.

Marcus's finger was back up my pussy, and he was teasing my anus with his thumbnail. When he put his wine glass down I knew what was coming and opened my thighs obligingly. Sure enough, his other hand went between them and he began to wank me. Annabelle snapped at Sophie to keep still and once more measured up her shot, tapping the quivering bottom in front of her, once, twice, before lifting the cane and bringing it swishing down on to Sophie's flesh.

Sophie jumped and squeaked, once more going through that ridiculous little dance, with her legs kicking out and her boobs bouncing about under her chest. For a moment she lost her balance, regaining it with a series of still more ludicrous postures. I felt for her so badly, but I couldn't help but find it funny, while Marcus's fingers were busy with my clit and I knew it wouldn't be long before he brought me off. He was starting to open my bumhole too, and I wondered if I was going to be buggered as Annabelle lined up for the third stroke.

The cane came whistling down, harder than ever. I felt my pussy muscles jump as it bit into Sophie's rear. Suddenly I wanted to see her beaten more than anything else, really thrashed, until she was a sweaty, bedraggled, blubbering mess, her bottom stripy with burning red welts, her pussy gaping and dribbling juice.

My anus popped at that moment and as Marcus's thumb pushed up into me, I was starting to come. He was merciless, rubbing and jabbing with his fingers, as my pussy and bumhole tightened on him. I was gasping, squirming my bottom on him and crying out for Annabelle to beat Sophie, hard, mercilessly.

She obliged, and right at the peak of my orgasm I saw the cane strike down on its fat, wobbling target. I shut my eyes and the image just held, a plump, bare schoolgirl bottom, ripe with puppy fat, under a woman's cane. Nothing else mattered, just Sophie's glorious behind and what was being done to it; that and the fingers in my body.

I was still coming down when the fifth stroke landed, and by the sixth I was on the floor, lying limp and panting at Marcus's feet. He took me by the hair, pulling me up as I heard the meaty smack of wood on flesh and Sophie's muffled scream. I thought I was going to be made to suck Marcus, but it was his fingers and thumbs that went into my mouth, one at a time, licked clean of my own mess. I heard the last strokes as I did it and was still sucking when Annabelle's boot was applied to my bottom.

She was still trying to look cool, but failing, obviously aroused, with her face and neck flushed pink and her nipples really straining out the rubber. As with Marcus, I thought she'd make me bring her off, but she simply gestured to Sophie and passed me the vibrator and butt-plug. I nodded, taking both and crawling quickly over to my friend.

Sophie was a mess, streaming tears and snivelling, her whole body shaking with reaction to the caning. Eight sets of tramlines decorated her bum, all neatly laid across the fleshy cheeks. Kneeling up behind her, I kissed her bottom, once on each cheek, then pressed my face to her skin, feeling the heat of her spanking and the roughened skin.

Using my lips and tongue, I began to attend to her punished bottom, kissing her hot skin and licking along the length of her welts. I could taste the salt of her sweat and I could smell her too, musky and feminine from her sopping pussy. I heard the sound of a zip behind me but didn't look around, lost in the pleasure of Sophie's bum and sure that if Marcus wanted to stick his cock up me he would do it anyway.

When Sophie stopped snivelling I began to lick her crease, feeling the plump, resilient flesh against my tongue and tasting her skin. She knew I had the little cock-shaped plug, and she knew where it was going. I readied it, kneeling back to admire her bum. It was stuck out, her cheeks wide, her bumhole loose and wet with sweat. I kissed it first, puckering up to press my lips to the tiny hole and thinking of how Marcus and Annabelle were looking, watching me kiss another woman's anus. Sophie moaned and stuck it in my face, so I began to lick, moistening the hole with my saliva until I could get the tip of my tongue in.

As I licked I put the plug to her pussy, sliding it up the hole and bringing it out, slimy with white juice. Her bumhole was ready so I drew back, poking the little cock-head to the hole. It was impossible not to smile as Sophie's anal ring spread around the rubber cock. I was just so rude, buggering a well-spanked girl, especially with her taste strong in my mouth.

I pushed it up, bit by bit, gently so as not to hurt her, until her hole closed on the narrow part and she was plugged. Her breathing had changed, from the pained little gasps after she'd been beaten to a steady, deep rhythm. She was moaning around her gag too, and obviously needed to be frigged off, badly. I was eager to oblige, turning on the vibrator and putting it to her pussy as I went back to licking.

Licking another girl's bottom is just so lovely, and if I couldn't burrow my tongue up her anus, then there was plenty more to enjoy. I began by tonguing her pussy, then put the vibrator in it and fucked her as I rubbed my face in her bottom crease. The vibrator was buzzing crazily, so that I could feel it through her flesh as I slid it in and out. She was getting urgent, wiggling her bottom and making little sneaking noises in her throat.

At last I took mercy on her, pulling the vibrator out and applying it to her clit, with my face still smothered between her chubby bottom cheeks. She began to make little treading motions, much like when she'd been paddled. I felt her buttocks tighten in my face, tensing hard, and she was coming, squirming and panting through her nose, in an ecstasy that went on and on until at last I felt her try to pull away.

I sat back, my face wet with her juice. She'd come, and so had I, but that didn't mean it was the end. Marcus and Annabelle were due their pleasure, and he at least was ready. As I turned I found him with his cock out of his leathers, a thick pillar of dark, hard flesh. I turned a look to Annabelle, wondering if I was supposed to suck him, even if I was allowed to.

She nodded and I scrambled over, eager to play the slut and bring each of them off in turn, if that was what they wanted. He took my hair as soon as I reached him, holding me by my bunches as I gaped wide for his cock. I was ready to suck, and swallow, or take it across my face if that was what he liked. What I didn't expect was to have my head fucked, not the way he did it.

Holding me hard by my bunches, he pulled my face into his crotch, forcing me to take his cock into my open mouth. I made a mouth pussy for him, pursing my lips around his shaft. He began to move my head on his cock, pulling at my hair, which hurt. It hurt more as he got faster and faster, until he was jerking my head up and down and ramming his shaft into my throat with each push. He came like that, suddenly, right down my throat, to leave me gagging and spluttering on the floor, with spunk dribbling from my lips and bubbles of it coming out of my nose.

Inevitably I was made to lick it up off the floor, but that was it. I'd thought Annabelle would want to come. Dominant or not, they usually do, and the ones who worry about losing their cool generally blindfold their playmate, or just sit on her face so she can't see. Annabelle didn't. She waited until I'd finished licking up Marcus's spunk and then went to untie Sophie.

After that I kept expecting her to do something, maybe wait until I was relaxed before taking me by surprise and beating me, so she could come over my shock and chagrin at being punished when I thought I'd got away with it. It didn't happen, and by the time I'd helped Sophie soothe the aches and pains from her body I'd decided it wasn't going to.

Washed and nude, I sprawled on the carpet, with Sophie using my bottom as a pillow. I was tired but happy, thoroughly content, but still wondering why Annabelle was holding back. In the end my curiosity got the better of me.

'Don't you want to come, Annabelle?' I asked. 'I'd do it for you.'

'I have, thank you, Penny,' she answered. 'While you were finishing Sophie off.'

'Oh, I didn't realise. You didn't even undress.'

'I never let a submissive see me come,' she went on. 'It doesn't do for a dominant to be seen out of control. I know Marcus does, but it's stronger for a woman, harder to keep control. It would make it hard for you to look up to me.'

'I don't know, you could blindfold me.'

'No, Penny. You should think of it as a privilege to see my sex. You'll never see me nude.'

'That's a pity. You're beautiful.'

'Nude is vulnerable, which is not an emotion for the dominant. You feel comfortable, don't you, just lying there naked?'

'Sure, in front of you. Why should I be shy after what we've just done?'

'You shouldn't, because you are a submissive and it's natural for you to be naked, especially at my feet.'

I nodded and tried to look thoughtful, not wanting to argue. There was silence for a while, each of us thinking her or his own thoughts, until Marcus broke it.

'What do you do, Penny?' he asked.

'I teach,' I answered, more or less truthfully.

'You're in your summer break then?'

'Yes, free until September, more or less.'

'I see. Could you excuse us a second?'

I nodded and they got up and walked over to the kitchen area, where they held an intense conversation in whispers.

'I think they want you to come up to their place in the country,' Sophie said quietly. 'Could you, if they ask, please?'

'Sure. You're going, I suppose?'

'Yes, but I'd really like your company. They're fun but, you know, a bit heavy. I'd rather not be on my own.'

'Fine.'

They came back, sitting together again, but much more formally, as if I were being interviewed. It was Marcus who spoke.

'It was good, this evening,' he began. 'We really enjoyed you, and you do seem to have an instinctive feeling for submission, even if you are a bit inexperienced. As you saw, we're selling up here, and we've already bought the new place, in Buckinghamshire. It's a farm, well away from anywhere else, so we can do as we like.'

'We're trying to create a perfect environment for D and S sex,' Annabelle added. 'Somewhere it can be real, away from all the crap you get in London, taking care not to be seen, hiding it from people at work. You understand, I'm sure.'

I nodded.

'Sophie's coming,' she went on, 'next weekend, and we'd like you to come too, if you can spare the time, and if you're serious about it. That's important.'

'Naturally you'll be free to leave if you want to,' Marcus added, 'but something tells me you won't.'

'I . . . I'm flattered,' I answered. 'Yes, I'd like to try.'

# Two

I don't really know Buckinghamshire, despite having been brought up in the Thames Valley, or at least not the northern part of it. Annabelle and Marcus had certainly found a quiet bit and had really hidden themselves away. The farm was in a dead end at the head of a valley, somewhere near a village called Mursley, which I'd never heard of.

I drove up on the Friday, using a map Marcus had emailed across to Amber's. Amber herself wasn't too happy about losing me for a weekend, and it took a very red bottom and a lot of licking before she got over it. Even then she insisted on Vicky coming to stay, so that it was Anderson who got left out and not her.

When I arrived I quickly realised that it wasn't just the remoteness of the place that made it so good. It looked like it had been abandoned for years, with overgrown orchards and the land turning to scrub. I'd known it was a struggle to farm profitably, but this was the worst I'd seen. Or the best, if you happened to be a well-off sadist looking for somewhere you can play in private. The buildings were down a long track, with thick hazel and birch to either side, leaving them completely invisible. The gate was alarmed, presumably to warn them of locals coming round to sign them up for the local Young Conservatives, and I had to be buzzed in.

If the gate was modern, it was more than could be said for the rest of it. The house was worn, red brick, green with algae in shady places, while the blue paint on the woodwork was cracked and peeling. There was a barn too, as high as the house, wooden, dilapidated and stacked with mouldering straw. Lower outbuildings formed a square around a cobbled yard, including a stable and a pigsty. The pigsty was empty, rather to my relief, but the stable wasn't, containing a single massive carthorse.

Marcus was alone when I arrived, Annabelle having driven in to Bletchley to pick Sophie up. I was glad of this because he was easier to get on with than her, and not so worried about constantly exerting his dominance. He showed me round, introducing the horse as Mabel and joking that I was lucky there wasn't a stallion.

They'd bought the farm at auction, pretty cheaply, and all they knew about the previous owner was that he'd been unable to make it pay. That much was obvious, and it didn't seem as if he'd made any effort to keep up with the times either. He'd been old too, and either died or gone into a home, after which his son had decided to sell up.

Inside the house was big and airy, with high-ceilinged rooms full of expensive but old furnishings. At the front was what I suppose had been the best parlour, which looked as if it hadn't been used since the war, and a dining room, which obviously had but felt older still. Between them was the hall, with a staircase leading to the upstairs, which Marcus said we could see later. At the back there was a big kitchen, with a scullery leading off it. All of it was old, except for a modern telephone and a few things Annabelle and Marcus had already installed, but that was it.

We were still in the kitchen when the gate bell went, and a minute later we heard the car. Going to the front door, we greeted Annabelle and Sophie. Both looked very different from the last time we'd met, which I was used to with Sophie but not Annabelle. She was in tweeds, very much the well-off country girl, without a hint of anything kinky. She kissed me, but wasted no time, ushering us into the kitchen where we were told to sit down. After the minimum of preamble she began to explain how things were going to be.

'This is how it works,' she said. 'There's going to be a real hierarchy. I don't want it to be the way it is in the clubs, were everybody knows it's a game. Here, you do as we say, or you leave. You obey me, and Marcus, or you get punished. When you get punished it's for real. There's no opting out, no stop-words, nothing like that. It's genuine physical discipline. That's the only way to really appreciate your submissive identities. It's no good if you can duck out of a punishment, or stop it, or choose how it happens. Here it happens, and it happens when I want it to and how I want it to. Do you both understand?'

'So what role do we take?' I asked as Sophie nodded her agreement.

'It's not a role, Penny,' she went on. 'While you're here, all weekend, you are our servant. You do the menial tasks about the house, you wait on table, like any housemaid, except that you are expected to provide sexual entertainment as well. Do you think you can accept that?'

'Yes,' I answered. 'I'd like to try anyway.'

'Good,' she said. 'That's good, not too much confidence.'

'Do we do it naked?' Sophie asked. 'I'd love to be naked here.'

'Sometimes you'll be naked,' Annabelle replied. 'You'll wear uniforms most of the time. They're on your beds. You're sleeping in the attic dormer, together. You'll keep your room tidy and yourselves clean, and there's to be no touching each other unless Marcus or I say so.'

'Oh!' Sophie complained.

'Right, that provides the perfect excuse to show that I mean what I say,' Annabelle snapped. 'That sort of thing calls for a spanking, plain and simple. Sophie, get over my knee.'

Sophie went, a bit hesitantly, but without answering Annabelle back. She was in tight jeans, which made her bottom into a beautiful denim-clad ball as she went down over Annabelle's lap. She was spanked quite hard, until it began to make Annabelle's hand sting. At that point she was told to take her jeans and panties down and she was given it on the bare, with her cheeks bouncing to the rhythm of the slaps until her bottom was a nice glowing pink all over.

I could see the game, because it was a game, no matter what Annabelle said. The discipline was as close to genuine as it can get without breaking a girl's consent. We'd be beaten, properly, and if we didn't like it our only choice was to leave – all or nothing. It was really quite scary, and my stomach was tying itself in knots as I watched Sophie being punished. If I was told to take the same, I had to do it. There was no 'maybe later' or 'just on my jeans – I'm not really in the mood'. It would be done, then and there, hard, and there was nothing I could do about it.

Unless, of course, I wanted to miss out on everything, and I was determined not to. With Sophie spanked and contrite, we were sent upstairs, not by the main staircase, but by a narrow one that came down in the kitchen. The steps were bare wood and it was really gloomy, leading up first to the end of a passage and then to the attic landing, off which our room opened.

This was long and low, so that even I felt I wanted to duck for the beams. There was no carpet, just bare boards, and a single ancient bed, which creaked as I sat down on it. We had a single chest of drawers as well, and a mirror, and that was it.

37

Sharing a bed with Sophie and not misbehaving was completely beyond me, and I could already see the punishment coming. She was still feeling a bit sorry for herself, rubbing her bum as she peered out through a cobweb-covered window. I wanted to comfort her, but I could think of no better way to lead up to my own punishment.

Our uniforms were on the bed, as promised. The dresses were grey, ankle-length things, not really much more than smocks, and totally without style. Their material was coarse, like calico, which was going to make them uncomfortable as well as shapeless. They were also the same size, and while I'm only two inches or so taller than Sophie, she has enough extra on her bust and bum to make a difference.

Underwear had been provided too, big white panties and vests to match, which were at least cotton. There were girdles too, again big and plain, and flesh-tone stockings, which I hate. They had even provided shoes, square-toed black ones with only an inch of heel. Lastly there was a packet of hairpins.

We set about turning ourselves into maids. It was an odd feeling, exactly because it was so genuine, with nothing a real maid might not have worn, even if it would have been several decades previously. It was all right with the underwear, which was the sort of thing my mother wore, albeit plainer, but it was the dress that really made the difference. It made me feel vulnerable, shorn of protection, which of course I was with Annabelle waiting downstairs. Oddly enough it made me feel guilty too, and spoilt. An awful lot of women have been maids across the years, and a good number must have had their bottoms whacked, both for genuine discipline and so that some bastard or other could get off on it.

Not me though, not Penny. I've taken a lot of pain, often in ways that would have old-fashioned feminists screaming in outrage. I've done a lot of rude things too, and again a lot of people would have classified many of them as abuse, maybe most. It had all been voluntary though, my choice, or at very least what I had wanted. I was still playing, whatever Annabelle said, but at something that had been real for other women, and that was what made me feel guilty.

Not that the cane or strap hurts any less across a willing bottom, but the mental feelings in the victim's head can never be the same. Of course it was what Annabelle was trying to achieve for me, real fear and apprehension, genuine contrition, and in the end that strange dependence that can come to those under a punishment regime. Nothing arouses me quite like those feelings, and I could see her way of thinking.

Sophie looked cute in her maid's outfit, a lot cuter than I'd have expected. Her curves showed despite the shapeless dress, and having a vest instead of a bra left her boobs free to move, which was good. She was going to put make-up on, but I'd warned her that Annabelle would just use it as an excuse to punish her. Without it she became innocent, very sweet, and even younger. She was equally complimentary to me, although personally I felt I just looked a pathetic little waif.

That evening we learnt what it felt like to be servants. Annabelle and Marcus had us doing everything, cooking, serving at table, washing up, then more serving as they sat in the parlour, smoking and sharing a bottle of wine. We weren't allowed any wine and had been told we wouldn't even eat until they had gone to bed.

When the time came I was ravenous, and also seriously frustrated. All evening I'd been expecting the game to turn to sex. I'd imagined how it would be, with Annabelle picking fault with Sophie or me, probably me because Sophie had already been spanked. I'd have gone down over her knee, or maybe bent for a slapping with Marcus's belt. Either way I'd have been given the delicious indignity of having my bum stripped, with the dowdy grey dress piled up on my back and my big white panties pulled down. Once I'd been beaten it would start to get rude, perhaps with Sophie and me performing for them. Marcus would fuck us, or we might even be given the privilege of licking Annabelle.

None of it happened, and at very nearly midnight they went to bed, leaving us to clear up before we were allowed our supper. We'd cooked it earlier, to Annabelle's instruction. The pork chops were cold and greasy, while the mashed potato had been made up with water and lard instead of milk and butter. It went with boiled cabbage, unsalted. That sort of meal is better dumped down another girl's panties than eaten, but we just didn't have the energy. We ate it instead, then went to bed, exhausted and more frustrated than ever.

If Annabelle really thought we were going to leave each other alone, she was wrong. There were nighties for us, big, shapeless cotton things that covered everything. If they were supposed to be sexless then Annabelle had been wrong twice, because being cuddled into Sophie's arms while she inched the thing slowly up my body was even better than being nude. Neither of us had kept our panties on and we quickly had each other's bottom bare, kneading and patting at the soft, fleshy cheeks.

The nightie ended up under my armpits; hers too. It was nice, cuddled together in the dark, stroking each other's bodies, tired but excited, drowsy but all the better for it, because there were no inhibitions. After plenty of groping at boobs and bums we went head to toe, licking each other. It was warm and we had the covers back, writhing and squirming together, our fingers and tongues everywhere. I cleaned Sophie's bottom for her while she did the same and it just felt so good, wanton and dirty, with my tongue burrowed as deep into her bumhole as it would go.

With our bums clean and wet with saliva, we turned our attention to each other's pussies, now frantic, licking and clutching at soft flesh, eager to come. I was going to come, really close, when the door slammed open and the light came on.

Annabelle was standing in the doorway, her face set in anger, a coiled leather belt in her hand. She was in a black silk nightie, thigh length, which showed more of her legs than I'd seen before, but I didn't have a chance to enjoy the view. She strode into the room, her eyes blazing, lifting the belt.

Sophie squeaked in alarm and we pulled apart, scrambling over to spare our thighs. She grabbed me, by the wrist, twisting it hard up into my back and wrenching me the rest of the way on to my front. I was held there, bum up, shivering with fear.

'What did I say?' she demanded.

'I'm sorry,' I managed, 'I'm sorry, I . . .'

'Shut up!' she snapped and brought the belt down across my naked bottom.

God it hurt! Smack after smack after smack, delivered in furious succession to my body, on my bum and thighs and hips, until I was screaming and struggling dementedly on the bed. All my reason was gone, and all my dignity, mewling and sobbing in my pain, kicking and writhing under the blows, until at last it was all too much and I burst into tears.

She left me like that, sobbing brokenly into the pillow, and went to attend to Sophie. I just lay there, without the will to even cover my whacked bottom, just thoroughly sorry for myself and wishing Sophie and I had been a bit quieter.

Sophie was caught in the corner of the room, where she'd retreated during my belting. She was made to turn around and kneel, with her bottom stuck out, then to pull up her nightie. I watched, still shivering from my own beating, as Sophie was given a dozen firm swats across her naked buttocks. She was snivelling by the end, but she didn't break down like I had. It stopped suddenly, Annabelle's anger gone, to be replaced by a cold, matter-of-fact attitude.

'Get up!' she ordered as she stepped back. 'Right, if you two can't be trusted to behave yourselves, you'll have to sleep with your hands in mittens – that should put a stop to your dirty games. On the bed, Sophie. Turn your backs to me, both of you, and kneel up.'

We obeyed and, as I got into position, I caught a glimpse of her pulling something from under the side of her knickers. It was just a glimpse, and only of her hip and a few inches of black lace, but it was a real thrill, a glimpse of something forbidden to me.

What she had weren't really mittens, but simple tubes of rough wool. We were made to put them on, like gloves, only reaching nearly to our elbows. She had cord as well, so I knew what was coming and crossed my wrists meekly behind my back.

'That's right,' she said, 'come on, Sophie, put your hands like Penny's.'

Sophie obeyed, throwing me a miserable look as she did it. She was done first, her crossed wrists lashed firmly together and tied off, leaving her pretty well helpless. My own followed, with my feelings of submissive pleasure rising as I was tied. I'd been just about to come, then beaten, and now I was to be tied and left, still with my nightie up. Sophie, I knew, would be feeling much the same, and if our hands had been taken care of, our mouths hadn't.

'You'll be gagged too, or I know what you'll be up to,' Annabelle said, as if she were reading my mind. 'Right, panties first. Mouths open, the pair of you.'

I opened wide with an awful sinking feeling. It was all very well being put in bondage, but I wanted to come, so, so badly. I wanted to soothe my bottom as well, which was smarting from the belt, while my beaten flesh had started to prickle with sweat, which tickled.

We had our panties stuffed in our mouths. Sophie's went in mine and vice versa, but Annabelle either didn't notice or didn't care. They were dry, and I had to chew on them to be able to bear it, only to get my face smacked for my trouble. That nearly made me cry again, and with the panties tied into my mouth with a piece of cord I was feeling very, very sorry for myself and more frustrated than ever.

Sophie was served the same way and we were left, in the dark, still with the bedclothes down and our nighties rucked up high so that our hot bottoms were naked to the air. I didn't dare try to get the gag out, or do anything but lie as I'd been left. They would be able to hear us, I was certain of it. I even wondered if they'd bugged the room in some way, even visually, infra-red perhaps, in which case they might have watched us making love. It accounted for Annabelle arriving at the worst possible moment.

If I was cowed, not so Sophie. No more than a minute after Annabelle had gone I heard the bed creak and felt her body pressing to me. I tried to pull back, but she cocked one thigh up, over mine, pressing her warm, wet pussy to my leg and starting to rub. It was too much; I had to let her do it, and I was going to have her return the favour when she'd finished.

She got faster quickly, her wet, slimy sex pressed hard on my thigh, rubbing, like a dog fucking someone's boot. The bed began to creak as she got more urgent and I was praying she'd be quick, so that I could have my own go. We were going to get caught, I knew it, and punished, our bottoms smacked again, then doubtless put in yet tighter bondage so that we really couldn't do anything at all.

I pushed my leg hard into Sophie's crotch, giving her better friction. Her motion changed to a fast bucking, jamming her pussy over and over on to my leg. Her breathing was getting fast, then urgent, and suddenly she had come, holding herself tight against me, her thighs locked on mine. We swapped immediately,

Sophie letting me get my legs around one of hers and my pussy pressed to her flesh. I began to rub, urgently, trying to ignore the creaking of the bed and focus on the state I was in, tied and helpless with my bare, spanked bottom stuck out behind.

I never even heard the door, but I nearly jumped out of my skin when the light went on. I rolled off Sophie with a feeling of sick fear welling up inside me. I expected to see Annabelle, belt in hand, but it was Marcus, in pyjamas, with his erect cock sticking out of the fly.

'Time to have your cunts fucked, girls,' he drawled. 'You first, Penny Birch.'

He just took me by the ankles and spread me out. I managed a muffled squeak, but there was nothing I could do. He just held me like that, legs up and wide apart, and knelt between them. His cock was lying on my pussy mound, and he spent a moment rubbing it in my pubic hair before adjusting himself so that he could put it to my sex.

I felt my hole open to the pressure of his cock and that was it. He was up me, fucking me and leering down at my body. My tits were still out of my nightie and he was really staring, the face set in a really dirty expression, enjoying my naked body without the slightest regard for my feelings. He got faster quickly, until I was chewing on Sophie's panties and breathing hard.

The bastard didn't even give me a decent fucking, let alone make me come. Instead he withdrew once he'd had a good poke and crawled over to where Sophie had been lying on her side, watching us. Taking her by the legs, he began to manhandle her into a kneeling position.

'This is what gentlemen used to do to their maids,' he said as he pulled Sophie up to the level of his cock. 'Especially if the wife wasn't up for it. Upstairs, down with the bedclothes and up their cunts, no fuss, no bollocks about respect. Back in, Sophie, arse up, let's see that tight little cunt.'

She did it, rounded her bum out into the most beautiful ball of girlflesh, the sight of which had him licking his lips. He took her by the wrists, holding the binding, and used his other hand to guide his cock to her pussy. I saw the expression on her face change as his cock went up, and then he was fucking her and she was mouthing on her gag with her eyes closed in bliss, just like I had.

It was too much for me, watching, but all I could do was lie there with my legs open, wishing someone would attend to my aching pussy. Sophie's body was moving to his pushes, her bottom bouncing and her little tummy quivering; such a horny sight, which I would have been quite happy to enjoy while I brought myself off. She'd come, I hadn't and now she was getting the best of the fucking. It just wasn't fair!

Marcus didn't come up her. He pulled out and jerked himself off over her bum cheeks, coating the flesh his girlfriend had beaten so red with thick streamers of white spunk. As he finished she slumped down, beneath him, her legs wide around his. He finished, pushing his cock down to wipe the last little blob of spunk on to her bottom.

I was still watching, and making eyes at him, hoping he'd take mercy on me. He grinned back, beckoning with one finger. Thinking he wanted to make me suck the juice off his cock, I sat up. Immediately he grabbed my hair, wrenching me down, right on to Sophie's bare bottom.

He held me there, rubbing my face into her bum so that his come was smeared all over it. It went in my hair and up my nose, all over both cheeks and across my mouth. Some went in one eye too, so that when he finally pulled my head up I was blinking frantically and trying to blow the come out of my nostrils so that I could breath properly. Marcus just laughed.

I was shown my face in the mirror, smeared with spunk, a piece of wet panty material hanging out of one corner of my mouth, my hair plastered to my forehead. That was it. He just left us, turning the light out behind him.

My head was dizzy with arousal, my senses filled with the smell of sperm and pussy. I had to do it, immediately, and Sophie gave no resistance as I climbed on top of her, cocking my thighs across one of hers. I started to rub, thinking of how we'd been abused, whipped and tied, then just fucked, casually, as if we had no say whatever in having our pussies filled. That was all we were, two obedient little maids, not daring to protest as our bottoms were stripped and beaten, too meek even to try to fight when we were fucked.

I was rubbing hard, too excited to care about the creaking of the bed, my pussy pressed to Sophie's leg, my soiled face pressed to her neck, my boobs squashed against hers. I was bucking my bottom, urgent, desperate to come, thinking of my belting and how it had hurt, how awfully shameful it had been, how I'd been punished without the slightest regard for my feelings . . .

My orgasm hit me with the picture of Annabelle in my mind, standing tall and stern over me, holding me down as she thrashed my wriggling, defenceless bottom with the belt. It was the perfect way to beat a maid, hard and fast, without ceremony, without mercy. She might not be that experienced, but she knew what she was doing and she knew how to handle me.

I felt happy in the morning, and so did Sophie. It had been done well, and if our bums were sore, they weren't so bad that we'd be out of action. We were chatting happily as we washed and dressed, discussing how we ought to behave and what Annabelle and Marcus might have in store for us.

The morning was spent doing our tasks, fetching and carrying, cleaning the house, even feeding Mabel. Most of it wasn't all that submissive, although crawling as we scrubbed the floor and cleaning the lavatory on my hands and knees felt pretty degrading. Annabelle kept an eye on us, making sure we were kept on our toes but not choosing to punish either of us. Marcus read the papers and sipped coffee at the kitchen table, dressed in overalls and boots, which wasn't really in keeping with his masterful image. After a while he went outside, not returning until lunch.

We served at table: vegetable soup followed by a roast chicken, with apple pie afterwards. Annabelle hardly ate, which meant Sophie and I were able to have some scraps of chicken meat with our cold soup afterwards. After that we went back to work, polishing the furniture, while Marcus once more disappeared.

There was still tension, never knowing when I wasn't going to be hauled across Annabelle's knee for a spanking. It didn't happen, and as the afternoon went on I began to relax, getting more into what I was doing rather than worrying about my bottom. I'd made a few mistakes, and been told to hurry up once or twice, but nothing major, and obviously nothing serious enough to deserve punishment. By teatime I was beginning to feel a bit disappointed. After all, it was one thing for Annabelle to want to play it for real, but I'd at least expected her to be strict.

With tea finished and cleared away, we were told to go into the parlour. I expected more polishing but arrived to find two of the kitchen chairs set against the wall and Annabelle seated in an armchair. She had a piece of paper, which she was looking at, not even bothering to glance up as we came in.

'Sit down, both of you,' she ordered. 'Backs straight, chins up. Now pay attention.'

'Yes, Miss Annabelle,' we chorused.

'As you see,' she went on, gesturing to a clock on the mantelpiece, 'it is six o'clock. Six o'clock is restitution time, when your debts are called in.'

'Debts, Miss?' Sophie queried.

'Yes, debts,' Annabelle answered. 'It is when you pay for all the annoyance you've caused me, whether through stupid and clumsy mistakes, like Penny spilling tea into my saucer, or through lack .of respect, like failing to curtsey when Marcus or I enter the room. Turn around on your chairs.'

I'd known it was coming from the moment I'd seen the chairs. There's nothing quite like a hard chair for when a girl needs discipline. Everybody has one; they look completely innocent and they are very, very versatile. I turned at her order, scrambling up into a kneeling position with my bottom towards the room. Sophie had done the same, and we shared a worried look as Annabelle cleared her throat.

'Sophie first,' she said. 'Now, let me see. Seven counts of failing to curtsey for a start, and that is a very lenient assessment. Three counts of giggling during your work, four of not paying proper attention, eight of talking . . .'

'Just talking?' Sophie protested.

'Nine,' Annabelle went on. 'You're polishing is also poor. All that's bad enough but, worse still, you lack respect for your betters, an attitude that is going to have to be beaten out of you. So, that is twenty-three, say seven for poor work and ten for disrespect, making a nice round forty. That translates to forty strokes. I used a belt last night, which is not really a Lady's implement, but it was the first thing that came to hand. I should cane you now, but I've decided otherwise. I shall use a slipper on you, always a suitable implement for domestic punishment, don't you think?'

'Yes, Miss Annabelle. Thank you for not caning me, Miss Annabelle,' Sophie answered.

'You are learning,' Annabelle answered. 'Now, Penny, you chatter less than Sophie, but you are clumsy, and you're a dreamer, with your mind on anything but your work. You must learn that it is the work which is important. So, seven strokes for failing to curtsey, just two for talking, a dozen for your clumsiness and another dozen for your dreaming. You are more respectful than Sophie, but I don't want you getting above yourself. You will also get ten more, but you may have the comfort of knowing they are done not for disrespect but simply to keep you in your place. That comes to forty-three.'

I'd tried hard, and it wasn't fair, but I wasn't going to say anything. What was worse was that I'd thought I'd got away with it and I hadn't. Nor would it just be a spanking, but a full-blooded whacking.

'Yes, Miss Annabelle,' I answered, very meekly, but fighting to keep a note of rebellion out of my voice.

'Then I shall fetch the slipper,' she announced. 'You may both get in position, over the backs of the chairs, right down. Grip the legs to steady yourselves. Come now, thighs together, bottoms up, good and high.'

She might as well have added 'so that your cheeks part'. I've seen other girls in the same awful, hapless pose often enough to know what it looks like. It makes a girl's pussy pout, so that her sex lips look really fat. The bum cheeks come apart too and the hole shows, stretched wide, with every detail showing.

I got into it anyway, knowing full well what it was going to be like once my panties came down. It was awful waiting, just knowing what was to happen, and she seemed to be gone for ages, even though it was only a few minutes by the clock. When she came back I wished she'd taken longer, and my heart was hammering as she came to stand behind us.

Her hands went to the hem of my skirt. Up it came, high on to my back, leaving me shivering, with my eyes tight shut in anticipation of that awful moment when I'd be exposed. That is always the worst moment for me, and the best, when my panties come down and I'm bare, waiting to be punished. It's even worse than the punishment in ways, despite the fuss I make.

Annabelle hooked her thumbs into the waistband of my panties and down they came, just tugged low as if it didn't matter. I could already feel the tears starting to well up in my eyes, and there was a huge lump in my throat as she settled them around my thighs. My pussy was showing, plump and hairy between my thighs, I knew it, my bumhole too pink and shiny with sweat in her little nest of hair. I could smell my own excitement too, and I knew they could as well.

I thought she'd inspect me, maybe have a feel, but she went straight to Sophie, stripping her bottom in the same matter-of-fact way. That really brought home the difference between us. I'd felt I was lucky just to see her legs and catch a glimpse of the side of her fancy knickers. Now I had every detail of my pussy and bumhole bare in front of her, and she couldn't even be bothered to look.

Sophie gave a little sigh and I risked a glance, finding her with her panties already down and her chubby bottom stuck up and bare, ready for the slipper. Annabelle had stood back and was looking at us, choosing who to punish first. She stepped towards Sophie and I felt relief.

It didn't last long. As Sophie was slippered I quickly found myself wishing it had been me first. That way I'd have got it over and done with, instead of having to watch her beaten, knowing all the while that I was about to get the same. The swats were firm, regular, making her cheeks bounce and sending ripples through her flesh. She started with her eyes screwed up tight, but they came open after six, then her mouth, gaping and gasping as her bottom jumped to the slipper. I could see her boobs quivering under her dress and see the tension in her muscles. She took about twenty before she began to lose control, kicking her feet and wriggling, squealing as well, until Annabelle told her to hold still and shut up.

She still squeaked a bit, but she was quite brave really, and she didn't cry, even after all forty smacks.

That made it worse for me because if she'd cried I could have done so without feeling quite so pathetic. I'd counted every one, listening to the horrid smacking sound of rubber on flesh and knowing I was next, my anticipation rising with every stroke.

I was close to tears when Annabelle finished with Sophie, and I was gripping the chair really hard. She came behind me, I found myself wondering how I could ever have been so stupid as to let myself end up in such a position and then it started, as the horrible slipper smacked down on my poor bare bum.

Unlike Sophie, I cried. In fact I was in tears before the shock of the first few strokes had even worn off. It was the pain, and the awful humiliating position too, but it was mostly because I'd had to wait so long for it and the sheer misery of being a maid, with my nasty cheap uniform and huge pants and not even a bra to hold my boobs in.

Annabelle took no notice of my tears but went on with the punishment, smack after smack on my burning bottom. Sophie had been allowed to get up and was watching, right behind me so that she could see everything, and doubtless really enjoying the show. I was certainly making an exhibition of myself, but I couldn't stop it, kicking and wiggling my bum and snivelling as the tears ran out of my eyes.

I couldn't count and when it stopped I was actually quite surprised. My bum was so hot and felt huge, really fat. It was throbbing and I could feel the shameful heat in my pussy, giving me a dirty, sneaky thought, wondering if I'd be allowed to come. I didn't even get up but stayed in my rude position, blubbering softly to myself but hoping Sophie would be made to lick me, as I'd been made to lick her in London.

Maids don't do that sort of thing and I was told to get up and cover myself by Annabelle, and that if we didn't hurry dinner would be late, as if it was our fault!

As we scampered into the kitchen, still trying to get our panties up under our skirts, she gave us the bad news. We'd only been slippered because so many cane strokes would have made us good for nothing. The next day, at six, it would be restitution time again, a final punishment before we went home, and it would be the cane.

I was very good after restitution time, very good indeed. If I didn't improve my behaviour I was going to get forty or more strokes of the cane, which is an awful lot. Six is usually as many as I like to take, and if that makes me seem a bit of a cry baby then maybe I'm just more sensitive than most girls. It's just the way I am, and it's not for lack of practice either.

I'd taken thirty-six before, but that had been from Amber, who's very skilled and really understands me. Somehow I was sure Annabelle lacked that caring touch. The idea of forty strokes from her terrified me, but I couldn't back out. Instead I did my best to be an angel; polite and efficient, very demure, and very, very obedient. Sophie tried too and between us we managed to get through dinner without making any obvious mistakes. It wasn't easy because the slippering had brought me back on heat and I badly wanted to come.

I was feeling confused and vulnerable, with so many tasks to do that I couldn't think clearly. In the back of my mind I knew that they were trying to keep me off balance, but that did help. Annabelle was worse than Marcus, far worse. She was a real textbook sadist, while it seemed to me that all he really wanted was to have a couple of girls who'd do as they were told when he wanted to get his kicks. Certainly he was friendly to us when she wasn't around, and he hadn't beaten either of us.

By bedtime I was even more frustrated than the night before. I was sure our room was bugged, at the very least with a microphone, and as I dried up the plates a genuinely awful realisation came to me, that everything we'd done might be going straight out on a webcam. I immediately felt stupid for not thinking about it. After all, I'd been caught before, by a miniature camera hidden in a toilet soap-cage. The resulting pictures of me peeing, taken about six inches from my pussy, had been horribly embarrassing, but at least there had been no clear image of my face.

I couldn't say anything to Sophie, in case the kitchen was bugged as well. It was where she'd been given her welcome spanking, so it seemed quite possible. The obvious place was the parlour, and I remembered the way the chairs had been placed for our slippering. The thought had me blushing yet, even if it were true, there wasn't really anything I could do.

I'd wanted to have Sophie give me a quick lick before we went up to bed, thus avoiding Annabelle's wrath. Now I didn't dare, and when she asked me if I'd do it for her I said I was too tired and gave her a wink when I was sure it couldn't be seen. She answered with a puzzled frown, so I gave her a hug, which I hoped wasn't going to earn me a belting, and whispered in her ear.

Her answer was a look of near panic. I wasn't surprised. She was studying law, and pictures of her having her bum reddened were not going to go down well. It was just as bad for me, as the authorities at the university knew nothing whatever about what I got up to in my spare time.

I went to the parlour, feeling worse about what I might find than I had when waiting to be beaten. There was nothing there, or nothing that I could find, but that wasn't altogether reassuring. I went back to searching, very methodically, checking every possible place that could have given a good view of the chairs. I was still looking when I heard Annabelle's cough from behind me, and I nearly dropped the clock I'd been trying to get open. She was in her black silk nightie, leaning on the door frame, looking at me in surprise. It was not the time to lie.

'Look, seriously,' I said, 'Sophie and I have respectable jobs. Well, she will have. We were worried. We thought that . . . you know, that you might be putting it all out on the net.'

'You don't trust me?'

'Well . . . yes, I do trust you, Annabelle. I'd like to anyway. Be fair though, I've hardly known you five minutes. I just need to be sure.'

'Do you really think I'd let a load of dirty little wankers see you the way I've had you?'

'Well, maybe. I mean . . . it might turn you on to have an audience, or to know I'm showing off to so many people. I don't know, Annabelle; I'd like to be punished with an audience, and the more excited they were, the better. Maybe you're the same, or Marcus. It's just the idea of images being kept that I can't accept.'

'I want you to be mine, Penny,' she answered. 'I don't want other people to see. Only Marcus. I'm hurt that you could think I'd do that to you, but you can search all you like. When you don't find anything, that's going to be twelve strokes of the cane at tomorrow's restitution. Do you agree?'

I nodded, unable to speak and feeling really bad. I searched though, thoroughly, and when I'd finished I insisted on accessing their system and checking through it, equally thoroughly. There was nothing, or if there was it was incredibly well hidden. They watched me, and Sophie too. By the end Marcus was grinning at the way I'd let myself in for punishment after trying so hard to avoid it. Sophie was sorry for me and gave me a kiss and a squeeze to try to compensate. Annabelle looked genuinely upset.

What it did mean was that I had a chance to check our bedroom. That was clean as well, which left me feeling really stupid. I'd earned myself twelve strokes of the cane, for nothing.

I got my orgasm in the end, cuddled together beside Sophie with our fingers busy between each other's thighs. It was nice, but nothing special, because I couldn't focus on what I was doing. I kept expecting Marcus or Annabelle as well, either to belt us or fuck us, which was a serious distraction. Neither came.

I was still feeling confused in the morning, and worse because it wasn't so much that they'd managed to put me off balance as that I'd managed to do it myself. Not that it stopped me thinking of the caning that was coming at restitution time, so I was on best behaviour all morning.

Annabelle was lapping it up, ordering us to do this or do that, watching us work or just relaxing while we scurried about like frightened mice. She'd said that a true submissive should take pleasure in her mistress's feelings without thought for her own, and she certainly seemed to believe it.

Marcus was out all morning and when I went to see to Mabel I could hear heavy machinery somewhere out of sight, a buzz-saw and some kind of engine. He was obviously working, and I felt a bit cheated at that because, however much I like other girls, I had been looking forward to some cock.

Lunch was everything an English Sunday roast should be, a rolled sirloin of beef, Yorkshire puddings, roast potatoes, vegetables, then Eve's pudding with cream. At least it was for them; Sophie and I ate beef fat and cold, dry cauliflower in the kitchen after nearly four hours of cooking, serving and washing up. The only good thing was that it kept my mind off the time, which had reached four o'clock by the time we'd finished.

The butterflies in my stomach were beginning to flutter. I had my twelve of the cane coming for certain, and I was sure Annabelle was going to find something to pick fault with as well. It is a good idea to tell a girl she's going to be beaten a good while before it happens because it makes the punishment far worse. Knowing it could happen at any moment is bad enough, but having to wait until a predetermined time is really awful. Normally I rather enjoy that dreadful jittery feeling of knowing it's coming, but for some reason this was different. I just didn't feel I could face it. My stomach felt weak and I kept having to go to the loo. I was telling myself not to be stupid, that I'd been caned before, and that the feelings afterwards were worth the pain.

The worst thing was that every time I went into the parlour or dining room I could see my car in front of the house. I knew I could go, any time I wanted, but I didn't dare. I'd already come close to spoiling everything with my little bug-hunting expedition and I was sure that if I backed out now that would be it, the end.

I didn't, and five o'clock passed, then half-past, with Annabelle quietly reading a book and Marcus dozing in an armchair. By a quarter to six I felt I was about to wet myself, despite having been half a dozen times. We'd tried to be good, really hard, and Sophie was confident, and equally sure, that once we'd been caned Annabelle would let us break role and do something rude with her, or at least each other. I wasn't so sure because, for Annabelle, the whole thing seemed to be more of a head trip than anything overtly sexual.

At five to six we trooped into the parlour and stood by the two hard chairs with our heads bowed and our hands folded in front of us. Annabelle didn't even look up, and I watched the minutes tick away, then the seconds until at last the clock struck six. I was so scared. Annabelle was good. Two days of service and I felt as if it was real. Suddenly I realised that the drab uniforms, the long hours of work, the absence of anything ordinary people would have regarded as sexual, all of it had been necessary, to make me feel the way I did, genuinely frightened.

As the last chime died away Annabelle put her book to one side. She had a slight frown on her face, as if about to undertake some irksome but necessary task. Marcus stretched and yawned, pulling himself up in his armchair. I swallowed the lump in my throat, thinking of the number twelve. It was going to be more, but it was the twelve that mattered, the twelve I'd so stupidly brought down on myself.

'Restitution time,' Annabelle said. 'On the chairs, both of you. Skirts up, panties down.'

We hastened to obey, bumping together in our hurry to get into the awful, degrading position. I knelt, fumbling my skirt up on to my back as I bent. Sure it was best to get it over with, I quickly peeled down the big white panties at the back, just enough to leave my bottom completely bare.

'Bums well out; I want to see those cracks,' Marcus added.

I pushed out my bottom, unable to hold back a sob as I felt my cheeks spread and the cool air on my pussy.

'Knickers down all the way, Penny,' Marcus said. 'Come on, let's see that hairy little cunt of yours.'

Before I could reach back Annabelle had jerked my panties down around my knees, leaving Marcus with the view he wanted. I hung my head, thinking of what I was showing and waiting for Annabelle to speak.

'Well,' she began, 'I am glad to say that your behaviour has shown a remarkable improvement. Sophie, you failed to curtsey only once, and four times spoke without being spoken to or for frivolous reasons. Your work has improved as well. A traditional six of the best will serve you, and you can be grateful for my leniency.'

'Yes, Miss Annabelle. Thank you, Miss Annabelle,' Sophie squeaked.

'Penny's behaviour has been better still,' Annabelle continued, 'aside from her little outburst last night. Without it she might even have been let off, except that I suspect she has come to need her discipline. How many extra do you feel you need, Penny?'

She understood me too well. Sophie was grateful, genuinely grateful; I'd heard it in her voice. So was I, but not for the same thing. With Sophie it was because she was only getting six, which is about right for a good, hot pussy without too much pain. For me it was because she was going to punish me, to give me what I genuinely felt I deserved, I needed. At least, half of me felt that way. The other half was screaming at me not to let it happen, to keep my dignity, that I was a modern, independent woman and that even the suggestion that I be caned should be greeted with utter outrage.

I couldn't stop it any more than I could stop myself feeling hungry or tired. She was making me choose my own pain and I hated her for it, but I was grateful too, pathetically grateful.

'Twelve please, Miss Annabelle,' I said, with half my mind still screaming at me to pull up my panties and run.

She gave a little snort, expressing both amusement and contempt. She knew what was going on in my head, she understood, because the same feelings were mirrored in her own.

'Twenty-four it is then, Penny,' she said, 'and six for little Sophie. Right, you will be beaten, then sodomised. Sophie first.'

I caught the word 'sodomised' and my heart gave a jump. She'd said it so casually, as if having a cock stuck up our bottoms was nothing, just an inconsequential detail because Marcus was going to get horny over the sight of us being caned. It mattered to me though, a lot, and I was already thinking of how his fat, meaty cock was going to feel as it was pushed up into my bottom.

Maybe it's because I tend to draw attention to my bottom during sex, or maybe it's just the way I'm built, but men always seem to want to bugger me. Maybe it's just because they're a bunch of dirty bastards who love making girls take cocks where they're not meant to go. Whatever way it was, Marcus was obviously no exception.

There was a grating noise, which I knew came from Marcus pulling down his zip. I didn't dare look and it came as a complete shock when his hand closed in my hair and my head was pulled around so that he could stick his cock in my mouth. I took it in, sucking him as he watched Sophie get the cane.

I heard the smack and her answering squeal as the first stroke came down, then a gasping, panting sob in reaction. Marcus was quickly growing hard in my mouth, and he was stroking my bum too, having a good, leisurely feel of the cheeks. His fingers went to my pussy, tickling me before one was slid up my hole.

Sucking busily while my pussy was groped, I listened to Sophie being beaten. The cane would whistle through the air, landing with a smack to make her cry out, and with each smack her cries got louder and her sobbing more plaintive, more broken, until on the fifth she started to sniff and I knew her tears had come. The sixth smacked in and it stopped, leaving her snivelling gently and thanking Annabelle in a tiny, cracked voice.

Marcus kept me sucking, waiting until he was rock hard before pulling my head off his cock. I hung it down again, pushing my bum out and bracing myself for the cane. I was trembling inside and my bowels felt weak, while it took all my will-power to stay still on the chair.

Sophie had not moved and was still bent over, showing everything. Risking a glance, I could see the ends of the six red lines that now decorated her bottom, lines that would last a week or more, keeping her constantly in memory of her punishment. She was very still, her blonde hair hanging down around her face, her boobs hanging in her dress, the nipples showing as little taut humps. Her back was still in, giving her full bottom a lovely curve from the rucked up dress to her lowered panties, everything showing, everything ready for Marcus's cock.

'Head down, Penny,' Annabelle ordered and I obeyed, closing my eyes and telling myself I'd take the punishment well, like a grown woman and not some squalling little brat.

I always think that before a punishment, and it never works. I do try, but the pain is always too much, even from a hand-spanking. As for the cane, I just don't have a hope. I heard it whistle through the air and got a last moment of pure terror before it hit and my bottom exploded in stinging, burning agony. I cried out, misery and anger flaring in my head, my feet kicking, my muscles jumping in pain. I struggled to control myself, the lump in my throat choking me, my head already full of a dizzy, swimming feeling.

The second came down before I was really ready and I jumped up, screaming out in shock and clutching my bum. Annabelle waited patiently as I got back in position. The strokes had been hard and both the cuts were really smarting. I knew I'd be quite badly bruised, marked, to keep the shame of my punishment in my head and to make sure that anyone else who saw also knew.

With my bum stuck out once more, Annabelle gave me my third. I jumped up again, my hands going straight to my bottom, squealing stupidly as I kneaded my hurt cheeks.

'Stop behaving like a baby, Penny!' Sophie chided.

'You were crying!' I answered her.

'Do try and show some self-respect, at least,' Marcus added.

'I don't have any!' I bawled. 'Not now, not like this!'

'Nor should you,' Annabelle said. 'What respect you do have is due to me!'

With that she brought the cane down across my bottom with all the force of her arm. I screamed as it hit, the force of it jamming me forward against the chair. It was agony and I jumped up again, squeezing my bum cheeks and dancing up and down on my knees, all the time giving a series of pained squeaks that I just couldn't hold back.

'For goodness' sake!' Annabelle snapped. 'Marcus, be a dear and tie her wrists to the chair.'

'Pitiable,' he remarked. 'What a fuss over a few cane strokes. You'd better not behave so badly when I put my cock up your arse.'

'I won't,' I snivelled. 'I promise.'

I looked back to find him undoing the laces from his work boots. He was still stroking his cock as he came over to me, and he popped it in my mouth as he tied me up, with my crossed wrists bound to the back of the chair. My bum was starting to glow, with the pain giving way to pleasure while my pussy was starting to juice.

Once I was secure I stuck my bottom out again and Marcus stepped back, pulling his cock from my mouth. He didn't go to the chair, but to Sophie, who took his cock in her hand and tugged at it as they watched me. I braced myself again, glad I was tied because it was going to stop me making an exhibition of myself and because I didn't need will-power any more. I was going to be beaten and I really had no choice.

The cane tapped on my bum and I hung my head, my teeth gritted. The fourth stroke came down and I screamed and bucked, kicking too, but I couldn't get up because of my tied hands and I was back in position a lot faster than I would have been.

'Good girl,' Annabelle said. 'That's better, isn't it?'

I nodded, turning to meet her eyes. My own were wet, with tears of misery and contrition welling up in them.

It was better, so much better, and my gratitude was growing stronger, and I wanted to cry, and I wanted to be caned.

She gave me the fifth and the tears started from my eyes with my yelp of pain. As I steadied myself they began to roll down my face, one from each eye, heavy and slow, only to spatter on to the floor as my body jerked in reaction to the sixth stroke. The seventh came down and the eighth. I was in a dizzy haze of pain and heat, the tears running freely, my vision blurred. She went on, nine and ten, ignoring my sobs and gasps, bringing the cuts in with hard, precise movements, full across the cheeks of my out-thrust bum.

By twelve my breathing was deep and even, my bottom throbbing, my pussy swollen and hot, with juice trickling down the insides of my thighs. I didn't even want it to stop any more and, instead of wondering how I could possibly take it, I was thinking of what a baby I'd been at first and how right I'd been to ask for another dose of twelve. I was sticking my bum out, moaning, wanting the pain, my tears drying on my cheeks.

I'd lost count, just jerking to each stroke, crying out, but more in ecstasy than pain. Sophie called me a slut but I hardly heard her, sticking my bum out now with my knees apart to let the air caress my pussy. I'd have been masturbating if my hands hadn't been tied, and I was thinking of the thick, hard cock which would shortly be forced up my bottom and wishing I could be caned and buggered at the same time.

It stopped, although I had no idea of how many strokes I'd taken. I was a bedraggled mess, my head hung in utter surrender, my face and hair soaked with tears, my bottom burning and prickly with sweat. I was wet between the legs, soaking, ready to take a horse, or at least to try, mentally as well as physically.

I felt so lewd, so dirty, a grovelling, punished little slut, beaten into submission and ready to be fucked, utterly in thrall to the people who had punished me. Annabelle had stood back, Marcus too, both watching us in our disgrace as he nursed his erection in readiness for our bumholes. He was grinning, his eyes flicked between our open, ready bottoms, choosing who to bugger first and who he wanted to come up. I wiggled my bottom, not wanting to wait, but he gave a decisive nod and stepped behind Sophie.

She was as bad as me, sticking it out in readiness. Her head came up as he settled his stiff cock between her buttocks, her eyes closing in expectant bliss. I watched him delve into the pocket of his overalls, bringing out a squat can labelled as tractor grease, a really humiliating thing to use to lubricate a girl's bottom hole. I smelt it as he twisted the lid open, a heavy, oily scent that reminded me of garages.

Grinning more broadly than ever, he dipped a finger into the can, pulling out a lump of thick, yellow-brown grease. Reaching forward, he showed it to Sophie, under her nose, which she wrinkled in disgust at the smell. Marcus laughed and took hold of his cock, spreading the disgusting grease over the head before pressing it down between Sophie's open buttocks.

Her expression turned to ecstasy as he began to rub his cock in her cleft, smearing the grease around her bumhole. Marcus was watching it, holding his cock by the shaft and grinning, thoroughly enjoying himself. I knew he was going to put it up her when his mouth suddenly set in a firm line. Sophie gave a pained gasp and her breathing changed, becoming deeper and faster. He was in her, up her bottom, jamming his greasy cock past her ring and up inside her, bit by bit.

She took it, panting and clutching at the chair, mouth wide, eyes tight shut. With most of it in he let go of his cock and took her by the hips, buggering her to a slow, easy rhythm. Her hand went back, between her thighs, her expression turned to a dopey smile and she was wanking; caned, buggered and now getting off on her own degradation.

Marcus kept it slow, very controlled, as Sophie got more and more excited. She was rubbing her clit, her eyes tight shut, gasping in pleasure. She started to mumble, then to talk, babbling in her ecstasy.

'Use my bum, harder, deeper, use it, Marcus, right up. Hurt me, bugger me, spunk in me and take out your lovely, lovely cock and make me suck it . . .'

She finished with a scream, her head thrown back as she came in absolute ecstasy, with her beaten bottom full of cock, begging him to spunk in her bumhole, the selfish little slut.

'No, don't . . .' she mumbled as she finally went limp.

He just laughed, spreading her bottom with his thumbs and easing himself slowly out. It hurts as much coming out as it does going up, sometimes, and Sophie squeaked a bit as he withdrew. As his cock left her hole it jerked upright, to stand proud out of his fly, slimy and glistening, with a blob of sticky brown grease on the tip.

Stepping round to her head, he prodded it at her face. Sophie shook her head, her mouth closed tight.

'Suck it, you little bitch,' he said. 'That's what you wanted, wasn't it?'

Sophie shook her head again and then suddenly her mouth was open and she was sucking on the cock that had just been up her bottom, gulping on it, swallowing her own taste and the grease as well. Marcus's eyes closed in pleasure and I really thought he was going to come in her mouth.

'No, don't, that's not fair!' I protested. 'I want to be buggered! Come on, Marcus, that's not fair!'

'You filthy slut!' Annabelle spat. 'You're supposed to be ashamed, not eager!'

'I can't help it! I want my share, and I want to be made to lick you while he does me. Come on, Annabelle, enough is enough, I want your pussy! I beg you! Now come on, Marcus, you're being unfair!'

His cock was still in Sophie's mouth, but he withdrew. It looked a lot cleaner now, but wet and shiny with her saliva. I could only sigh as he got behind me and I felt it rested between my bum cheeks, with the hair on his balls tickling my pussy. I turned to Annabelle, who hadn't moved but was still watching. I tried to plead with my eyes and at that she stepped forward, her hands going to her dress. That made me feel so good, really triumphant, and I was grinning as she came in front of me.

She turned her back and I realised I was going to be made to lick her bottom, or at least have my nose stuck in her bumhole while I tongued her clit. Marcus was greasing his cock and, as Annabelle's pretty black silk panties came on show, I felt the firm, round head squashed down between my buttocks.

Annabelle stuck her bottom in my face, panties still up. It was lovely, pert and small and firm, encased in slippery black silk. I began to rub my face against her, in the crease, hoping she'd take her knickers down but enjoying it anyway. Marcus had his knob to my bumhole, pushing. I relaxed my ring to the pressure, and up it went, the head anyway, with a disgusting squashy noise that made Sophie giggle.

'Frig me, Sophie, please!' I begged and went back to nuzzling Annabelle's bottom.

She obliged, holding me around my tummy and sliding her hand back between my thighs. Neither of them objected and her fingers found my clit as another inch of cock was rammed firmly up my bottom. Marcus put it all in, bit my bit, until my whole gut seemed to be full of huge, bloated cock. I was panting into Annabelle's knickers, breathing in her musky scent and rubbing my face on her. Her cheeks started to jiggle and I knew she was masturbating, which added the final, glorious touch to my pleasure.

I was coming, smothered in my Mistress's bottom, my Master's cock jammed well up my bumhole, my friend attending to my pussy. I'd been made to work, made to clean, made to scrub and grovel on the floor, made to clean a toilet bowl on my hands and knees. I'd been abused and molested, tied up and fucked, given the belt and the slipper, and now, better, caned hard and then buggered, made to beg for the privilege of kissing my Mistress's bottom.

That was what got me as my climax came: the state that I was in and the way it contrasted with Annabelle, who hadn't even let her knickers down. It made me feel so submissive, such an utter slut, even more than having a man about to spunk up my bottom. My hole was contracting on his cock as I came and I knew it was going to happen. Sure enough, I felt him jerk and heard his grunt of ecstasy and I knew he spunked up my bottom. That was enough to give my orgasm a last, lovely peak, and then it was fading, slowly, as I heard Annabelle's own, muted sigh of ecstasy.

She had her bottom pushed firmly in my face, and I could feel her muscles clenching and her cheeks quivering as she came. I want to lick her properly, to show her how much I'd do for her. I tried, but she reached back to slap me away and then it was over. Sophie had already withdrawn her hand and Marcus was pulling out, leaving me gasping on the chair, suddenly sore and exhausted. My bottom was burning and I had spunk dribbling out of the hole, which felt really open and wet, while my cane cuts were wet with sweat and had really started to sting. I was going to be off punishment for days, and probably walking bow legged, but it had been worth it.

# Three

Annabelle said nothing about tattoos. I drove Sophie back and dropped her at the station in Hertford before going on to Amber's. We talked as we went, mainly about Annabelle. She explained how they'd met, at Rathwell's club, after she'd done her traffic warden cabaret. They'd been there before, and Annabelle had been a big hit with the male submissives from the start. Apparently she was happy to take on as many of them as asked, so long as they did as they were told and made no demands on her.

We both saw what we'd done as a game, albeit to stricter rules than we were used to. Like me, Sophie wished Annabelle had been a little less the formal dominant, especially when it came to allowing us to touch her. Both of us would have liked to show our appreciation by giving her a good, slow tongue bath, or whatever else appealed to her.

I could see the sense in it because she had utterly degraded me and I hadn't even seen her boobs, let alone her pussy. That really accentuated the difference in status between us and had added a lot to my experience; presumably hers also. I was still surprised she hadn't let me lick her, even when she was actually coming. Either she was determined to maintain her image and it had taken iron self-control, or she was hung up about her body. That also led us to question her dominance, whether she genuinely wanted only that role, or if she kept the image up as a shield for her insecurity. Having seen her reaction to Melody Rathwell I was fairly sure I knew which.

It had been good, but I was glad to be back with Amber, with whom I'm always equal except when we're playing, and even then I go dominant now and again. Vicky was still there and I told them everything, showing off my cane marks before we went to bed.

Annabelle had ticked me off for taking control at the end of my session as servant. I'd pointed out that I'd been tied up at the time and if she wanted me to shut up as well she should have gagged me. Other then that, she'd been pleased with us and had given another lecture on understanding our natural roles and so forth before we left. She'd also said they'd be in touch for another session if we felt we could take it, and we'd both agreed.

The email came in the middle of the week. It was quite long and explained that, while she felt I'd learned something important as her servant, I still had a long way to go and that she could provide a depth of experience that I'd never even dreamed of. If I was happy with keeping whatever role they set me and not breaking it until the end of the stay, I could come up in two weekends' time. I was determined to do it and Amber eventually accepted it, after a lot of begging on the floor and another lengthy session with my tongue.

What Annabelle hadn't said was what I was actually going to have to do. I could see living as a servant becoming boring after a while, even with her terrifying 'restitution time' every evening. Still, she had implied it would be something different, and it was fun trying to anticipate what. The obvious thought was a slave but then, as she hadn't actually paid me for my service, it was hard to see the difference. I might be made to go naked, maybe to sleep chained up, which would be nice, but I was hoping she would be more imaginative.

\* \* \*

To compensate for my behaviour, Amber made me go to a public swimming pool at the weekend. That may not sound like much of a punishment, but I'd been caned and the bruises showed at either side of my bikini bottoms. It was hideously embarrassing. There I was, a grown woman and it was quite obvious I'd had my bottom smacked.

I couldn't stand it for long, what with the little whispered comments, sniggers and knowing looks. The majority probably thought I'd been caned by my boyfriend or husband, either completely against my will or after being forced to accept it. Some knew, the ones who tried to hide their smiles as I passed, both men and women. They were the worst because I could easily imagine them all thinking about how I'd have looked bent over for the cane with my panties around my legs.

Even then the bruises were fading, which was exactly why Annabelle had wanted to wait two weeks. It would give her a fresh, unmarked bum to work on, which was another thing Amber wasn't too pleased about, as she had to content herself with hand-spankings for my discipline.

She put up with it though, and on the Friday I once more set off for Buckinghamshire. This time I went by train, having nearly taken off my sump on their badly made-up track. It had been raining and the fields and woods were still wet, sparkling in the sunlight. Marcus met me at Bletchley station and, to my surprise, he was in uniform, a brilliant red jacket and trousers in deep blue with a red stripe, also two pips on his shoulders. He looked really smart, and the idea of being dominated by him like that appealed to me immediately.

'Military?' I asked as we got into the car. 'An army fantasy?'

'Don't let Annabelle hear you use that word!' He laughed. 'Yes, it is, military dominance anyway.'

'Great! I love your uniform. Where did you get it?'

'It's real. I was in the guards for two years.'

'An officer too, I see.'

'First Lieutenant.'

'Good for you. I wouldn't even join the cadets at school, even though a lot of the girls were desperate to be in.'

'No? Maybe it's time you had a bit of military discipline then.'

'Maybe. How about Annabelle?'

'She's never had anything to do with it either, but she'd make a great sergeant. She's a natural.'

'So what's in store for me? Boot polishing? Drill? A good thrashing with your riding crop?'

'You'll see. How's your bum?'

'Better, thank you. Nearly all the marks have gone, except for one or two places on my right cheek where the tip caught me. She's good, Annabelle – there were no thigh shots or wrapping and nothing too high.'

'Thigh shots? Wrapping? You sound like you wrote the manual.'

'It comes of reading *Janus and Blushes*, that's all.'

I shut up, cursing myself for not remembering how inexperienced I was supposed to be. He was being so friendly that I'd forgotten who I was talking to, and I'd nearly put my foot in it. Fortunately he accepted my explanation.

'It's funny, you know,' he went on. 'I always used to think it was only dirty old men who read that sort of magazine. I'd never have believed a woman would read one.'

I just laughed, sure that explaining my opinions about my right to express my sexuality would give even more away. I was supposed to be the one exploring my feeling, after all.

'No Sophie?' I asked, changing the subject.

'Tomorrow morning,' he replied. 'She couldn't get away tonight.'

I nodded, thankful that I was going to have company, and especially Sophie's. We kept talking as we drove, very easily, much in the way I talk to Amber. I was glad of it because, however much I like submissive sex, I hate the feeling of genuine inequality. I also tend to need a cuddle if things get really strong, and I couldn't really see Annabelle giving me one.

She greeted us at the door, in uniform like him, but nothing like as smart. Not that she was unattractive, far from it, with her neat little bottom packed into tight khaki trousers and her nipples showing through her top. The cropped blonde hair suited the image too, much better than it had that of respectable country lady. She had a little cap on too, and brilliantly polished boots, which amused me, because I could imagine her doing the polishing. There were three chevrons on her sleeves, making her a sergeant, which, as Marcus said, seemed to suit her, even if I was surprised that she'd taken a lower rank than him.

That set me wondering and, as I was in a mischievous mood, I asked if I was going to get to see her beaten if she didn't behave. That really put a scowl on her face and I realised I'd touched a very raw nerve. I apologised as we went inside, Annabelle ushering me straight into the kitchen as before. I began to make tea, taking up my servile role more or less by instinct.

She explained their choice as we drank tea. I'd been obedient enough, they felt, but not in the right way. My problem, apparently, was that I thought too much, obeying in order to avoid punishment when I should have been doing it by instinct. I was also too inclined to make my own choices, as I'd shown at the end of my time as a servant, trying to take over the situation when it got heated. I'd actually succeeded, more or less, but I didn't mention that.

Annabelle went on, explaining that she disagreed with the idea that the submissive partner should have ultimate control. She felt this was an absurdity and no more than a piece of political correctness that had managed to creep in to the world of dominance and submission. To her mind the dominant should have real control, with the submissive given a simple choice of obeying or getting out altogether. What she wanted was the perfect sex slave, whose only desire was to fulfil her needs.

She was pleased with me and had decided that I might just be good enough, if my attitude could be improved. They discussed it during the week and decided that the cure was a little military discipline. That way I'd have to obey orders, promptly and without hesitating. It was something they were into anyway, Marcus having served his time, which conjured up a very pretty picture of Annabelle with her army trousers down getting a thrashing across her pert little bottom, another thought I kept to myself.

I nodded as I listened, never disagreeing with her but all the time wondering what the discipline was going to involve. She had hit a bit of a nerve though, especially when it came to physical things. There were two reasons I'd refused my chance to join the cadets at school, well, three really, but the third was that I was a little swot so that didn't count. The first was my hatred of anything organised and a total lack of team spirit. The second was that I hate being made to compete, physically, because I'm small and lightly built so I invariably lose.

The first problem I'd avoided ever since. The second I'd got over by linking it to my need for sexual punishment and humiliation, so that I can go pony-girl racing or whatever and not mind being useless. What I'd never got over was the fear of anything military, and they had brought it back to the surface very effectively. I'd put on a brave face in front of Marcus, but the more I thought about it, and the more I tried to tell myself that I was being irrational, the worse it got.

There's only one thing to do with feelings like that, which is to turn them into fantasy and masturbate over them. That's what I always do when something gets to me sexually and I can't shake it off. The orgasm diffuses the tension and afterwards I'm all right again. The best example was after seeing a stallion with an erect cock. It was so big, and I just wanted that huge, thick shaft in my body. Not that I was actually going to do it, but the thought wouldn't go away, and so I imagined myself in my pony-girl gear, being put to stud. It was a great orgasm and afterwards I could look at a horse again without getting hot flushes.

Annabelle sent me to bed early and I tried to do the same over the army thing. Lying in the dark and quiet, I let my mind wander, wondering what they could do to me. At school it had always been the idea of being shown up in front of other people that scared me. I've always been too much of a dreamer to be good at things like drill, and too small for heavy physical stuff. Inevitably I'd have ended up getting singled out and picked on by the corporals, probably bullied by the other cadets as well.

I imagined being made to drill, not officially, but with some of the other, weaker girls, lined up in the changing rooms at school by the bigger, tougher ones. I'd have done as I was told, even though I didn't understand the submissive part of my nature. My tormentors wouldn't have understood themselves either, but bullies don't need to.

They'd have started by making us drill, only before long they'd have decided it was amusing to make us pull our tops up and do it with our boobs showing. They'd see our embarrassment in our flushed faces and trembling lips as we stood there with our bras and tops tugged up over our breasts. Our trousers would have come down next, adding to their amusement, not off, but down, around our ankles, so that we couldn't try to run away without tripping up. They'd think it was hilarious, but it wouldn't be enough. Before long our panties would come down, jerked to our knees to leave a line of us, bare boobs, bottoms and pussies all on show.

I'd be shivering, standing to attention, my nipples hard because it was exciting me and I couldn't help it. They'd notice and laugh at the sight, calling me a tart and a bitch. I'd be made to strip completely, stark naked, then stand there, at attention, nude while the others were allowed to dress. They'd send me into the lavatory and make me clean the bowl with my tooth-brush, kneeling naked on the pee-soaked floor while they stood over me, gloating.

Even that wouldn't be enough for them. They'd pee in the bowl, one by one, making me watch, each dabbing her pussy with a piece of loo paper when she'd finished. When they were done one would take me by the hair and drag my head over the bowl. I'd be forced down under the water, and then they'd flush it, laughing at me as I gagged and spluttered, my hair sodden and full of bits of lavatory paper, their piddle in my mouth and running out of my nose . . .

I came, thinking of myself utterly, totally soiled with my head down a lavatory and three army girls laughing at me. It was good, really good, as good as when I'd come over the stallion's cock. Unfortunately there was one major difference. I'd escaped the stallion, whereas I had to face Annabelle and Marcus's army fixation, and it was the next day.

Morning came with Annabelle screaming at me, jerking my bedclothes off and dumping me hard on the floor. I came down on my bum, squeaking in shock. She kicked me, her big army boot smacking into the flesh of my thigh, then grabbed me by the hair and wrenched me to my feet, still yelling, right in my face.

She had a stick, which she hit on the bed as I struggled to get up. I was bleary eyed with sleep, but not for long. She took me by the scruff of my neck and dragged me over to the stairs, which she helped me down with another kick, this time to my bottom. I ran, tumbling down the stairs as fast as I could with her behind me, screaming at me to hurry and get out into the yard.

It was barely light, and cold. All I had on was a string vest and little khaki panties, which were what she'd given me to sleep in. The cobbles were wet with dew, and the carthorse, Mabel, was looking at me as I huddled into myself shivering and wishing I had the long nightie I'd been made to wear as a servant.

Annabelle came striding out after me. She was in full uniform, immaculate, except for a slight smudge where her perfectly polished boot had come into contact with my flesh.

'Stand to attention! Shoulders back, chest out!' she roared. 'Get your arms away from your tits!'

I obeyed, fast. My thigh was already smarting and I was sure there'd be a bruise coming up. Kicking me seemed really unfair, but I wasn't going to complain. She walked up to me, looking down at my near naked body with an expression of disgust. I was shivering with shock, cold too, and I could feel my nipples poking out through the holes in my vest.

Her stick was about three feet long, of polished wood and thicker than the cane she'd used on me. She began to poke me with it, adjusting my stance until it was to her satisfaction, then she walked around me, inspecting me. I kept thinking she was going to hit me with the stick, but in the end she put the brass tip under my chin, tilting my head up until I was looking into her eyes.

'You will remain here,' she said. 'You will remain here and you will not move until your are ordered to do so. Is that clear?'

'Yes, Miss,' I answered.

'Yes, Sergeant!' she screamed and brought the baton around, really hard, on to the back of my thighs.

I went down, clutching at my legs and gasping with the sudden pain.

'Get up!' she yelled. 'You are pathetic, Birch, a grovelling little worm! What are you?'

'Pathetic, M– Sergeant, a grovelling little worm.'

I thought she was going to hit me again but she stopped and once more tilted my chin up.

'You will obey orders,' she went on. 'You will obey them without hesitation or comment. You will do what you are told, when you are told to do it. For now, stay here.'

'Yes, Sergeant,' I answered.

She ducked quickly down, snatching hold of my panties and jerking them to my knees to leave my bum and pussy showing as well as my boobs, just as I'd imagined it in my fantasy. With that she left, walking briskly back into the house. I stayed still, feeling bewildered, and silly too, standing there in my vest with my panties at half-mast. My humiliation was welling up, fast, and I already felt close to tears.

My only consolation was that there was nobody to watch me in my embarrassment – well, only Mabel, but that was bad enough, with her huge brown eyes staring placidly at my near naked body. On the other hand, I was pretty sure that if Annabelle wasn't watching me from the house then Marcus would be.

I had no way of gauging the time, except to watch the sun climb slowly into the sky beyond a bank of scrub. It was still cold and I was covered in goose-pimples, while my nipples just wouldn't go down. I needed the loo too, and was wondering if Annabelle's sadism extended to expecting me to do it into my lowered panties. I was fairly sure I knew the answer, and I wouldn't have dared move, but Marcus appeared before it was too late. I stiffened up, trying not to squirm, my thighs together.

He was in the same smart blue and red uniform as before and, like Annabelle, he had a baton, shorter but even thicker. I tried not to look at it, expecting it to be applied to my bum or legs at any moment. He didn't hit me but gave me the same lingering inspection as she had, walking slowly around me. My bladder was getting bad and, worse, I could feel pressure up my bottom, which was bad news.

I could imagine it all coming out and the thought was making my face burn, but I was determined not to give the game way. One thing I was pretty sure of: if I asked to relieve myself he'd let me, in my panties. He'd also probably leave me standing there in a puddle of my own mess and call Annabelle out to see. Then I'd get punished for it.

So I stayed still, staring dead ahead and trying desperately not to squirm. Twice Marcus walked around me, peering at my naked body from inches away. When he was behind me the second time he took a handful of my bum, squeezing it and kneading the flesh before slipping a finger down between my cheeks to tickle my anus and push briefly into the little hole. I held still, my face scarlet with blushes, praying he wasn't going to decide to sodomise me, not with the state I was in.

He didn't, but came around to my front and put his finger in my mouth. I sucked. With his finger clean, he began to molest me, exploring my breasts and tweaking my nipples through the string vest. Because I'd been fingered, my bottom hole felt loose, and I knew I really couldn't hold on much longer. He went on exploring me, pushing the tip of his swagger stick into the groove of my pussy and rubbing directly on my clit.

If he made me come I was going to wet myself, probably worse. I struggled not to think of sex, or water, staring at the stable roof with tears of frustration and shame welling in my eyes. It was so cruel, and what was about to happen to me so unbearable, that it was impossible to stop myself and the tears began to roll

77

down my cheeks as his baton probed deep between my sex lips.

I cried out, I couldn't stop myself, a desperate sob, my lips coming apart of their own accord. Immediately he stopped masturbating me, gave me a final leer of contempt and turned on his heel.

'Breakfast, Birch, look sharp,' he said as he reached the door, not even bothering to turn around.

I ran, not to the kitchen, but to the loo, tripping over my panties and kicking them off because there was no time to pull them back up. Inside I let go the moment I was on the seat, with my mouth wide open in sheer, blissful relief. It felt so nice, with my pussy gushing pee and my bottom hole wide open to let it all slowly out. I already wanted to masturbate, just from the strength of feeling they'd given me, especially after the way Marcus had handled me. I would have done as well, but I heard Annabelle's footsteps outside and hastily finished up, not wanting to be caught.

She tapped on the door with her stick, ordering me to get on with it. I cleaned up and went into the kitchen, where breakfast had been laid out for me. There was a great bowl of porridge, covered with sugar, already on the table. A frying pan was ready too, with a big blob of lard in it and food laid out on the side – three great fat sausages, four rashers of bacon, four eggs, about half a black pudding, a loaf of bread, butter and a large can of beans.

My immediate reaction was to say that I'd rather have a bowl of cereal, but I kept it to myself. If they wanted me to eat the sort of breakfast a long-distance lorry driver would consider heavy, then it was best to do it and not complain. The alternative was undoubtedly a smacked bottom and probably some sort of humiliation too, after which I'd be made to eat it anyway, only out of a dog bowl or off the floor.

I was learning, learning to behave the way Annabelle wanted me to, and I knew it, but I did as I was told anyway. The porridge was all right, but filling, and I'd already had as much as I wanted before the end. I tried to take my time over the frying, but I kept thinking Annabelle was going to come in and find fault and ended up cooking it all together in the pan, which made a real mess. I ate it anyway, feeling more and more bloated until, by the time I'd forced the last forkful down my throat, my stomach was swollen into a hard ball and very uncomfortable. A mug of coffee only made it worse and I ended up clutching my bulging tummy and praying that they were going to make me polish boots, or anything, so long as it didn't involve moving around. I was still sitting like that when Annabelle came back.

'Come on, you pig, get your face out of the chow,' she snapped. 'And where in hell are your panties?'

'Outside,' I answered, 'sorry, Sergeant, I –'

'Over the table, now!' she barked.

She didn't give me any option, grabbing me by the scruff and throwing me face down on to the table. My boobs had gone right in the plate I'd been eating from and I felt them squash in the mess of grease and egg that I'd left. An instant later her stick came down across my bottom and I yelped in pain, then again, and a third time and she gave me my sudden, perfunctory beating.

'Outside, get them on, clean up,' she ordered. 'Dormitory, two minutes.'

I ran for the yard, scrambling into my slightly muddy panties before making for the bathroom. My boobs were smeared with egg and cold fat, which I tried to get off with soap. I was still trying to get enough lather when Annabelle appeared in the doorway, looking more disdainful than ever.

'So, we have a slow learner, do we?' she said. 'Are you stupid?'

'No, Sergeant, I –'

'You are stupid,' she cut me off, 'very stupid. Two minutes I said, and two minutes I meant. Attention!'

I jumped, standing rigid as I had before, wondering if I was about to get the degrading fate I'd imagined in my fantasy and have my head flushed in the toilet.

'Eyes front!' she snapped. 'Now stay still and do not move so much as a millimetre. Do not speak, either.'

She put her stick down and went to the cupboard, pulling out a heavy scrubbing brush, which looked more suitable for the floor than human skin. A bar of carbolic soap followed. I could only watch as she went to the sink, ran the cold tap on to the brush and smeared soap on to the bristles. Coming back to me, she put the brush down and tugged up my top, over my boobs and then off. My panties followed, leaving me nude, my chest still smeared with soap and food.

I was scrubbed down, hard, between my breasts and over them, even on my nipples, which hurt crazily as the coarse bristles scraped across them. She did my belly too, pressing on the bulge, which nearly made me sick, and my pussy for good measure. By the end, my whole front was tingling, but she wasn't finished. Pushing the horrible brush into my face, she scrubbed that too, leaving it stinging worse than my breasts.

I did manage to stay still, or pretty still. By the end, I'd been forced to close my eyes and I had no idea what she was doing, until a wet, freezing flannel was slapped across my chest, right over both boobs. I yelped at that but she took no notice, smacking me again, this time right in my face. It hurt and I squeaked but was told to shut up and had to endure having my breasts, belly, pubic hair and even my face whipped until she was satisfied.

When I finally opened my eyes I found that the whole front of my body was bright pink from face to thighs. I was trembling and very hot, wishing I'd tried harder to obey properly. I also expected a beating, but she turned her back on me, pausing only to wash her hands before collecting her stick and marching out. I followed, quickly, up the back stairs to my room, where I saw that fresh clothes had been laid out on my bed.

'Dry yourself,' she ordered, flicking her stick at a ridiculously small towel. 'Into panties and vest and stand to attention by the bed. One minute.'

This time I didn't linger, just dabbing at my wet body with the towel before scrambling into a fresh pair of the tiny khaki panties and a string vest identical to the other. She nodded as I got to attention, checking her watch. Her hand went to her top pocket and she took out a small yellow notebook, in which she made a mark.

'As you know,' she said, 'I believe in the benefit of knowing a punishment is coming, and of waiting for it. Every error you make will be entered in this book. In due course you will be made to regret your stupidity and laziness. Understood?'

'Yes, Sergeant.'

'Good. I think you are learning. Already you have three marks, one for making odd noises while being inspected by Lieutenant Yates, one dress misconduct and one time-keeping error. It will be a long day, Birch, so I suggest you do your best to improve.'

'Yes, Sergeant. I will, Sergeant.'

'We shall see. Now, pay attention. You have four uniforms. First, your number one dress uniform – scarlet jacket, blue skirt – here.'

She pointed her stick to the first of four sets of clothing laid out on the bed. It was the same as the one Marcus was wearing, only a female version and, as far as I could make out, my size. A beret went with it, and there appeared to be some quite smart underwear beneath.

'Second,' she went on, 'number two dress uniform; third, barrack dress.'

These were less smart, khaki and dark green respectively, but as neatly pressed and folded and also with berets and underwear. The last set was different, a cotton shirt and trousers in dull green, no underwear, but a pair of boots set out on the floor in front of it.

'Denims,' she said, 'which you will now put on. Two minutes, look sharp.'

She stepped back and I began to dress, as fast as I could. It fitted me, and I realised that they'd had it all made up to order, which gave me an odd feeling of gratitude that they should go to so much effort and expense just to bring me to my knees.

I managed to dress in the two minutes I'd been given, only for Annabelle to criticise my bootlaces and the way I'd buttoned my collar. Another mark went in the book, which I watched ruefully, wondering just what sort of punishment they had planned for me. Ready, I was marched smartly downstairs and out on to the lawn, where Marcus was waiting with his hands folded behind his back. I was put to attention.

The sun was fully up, and it was getting hot. They spoke together for a while, ignoring me completely, until Marcus glanced at his watch and said it was time to collect Sophie from the station. The morning had gone so fast that I'd forgotten Sophie was coming, and I was extremely glad she was. With Marcus gone, Annabelle came back to me, again using her stick to tilt my chin up.

'So, it seems you're all mine for a while,' she said. 'Now, I'm supposed to give you a taste of drill, which I shall, among other things.'

I've always hated the thought of army drill. It always seems so facile, with the endless shouting and repetition. I'd also managed to avoid it, but not any longer.

Not that Annabelle's version would have gone down well at my school, except with the boys. For a start I was made to undress as I did it, losing a piece of clothing for every mistake I made. As I had no idea what any of the commands meant, this didn't take long. My top was off almost before I'd started – for moving off on the right foot, both shirt and vest. That left me with my bare boobs jiggling up and down as I was marched back and forth, round and round, with Annabelle yelling orders at me so fast that they were impossible to follow.

She seemed to like me topless and, despite several mistakes, I was left that way for quite a while. Not that I expected any leniency and, sure enough, after turning the wrong way, off came my trousers. I was made to put my boots back on and drill in just my panties, which not only lasted a long time but involved a lot of fondling of my bum and boobs before they too came off. I was nude, or almost nude, and having the huge, heavy boots on and not a stitch beside left me feeling not only exposed but ridiculous.

When I was put at ease I thought it was over, only to discover the position was ideal for Annabelle to get a finger up my pussy. I was forced to stand stock still as I was finger-fucked, then masturbated, as Marcus had done. Inevitably I came and just as inevitably I got a black mark in her book for it.

Next it was something called beasting, forced PT, really fast, with press-ups, and all sorts of bends and jerks, most of which left me in thoroughly exposed and rude positions. Occasionally she would slap me across my bum or legs, sometimes on my boobs or even in the face. She also came behind me while I was touching my toes, pushing the head of her stick up my pussy and then making me suck my own juice from it.

When she finally grew bored of exercising me, I was running sweat and already exhausted. I was ordered indoors, which I was hoping meant the end of it, only to be taken up to my room and made to do something called change parade, which was equally beastly and nearly as exhausting.

It involved getting in and out of my uniforms as fast as I could, and being inspected each time I was dressed.

She made me use my number two dress uniform and my barrack dress, first given two minutes to dress, then three to change to the other uniform, then two to change back, and again, and again. Inevitably I got in a tangle, failing first to meet my time and then the inspection once I was ready. More marks went in the book.

At last I was ordered into the shower. Annabelle watched, gloating and occasionally prodding me with her stick. Back in my boots, I was marched outside and stood nude on the lawn for a while before at last being allowed to dress when we heard the sound of their car in the distance.

By the time Marcus appeared I was just as I had been when he'd departed, at attention on the lawn. Annabelle went off to deal with Sophie and I was left, sure I was being watched and not daring to move.

At last Sophie was marched out. Like me, she was in the green denims, which did look good, with her little fat breasts pushing out the shirt and the trousers tight around her bum and up between the lips of her pussy. She was drilled in front of me, but neither made to strip nor punished, and she was a lot better. It was obvious she had had some practice, which left me with the certainty of being the one who got picked on. Sure enough, when it came to drilling together she knew what she was doing. For some reason the commands were different and I messed up again. Yet another mark went into the book and I was made to stick my bottom out for a couple of swift swats of Annabelle's stick.

The day had turned hot and still, leaving me sweating and thirsty in the sun. Stood at ease with Sophie on my right, I waited, wondering what horrible punishment I was going to be given for my endless stream of mistakes. Whatever it was, I hoped they let me rest first, at least for a while, because what with the enormous breakfast and all the marching and jumping up and down I was feeling dizzy and slightly sick as well.

'Very well,' Marcus announced as he came to stand in front of us, 'I trust that has warmed you both up. Now, I think a little competition is in order. Follow me.'

Annabelle yelled at us and we went, marching down a gentle slope to the bottom of the valley, which was thick woodland. A track led into it, just two deep ruts in the mud made by caterpillar tracks, which opened out into a clearing. The first thing I saw was the digger, because it was brilliant yellow. Everything else was mud coloured.

It took me a moment to realise – because I hadn't seen anything of the sort since I was at school – that it was an assault course, with obstacles made of wood, and rope, and water, or rather mud. In fact it was mostly mud. There was a high wall, made by stacking old railway sleepers between two uprights, with a rope dangling down one side. There was a rope walkway, a good ten feet off the ground and over a pool of mud. There were telegraph poles across another mud pool. There was a great concrete pipe, with a little stream flowing through it. I knew full well who was going to be doing it – me – and it absolutely terrified me.

'This,' Marcus stated as we were once more lined up, 'is something I've been working on for the last couple of weeks. Since you first came up here, in fact. As it has been built for you, I trust that you are going to appreciate it. Certainly you are going to make full use of it. Sergeant, if you could explain the problem.'

'Sir,' Annabelle answered, stepping forward and pointing at a rope ladder suspended from a nearby tree. 'Right, Birch and Cherwell, this is what is going to happen to you. You are going to complete this course, twice. Whoever reaches the end first will then be dismissed to mess. The other will complete the course a third time before they are taught to try a little harder in future. Go.'

That was it, and it took me by surprise. Sophie had responded immediately and reached the rope ladder first, so I had to wait until she had reached the little wooden platform in the tree before I could even start. From then on it was hopeless. I was already tired, and when it comes down to it I suppose I'm a bit of a coward.

I nearly slipped off the rope walk, which would have meant a ten-foot fall into a pool of muddy water. That had me close to tears, and if swinging down wasn't too bad then the log was, because halfway across it twisted under me and set me headlong into the mud. I managed to save my face, but not much else. I was soaked, my top plastered to my chest, showing every contour of my breasts as if I'd been in a wet T-shirt competition, only run by perverts. My trousers were as bad, clinging to my bottom and tight up my pussy, leaving nothing to the imagination.

Annabelle was yelling at me, calling me pathetic and weak as I struggled up, then ordering me to do the log again. I went back again and fell off again, but on the third time I succeeded, by crawling slowly along on all fours and ignoring the taunts from Annabelle.

Sophie is smaller than me and maybe two stone heavier – facts which Annabelle kept pointing out, ignoring how hard she'd worked me before. That seemed so unfair and, as I slipped and stumbled through the mud, I could feel my tears getting closer and closer. I'd known it would be me who got picked on, it always is, but it's not my fault I'm no good at that sort of thing.

Annabelle was really screaming, but I just couldn't bring myself to do it fast. In fact I could barely bring myself to do it at all. I was scared and exhausted and the more Annabelle shouted at me, and the further Sophie got ahead, the worse it was. I was soaked too, wet through, and plastered with mud, while the sick feeling in my stomach was getting steadily worse.

In the big pipe Sophie was right behind me, and she reached the wall first, forcing me to wait to use the rope.

I was lost after that, confused and miserable and sick, staggering slowly on in blind obedience, back up the rope ladder, on to the rope walk, down the swing and the log and straight into the mud pool beneath, face first.

I just lay there, my face plastered with mud, my body aching and filthy. The tears had started to come and all I could manage was a broken sob as Annabelle came to stand over me. She reached down, grabbing my belt and pulling me up on to the side of the mud pool. A hand went under my tummy and my trousers were worked open, then jerked down, my panties with them.

Bare bottomed in the slimy mud, I was given six hard swats of her stick, leaving me tearful and more broken than ever. She lectured me as she did it, calling me useless and stupid in between whacks at my bottom. With my bottom burning from the strokes, I was made to stand still with my trousers and panties around my knees.

I was told to pull them up but not to fasten them. She then soiled me. I was made to hold out the back, down which she dumped several big, double handfuls of slimy mud, right into my panties. My front was then given the same treatment and the filthy, lumpy mess rubbed into my bottom and pussy before I was sent back on the course with a slap.

It felt awful, with the mud hanging heavy in my panties as if I'd fouled myself and making disgusting squelching noises as I ran. It was dripping out too, down my legs and into my boots, making me even more uncomfortable. I could even feel it on my pussy, and when I slipped and sat down hard on my bum some went up, squeezing up the creases of my bottom and sex, and even up the hole.

Sophie had finished and was standing watching me as I went on, through the pipe and over the wall, which I only just managed. Annabelle simply flicked her stick at the rope ladder, indicating that I should continue. I staggered on, the muck squelching in my panties and dribbling out of my trouser legs. I climbed, shaking with exhaustion, clawed my way across the rope walk and swung down. The log I did with my legs cocked to either side, ignoring the extra mud being squeezed into my already stuffed pussy hole.

I still fell off, right in the mess, smearing my top to my breasts and soiling the last clean bit of my hair. I really felt that I couldn't go on, but there was no mercy, with Annabelle screaming at me to hurry up and threatening another beating if I didn't. I tried, struggling up out of the mud and back to the start of the logs. Again I tried, and again I fell in, and this time I knew that there was no going on.

All I could do was kneel in the mud, clutching the log with the tears streaming down my face and a huge lump in my throat. Every part of me was brown, head to toe, filthy with mud. Somewhere along the way my top had torn, the vest too, and one boob was showing, as brown and filthy as the rest of me. I could feel the mud down my trousers too, bulging obscenely in the seat of my panties, cold and soggy up my pussy. My head was spinning and I was mumbling to myself, repeating over and over that it just wasn't fair, until the lump in my throat rose up and I emptied my breakfast over my chest and into my lap.

That was the last straw. I just slumped into the mud. There was liquid trickling from the side of my mouth and I could feel my bare breast in the warm sick, but I just didn't care. I was completely limp, beaten both mentally and physically and no more able to get back on to the log than to fly.

I was vaguely aware of voices and the squelch of boots in mud. Something prodded me; Annabelle's stick. I rolled over halfway, staring at her and wondering numbly what she was going to do. There was a sneer on her face, showing amusement and contempt too. As I tried to turn over properly she spat, full in my face, catching me in one eye and across my nose.

'You know what you need to do,' she said. 'Do it.'

'I can't!' I whimpered.

'Do it!'

'I can't, An . . .'

I stopped. For one moment the corner of her mouth had twitched up, into the beginning of a smile. She had broken me, and she knew it, or she thought she did. I shut the only eye I could still see with and drew in a deep breath. I was in an awful state, but it was no worse than having my head down a lavatory bowl someone else had peed in, or not much.

Rolling over once more, I crawled slowly to the edge of the mud pool. As I opened my eye I found that Annabelle was watching, expecting me to get out, but I rolled over as I reached the edge, resting my head on firm soil. Marcus was approaching, with his arm around Sophie's waist, both looking down at me. I returned their stare. My hands went to my torn top, gripping the edges and tearing it wide before pulling up the tattered remains of my string vest to put both my breasts on show. Catching up mud in both hands, I smeared it on my chest, rubbing it over my bare boobs until the nipples were poking up through a mat of brown slime. More went over my stomach and I undid my belt and trousers, opening them and squeezing another handful down my already filthy panties.

I arched my back, lifting my bottom from the muck with a sticky, pulling sound. My trousers came down, pushed off my hips to my ankles. The back of my panties were full of mud and I could feel the weight of it with my bum lifted, an utterly disgusting and truly wonderful feeling. Keeping my bum up, I put my hands to my panty pouch, squeezing the thick, soft filling so that it oozed out of the side and up over my pussy. That left a big bulge over my sex, and I pressed it down, squeezing as much as I could up my hole until I could feel it bulging inside me.

They were watching, fascinated. Marcus was rubbing his cock, with one hand down the back of Sophie's denims. Annabelle looked disturbed, even annoyed. Her fingers were on her tummy, immediately above her belt. I took more mud, two big handfuls, smearing them over my flesh. My mouth came open, wide, to show them the inside, pink and clean in my filthy face. Taking another wad of mud, I crammed it inside, filling my mouth until I could no longer shut it, then more, which I piled on top.

The filthy mess was trickling down over my face, across my chest too, lumps falling occasionally as I breathed, or to the gentle squirming motion I had started as I rubbed my mud-packed panties into the ground. It felt gorgeous, but I wanted them off, so that everyone could see the filth in them and up my pussy.

I did it, rolling my legs up high and whipping them down off my bum to give everyone a good show of soiled, mud-smeared bottom and the packed entrance to my pussy. Only my bumhole was inviolate, and I was determined she wasn't going to stay that way. With my legs high and muddy water dripping over my face and chest, I spread my bum cheeks for them. I put a finger to the hole, finding her slimy with mud, moist and really quite open. The finger went in, in full view, and I began to bugger myself, opening the dirty little hole until I felt ready for a second finger, then a third.

There were round stones in the mud, I'd felt them, big, smooth ones, just right for girls' holes. I groped beneath the mud as I wanked my bumhole, found one, then another, bigger and wider around than the largest cock. Up they went, one after the other, squeezed into my dirty, open ring. It hurt, but I forced them in, stretching my hole until they went in, along with a good deal of mud. With the smaller up my bum it felt good, as if I were being buggered. With the larger it felt better still, bloated and rude. It wasn't properly up either, because my ring couldn't quite close over it. I could feel the smooth surface where it was keeping my bumhole stretched open, and I knew they could see it.

I was ready, and my fingers went to my sex, still with my legs high, showing them everything. I began to feel myself, stroking the mound of my lower belly and touching myself down between my sex lips. My pussy was clogged with mud, my pubic hair thick with it and a solid wad packed into the hole. I began to rub, one handed, putting the other to my chest so that I could smear the mess over my boobs as I masturbated.

My pussy was so hot under the coating of muck, really burning, while the rest of my body felt cool, even my bum, despite the whacking Annabelle had given me. That seemed the best thing to concentrate on, not just the beating, but the whole awful army experience; the humiliation of being made to strip, my fear on the assault course, the feel of having my trousers wrenched down for punishment. I'd failed too, in the end, as I'd known I would, and now I was in the dirt were I belonged, masturbating in filth, soiled and foul, with mud in my mouth and mud up my pussy, showing everything, a filthy, ruined mess for their amusement.

I was coming and, as it happened, the stone began to squeeze from my bumhole. My back arched and my mouth closed, squeezing mud out between my lips and down my throat. I felt my anus stretch, gaping, and I pushed, forcing it out of my bumhole even as the ring was trying to contract, a feeling so utterly wonderfully lewd, but no more so than the feeling in my pussy, with my clit burning under my finger and the mud squeezing from the hole in a fat, filthy worm, which I squashed out on to my sex as I started to choke on my filthy mouthful. I couldn't breath but I was still coming, in complete ecstasy, with the filthy, degraded state I was in not just good, but perfect, the source of the glorious erotic high burning through and through my head until my desperation to breathe finally got the better of me.

Jerking myself to the side, I spat out my mouthful, coughing and gagging until my airways were clear. I could breathe again and, for a moment, that was all that mattered, until I remembered my audience. A lot of embarrassment came with that, but I managed to turn them a shy smile. Sophie had Marcus's cock in her hand, with thick white spunk running down over her fingers. Her trousers were wet over her pussy too, and I doubted it was sweat. Annabelle was the best because she had her hand down the front of her trousers and a glazed expression on her face, with her eyes wide and her lips slightly apart. Suddenly the muscles of her legs tensed, she gave a low moan and I knew she'd come.

To my surprise she didn't look too happy after she'd come, as if she'd felt there was something wrong in allowing herself to show her feelings over what I'd done. She quickly regained her composure, once more the sadistic sergeant, calling me a choice variety of names and sending me to the pump to clean up.

I went gladly, because I needed it, and fast. The thing with that sort of really dirty sex play is that you have to sort yourself out properly afterwards. A wash was the least of what I needed, after having mud in my mouth and up my pussy. I went to the pump first, running over what I needed to do and reflecting that the cleaning up can sometimes be as humiliating and intimate as the act itself.

First I stripped, just dumping my soiled and ruined clothes on the ground. They had come up behind me and watched as I got under the pump, pulling the handle so that the freezing water gushed out over my body. It was cold, straight from the ground, but it was bliss too, at least at first. With my face done, I rinsed my mouth, then douched, which meant rolling up on my back in the trough to get at my pussy, a ridiculous position that made Sophie laugh. The rest of my body followed, revealing a fair number of little cuts and not so little bruises as the mud was washed away to reveal the pink skin underneath. Finishing with my hair, I climbed from the trough and made a weak effort to stand to attention in front of Marcus, saluting. He had a two-litre bottle of spring water, which he passed to me. Annabelle barked at me to get indoors, giving me ten minutes to parade on the lawn in my number one dress uniform.

Unfortunately that was out of the question. She could abuse me as she wished, but I was not going to hurry. Inside, I went to their drinks cabinet and found myself a bottle of over-proof vodka. I drank some, swirling it in my mouth and spitting it out into the kitchen sink before taking a second gulp and swallowing.

Upstairs, I got into the bath and gave myself a proper douche, then an enema. The treatment left my head swimming, but it was necessary. Mouthwash followed, a good scrub of my body and two hair washes, after which I stood in front of the big mirror and carefully cleansed every one of my scratches. I was in a sorry state, especially my bum and chest, while my pussy and bumhole were both sore. It felt good though, and my main feeling as I admired my naked body was pride. My endorphins had really kicked in and nothing seemed to hurt. In fact it just tingled nicely, even my bottom, which was not only scratched and bruised, but decorated with the six broad welts Annabelle had applied with her stick.

Only when I had completed my little health routine did I drink the water Marcus had given me, all two litres, which hardly seemed to touch the sides. Even that wasn't enough and I made a rapid and guilty trip down to the kitchen, for milk and orange juice. That done, I finally went to get dressed, wondering what was intended for me that needed such a smart look.

Smart it certainly was, even the underwear, with a bra, panty and suspender belt set in white, with plenty of lace, along with black stockings with a seam at the rear. The knee-length skirt, in dark blue with a scarlet stripe at either side, a perfect fit on my hips and just tight enough to make the best of my bum, was very demure too. Best of all was the scarlet jacket, which was exactly my size, tailored for me too, just right for my chest and cut to show off my waist and hips. Lastly there was the beret, in the same rich blue with a red cockade and a badge.

Dressed, and with my hair up under the beret, I admired myself in the mirror. I looked good, modesty aside, very smart indeed. With that I felt good, despite the nagging worry that they might have dressed me up specifically so that they could tear me down. On the other hand, the uniform had to have been expensive. I couldn't see them ruining it just for the fun of debasing me.

I knew I had a punishment coming and imagined that the uniform was something to do with it but, loaded with vodka and with my endorphins singing, I didn't really care. They could do as they liked with me, and if it had taken me over an hour to get ready instead of the allotted ten minutes then it was my hard luck.

They were on the lawn, amusing themselves with Sophie. She was nude except for her boots, doing press-ups with Marcus's swagger stick up her bumhole. They let her stop when I appeared and Annabelle started to yell at me, threatening me with all sorts of things. I did my best to stand to attention, but I was struggling not to giggle. Finally she stopped, threw me a last look of disgust and ordered Sophie to go and get into her dress uniform. Marcus walked over to me, Annabelle barking orders at me as he approached.

'Stand to attention properly, Birch! Shoulders back, hands by your side, chest out!'

I obeyed, standing ramrod stiff and staring dead in front of me, not even moving my eyes as he walked to the side. The tip of his crop touched my chin, tilting my head up another degree, then traced a slow line around my neck, tickling the sensitive skin at the nape.

'A disgusting display, Birch,' he remarked, 'really quite revolting. You will, of course, be punished. Also, you will be punished for failing to complete the assault course and for coming in last. A truly pitiful effort, all in all, which warrants chastisement. Don't you agree?'

'Yes, sir,' I answered, still trying not to giggle.

He stepped back, looking at me, more with satisfaction than anything, more like a man admiring a new car than one looking at a girl. Clearly he was anything but revolted, but I refrained from pointing out that he had come over my 'disgusting display'.

'We could beat you,' he went on, 'but I doubt a flogging would have the right effect. You must learn to obey, that is what is important. Therefore, you will stand here, to attention. That is an order. However, there may come a time when you no longer feel able to obey that order. If that time should come, you may return to the house; change and come to me, apologise to Annabelle for wasting her time and I will take you to the station. That is all.'

He strode away, Annabelle following, to leave me alone on the lawn. I stayed still, still buoyant from the drink and the abuse my body had taken. Underneath I could feel my exhaustion, but it no longer seemed to matter. My thoughts were actually clearer than they had been all day, and with nothing else to do but think, I tried to make sense of what Annabelle was doing to me.

She'd had me confused, in a panic, scared and unable to do anything except respond to her orders. It had been an odd feeling, and very submissive, which in the end was why the orgasm had been so good. Out of control can mean uninhibited, and I'd certainly been out of control. What I wasn't so sure about was whether I'd been under her control.

I'd done as I was told and masturbated in the mud, yet she had seemed unhappy about it, which was odd. She'd been excited, yes, and it might just have been that I'd forced her to show her arousal, which I knew she didn't appreciate. It wasn't that, I was sure. She'd been dissatisfied as soon as I'd started, as if it wasn't actually what she expected me to do, despite what she'd said.

So what alternatives had I had? Sexual choices are seldom simple, yes or no, black or white. Rather they exist as a continuum, ranging between practical limits. At one extreme I might have lost it completely, throwing a tantrum and calling her every name under the sun before demanding to be driven back to the station. If so, it would have been the end and she'd have lost me as a playmate. Considering the effort she'd gone to for the sake of my submission that hardly seemed likely.

I might have been cross but not gone so far, but again that was likely to have spoilt things. More likely I would have begged to be let off, pleading for mercy and grovelling at her feet. Beyond that was what I had done, responding to what we both knew I needed and masturbating in front of them. I'd been pretty rude about it too, and she had come over me, so how could I have been more extreme?

It was hard to see how I could have debased myself any further, save for a few really dirty details which simply hadn't occurred to me at the time. Anyway, her dissatisfaction had come earlier, before I'd really got into it. No, it had to be that she'd wanted me to make a different choice, and if it wasn't running away screaming, then it had to be grovelling to her. Suddenly I understood. The bit about obedience was a fake. She didn't want me pliable. What she wanted to do was break my spirit.

It hadn't worked so, instead of whatever piece of sadism they'd had planned for me, I'd been put out on the lawn for another go. The trouble was, I could only lose. They had set no time limit and eventually I had to give in and go back to the house.

I wouldn't be taken to the station when I did. That wasn't what they wanted. They knew I'd beg to stay, and that was exactly what they wanted. I'd grovel and plead and whimper, apologising for not being good enough and begging to be allowed another chance. Eventually they'd give in, probably after a good whacking and Marcus's cock up my bum, or whatever amused them. They risked losing me that way, but they had to. After all, if I wasn't prepared to beg to stay I was hardly going to get my pussy tattooed for her, was I?

It was a pretty wicked trick and my immediate instinct was to give in, only for a sudden stubborn urge to rise up in me. After all, I only had to stand still, and so long as I kept my circulation going by moving my toes in my shoes I'd be all right. At the very least I could make them sit up into the early hours of the morning for their plot to work.

So I stayed still, feeling gradually weaker and less confident, occasionally moving my fingers or toes. Before long I realised that there was no way I was going to make the night. It was hot, and the initial flush of the vodka was beginning to wear off. I was even beginning to tell myself that it was stupid to be so stubborn and that I'd be better off getting it over with when Sophie came out, dressed up in her smart uniform. She was carrying a small table, which she placed at the edge of the lawn, some way in front of me. As she turned back she smiled and winked, which I ignored, fairly sure that Annabelle or Marcus would be watching from the house.

She was laying lunch, French bread and ham, cucumber, baby tomatoes and a bottle of Mosel, which made me realise how hungry I was after all the exercise and losing my breakfast. I knew it was being done to torture me, but that didn't stop me wanting it, and I had to watch as Sophie laid it all out on an immaculate white tablecloth. There was silverware as well, and beautiful glasses, all of which started to bring back my feelings of inferiority. They even had candles, in silver sticks, tall red ones to match our uniform jackets, although it seemed a bit silly in the blazing midday sun.

When she was finished she went to stand at ease beside the table. Marcus and Annabelle came out, both in full dress uniforms, which did look superb, especially on her. I was ignored completely as they started to eat, slowly and daintily, occasionally ordering Sophie to pour wine. I could smell the food, the wine too, and my hunger was growing quickly, thirst as well, despite the amount I'd drunk.

In fact, all the fluid I'd taken in was starting to become a problem. I could feel the tension in my bladder growing, quite fast, and having to watch them was making it worse. For one thing there was the wine, with Sophie pouring out the pale yellow liquid, which made a painfully familiar tinkling sound as it filled the glasses. Another was water, which Sophie had forgotten and was made to fetch. It came in a large, crystal jug, which was stood on the table, twinkling in the sunlight, cool and refreshing. Watching it made me more and more thirsty, while every time Sophie filled their tumblers my urge to pee grew worse.

I was going to wet my uniform if I didn't give in, but I still didn't want to. After all, they hadn't made me drink all the water, never mind the milk and orange, so if I surrendered it wouldn't even be her victory over me, but my own stupid fault. Instead I struggled to hold it, trying not to squirm my thighs too obviously and wincing at the sharp pains in my bladder each time the bottle or jug was poured.

When they finished the Mosel I was so relieved, only to hear Marcus order Sophie to fetch another. She went, and somehow I knew I wasn't going to make it. With my toes wiggling frantically in my shoes I was trying to tell myself that it was all in my head and there was no reason why watery sights and sounds should make my bladder any harder to control. It just wasn't true and, as Sophie hurried back with the tall green bottle, I felt myself start to panic.

I was in pain as she drew the cork, my bladder stinging and my thighs locked tight in my struggle to keep it in. She lifted the bottle, poising the neck over Marcus's glass and out it came, a stream of clear yellow fluid, tinkling into the glass even as my own stream burst out into my panties. I just let go, stifling a sigh as my piddle sprayed out into my fancy underwear and over the front of my skirt, with tears of embarrassment and humiliation welling up in my eyes.

Just pissing myself was bad enough but I couldn't even slow it down and they heard the soft hissing sound, both Marcus and Annabelle turning at the same instant with looks of utter disgust on their faces. They watched me do it, with the stain spreading on my skirt, front and back, and the trickle of hot fluid running down my stockings and into my shoes. My face was burning with blushes, but I could no more stop it than a tidal wave and just let it all come, until my shoes had begun to overflow and it was trickling over the sides, while it was dripping from my sodden panties and the hem of my skirt.

They watched me until I'd finished, then calmly went back to their lunch, Marcus making some remark which I didn't catch but which I was sure was at my expense. Annabelle gave a light laugh in response, shaking her head in amusement and disgust at my behaviour.

I was left there with the pee-soaked material cooling against my skin, feeling utterly humiliated and very,

very sorry for myself. My shoes were completely full of it and I was wiggling my toes not just for the sake of my circulation but in discomfort, feeling the squashy, pee-soaked nylon around them. My brief burst of confidence had faded and I was back where I'd been before, vulnerable and small, very small indeed next to my mistress and master.

What seemed most unfair was that Sophie was getting a far easier ride. They obviously wanted her too, but Annabelle always seemed to favour her, or at least persecute her less. I'd been punished more, and degraded more, and now I was being made to stand to attention in clothes soaked with my own piddle while all she had to do was serve lunch.

I changed my mind when lunch was over. Marcus and Annabelle had sat back, sipping their wine and talking, never looking at me, but occasionally glancing at Sophie. Marcus said something which seemed to amuse Annabelle and she took out her book. I listened as all my faults were read out, then Sophie's. She had made far fewer mistakes and was looking smug as the shortlist was read out, at least until Marcus casually announced that, as I was in disgrace, she would have to take my punishment for me.

At that she complained, which was a big mistake. Annabelle stood up, suddenly, knocking her chair back. Sophie started back, but too slowly. She was taken by the scruff of her neck and forced down over the table, squealing frantically as Annabelle yelled at her. Her bum was towards me and I watched in delight as her skirt was pulled up, exposing her wriggling buttocks inside lacy white panties. It was great to see her getting it and I was trying hard not to smile as her panties were wrenched down and her wobbling, bare bottom was put on show.

I could see her pussy, shaved pink and bare as she usually is, as Annabelle started to spank her, still yelling at her, making the plump cheeks dance and spread. That made her kick and showed off her bumhole, which is so important for a beaten girl and made me yet more excited. Despite her struggles she was held down easily, and soon her bum was rosy pink, then red, at which point Annabelle stopped, exchanged glances with Marcus and nodded.

Sophie was taken by the thighs and humped up on to the table, her ample bottom pointing skywards and her panties in a tangle around her thighs. Annabelle held her tightly while Marcus extracted one of the candles from a stick, prodded it into the soft butter and stuck it unceremoniously up her bottom.

She squealed at that, like a stuck pig, but not nearly as loudly as she squealed when the first drop of hot wax landed on her bare pussy. Marcus told her to shut up and laid his swagger stick across her bum. The blow spattered wax across her bottom, making her squeal again and start to kick out. They took her by the thighs and hair and held her in place, forced her to stay still with her bottom the highest part of her body and the candle pointing vertically up in the air.

Her struggles subsided, but she was panting hard, and crying out every time fresh wax caught her skin. They let go after a moment and she stayed put, a human candlestick, as they went back to sipping their wine, their chairs pulled out so they could watch Sophie in her torment.

I was watching too, fascinated and horrified at once, sorry for her yet delighting in her pain, and also, deep down, wishing it was me in the same sorry pose. It was a thick candle and there was plenty of wax running down on to her punctured bumhole and dripping over her pussy. As each drop fell on her bare skin she jumped and squeaked, and at each squeak Annabelle brought the stick down across her bum, dislodging fresh drops of wax.

I knew she'd do it and, sure enough, before long she had reached back, rubbing at her little fat sex lips to bring herself off in her distress. They let her, watching, Annabelle using her stick, Marcus with his cock sticking out of his fly. With her masturbating the wax really started to fly, the candle shaking as her bumhole moved and flicking drips over her cheeks and on to her pussy. I saw a bit go right in her hole and another landed on her clit, just as she was dabbing her fingers down. That was too much and she screamed, bucking her bottom frantically up and down as she went into orgasm, shaking and quivering and babbling into the table cloth until at last it was over.

She stayed in position even after she'd come, once more fully obedient. The candle started to squeeze from her bum and Annabelle caught it, then nodded to Marcus's cock. He responded with a grin, catching hold of it as he got to his feet. They took Sophie, rolling her over on to her back among the remains of their lunch. Her jacket and blouse were pulled open and her fat little breasts popped free of her bra. Marcus's cock was put in her mouth, then up her pussy, fucking her as she lay spread on the table.

Annabelle took the candle and began to drip wax on to Sophie's naked breasts as Marcus fucked her, coating them in shiny red caps with the nipples making humps at each centre. I thought he was going to come in her, but he pulled out and, as he pressed his cock into the butter, I realised that he was going to bugger her.

Well he'd done it to me and he'd spunked up my bottom, so that was fine. Sophie moaned as a buttery finger was slid up her back passage but made no effort to resist, just jerking to the pain of the wax as it dripped on to her breast skin. He rolled her legs up, spreading her bumhole. I saw her expression change as the head touched her hole, then her mouth grow wide as it went up, stuffed, slowly but firmly up her back passage until his pubic hair was pressed to her wax-smeared pussy.

He had her by the legs, admiring her body as he buggered her. Annabelle had started to respond too, doing her sneaky little masturbation bit with one hand down the front of her dress skirts. I was being ignored completely, with Annabelle's back turned to me, and it was more than I could resist.

I tugged up my skirt, stuffed my hand down into my pee-soaked panty crotch and began to masturbate, urgently, to make sure I came before they saw what I was up to. It didn't take much, not with Sophie spread out on the table, her beautiful uniform in disarray, spanked, waxed and finally buggered, with a big, fat cock up her bottom while she writhed in a blend of pain and ecstasy.

I made it, moments before Annabelle, coming with as little fuss as I could manage. My knees buckled under me as my self-control went and I finished off on the lawn, kneeling, but still with my eyes locked to Sophie's body. Annabelle had dropped the candle and was coming too, the same way I was, on her knees with her fingers down her panties. That was good, and even with my orgasm still running through my head there was the delicious thought that underneath she and I were the same – sluts.

That didn't stop me getting up as fast as I could, and fortunately for me Marcus chose that moment to come, whipping his cock out and spraying it all over Sophie's tummy, which Annabelle watched, still rubbing at herself. By the time they became aware of anything other than their own pleasure I was back at attention, although once again struggling to keep a smile off my face.

If peeing myself had made my ordeal easier, the same was not true of masturbating. My legs hurt and by the time Sophie had tidied herself up and cleared away the lunch I was starting to feel dizzy. Annabelle watched me for a while, perhaps expecting me to give in, but eventually grew bored and went back inside.

I knew I couldn't last much longer but, oddly, there was no urge to surrender, or really to do anything at all, but just to stand there, with the world growing slowly less and less distinct until at last everything slipped away to one side. I'd fainted, and I never even felt the ground when I hit it.

# Four

I came round in the attic room, lying on the bed. Annabelle and Sophie were looking down at me, their faces full of concern. I managed a weak smile, raised my head a fraction and then collapsed back.

It took a moment to remember anything, but it came back, the army fantasy, my feelings of insecurity and fear, the exercises, masturbating in the mud, being made to stand to attention, wetting myself, watching Sophie punished, fainting. I sat up, expecting Annabelle to start yelling at me again. She just smiled, looking slightly guilty as she held out a mug of tea.

I took it, my hand shaking as I grasped the handle. I still felt weak, and very sore, but there was a feeling of triumph growing inside me, and of having passed a test, or a barrier. Drinking the tea, I let my senses slowly return to normal. I'd been out for a while because the light coming in at the window was butter yellow. I had vague memories of coming round before and of being undressed and put to bed, but I was by no means sure if that had been a dream. In any case I'd been put in a nightie, the long, warm one I'd worn as a servant.

My uniforms were gone, the military thing done with, for me anyway. Already it seemed like a nightmare, all my suffering and all my ecstasy unreal. Normally after a heavy scene my only regret is that my body won't be up to any more for a while. Now it was very different, and if I felt I'd passed a barrier then I also felt scared at the prospect of going back.

'Are you all right?' Annabelle asked.

'Fine,' I answered, 'just a little weak.'

She kissed me, and all of a sudden I felt utterly, pathetically grateful to her. All her cruelty, all of her stern, cold image was gone as she gave me a gesture of apology for pushing me too far, and I just melted. She was human, after all.

'Thank you,' I said, 'and thank you for the . . . for the military discipline as well. It was really strong.'

'Did you learn anything?' she asked.

'Yes,' I answered truthfully.

'About your nature?'

'You were right about my problem with obedience,' I admitted. 'I learnt that I can reach a point where I'll obey automatically rather then because I'll be punished if I don't.'

That was at least partly true, although other people had put me in the same state before, if not the same way. I was sure she'd meant to go beyond that though, breaking me so that I'd grovel and beg for her attention, not just without self-respect, but without self-will.

'You're learning, Penny,' she answered. 'You're learning to be true to your submissive nature, which is very important. There's a long way to go, but you are learning.'

She began to stroke my hair, very tenderly. I smiled and snuggled against her arm, feeling very happy for the way she was treating me and rather bad about not having told her the full truth. After all, she seemed to be genuine about wanting me as her plaything.

'One day, Penny,' she went on, 'you'll be able to surrender completely, with no guilt, or pride, or any of the emotions that get in the way of expressing your submission. There's a secret to it, a secret you can't be told until you're ready. You're not. Nor are you, Sophie.'

'No?' Sophie asked.

'No,' Annabelle said firmly, 'not yet, even though you're a step ahead of Penny. How do you feel when you're naked, especially in front of people?'

'I like to be naked,' she answered. 'It's always felt good, especially in front of other people.'

'And sex outdoors, where you might get caught?'

'That's half the fun. The only things I worry about are the creepy-crawlies.'

'You see, it's natural for you, as a submissive,' Annabelle answered her. 'For me, as a dominant, it is unnatural. Penny, how do you feel about nudity, or being stripped for a punishment perhaps?'

'Humiliated,' I answered without hesitation.

'Why?'

'I just do. I was brought up to believe it's wrong to be naked. My mother used to say I should treat my body as sacred, to be seen only by myself and my husband. I know that's nonsense, but I still feel ashamed of being naked.'

'How can you handle the things you do?' Sophie demanded.

'Easy,' I said. 'It's the humiliation which turns me on.'

'Why?' Annabelle demanded. 'Explain.'

'I can't,' I admitted. 'It's always been like that. My first fantasies were about being put in some sexually embarrassing position. Like tearing my skirt so that I had to walk home with my panties showing. I know it doesn't sound much, but it really used to get to me.'

'I'd have loved it,' Sophie put in. 'What a great excuse to show off to the boys!'

'It would have made me feel utterly humiliated,' I went on, 'but it would have turned me on, just like you, but for a different reason.'

'What if nobody saw you?'

'Oh I always got seen in my fantasies, it's no fun otherwise. Sometimes I'd imagine myself getting caught and having my panties pulled off for a souvenir, even being stripped completely and made to run home in the nude.'

'So you don't mind just being naked?'

'Not indoors, really. It feels naughty if I might be seen, and humiliating if I know I'm going to be seen or if I'm made to show myself off.'

'For me it's always naughty. I just love being naked and the bigger the audience, the better.'

'So I've noticed, slut.'

'It's your way of handling your mother's old-fashioned attitudes, Penny,' Annabelle said decisively. 'You need to get over that.'

I wanted to tell her that she was talking rubbish, that my sense of humiliation was the main drive for my sexual pleasure and that the last thing I wanted to do was get rid of it. After all, what did she think I'd come over in the mud?

The answer was obvious. She thought I'd come over her, the attention she was giving me, the extreme physical sensations she'd subjected me to. With Sophie it might have been true. Not me; I'd done it because she had totally and utterly humiliated me.

She had quite an ego, but I could see where she'd got it from, with a girl as gorgeous as Sophie wanting her, not to mention her devoted pack of submissive men in the clubs. I remembered what Bart had said about the man who claimed Annabelle was the centre of his existence rather than himself. He'd certainly got her number. I'd thought she was playing me so skilfully too, and all the time there had been a basic misunderstanding between us. Not that it mattered, not in terms of pleasure, but it was odd to think that we could really work together without either one of us really understanding what the other was thinking.

'That's the next step for you,' Annabelle said, nodding. 'A submissive woman should feel natural in the nude. For a start you're to come down naked tomorrow.'

She left it at that, taking Sophie with her as she left the room.

Both girls had still been in their uniforms when they'd visited me. Once downstairs they started again, as I could tell from the occasional barked order or squeak of pain or shock. When Sophie brought me my dinner on a tray she was wearing her number two dress uniform, hurried and flustered too. I ate mechanically, thinking about Annabelle and Marcus and my own sexuality, but mainly about Annabelle.

She wanted me in love with her, and more, while he really just wanted me as what Morris Rathwell calls a 'fuck dolly', a girl who has to be sexually available regardless of her own feelings. Annabelle was certainly compelling, making me feel very submissive, and also grateful for the effort and expense that was going into my training. She had really put me in my place, and if she didn't entirely understand me, then she certainly had a knack for finding my weak spots.

I'd felt the pressure on me to submit my will to hers from the first, but it had been a game, one I'm familiar with and which I play to lose. It had stayed that way even during the worst of the military fantasy, and had I gone crawling to her instead of fainting, nothing would really have changed, not for me. I had fainted and she had shown compassion. It was that which made the difference, and now I was no longer sure if I was playing or not.

When Sophie finally came up she was nude, and pink bottomed too, but absolutely exhausted. They'd beasted her, as Annabelle had me, belting her while she did her exercises, then making her do squats on Marcus's cock until he'd come. She was exhausted and flopped into bed, where we had a kiss and a cuddle but nothing more, both too far gone for sex.

* * *

When I woke up I remembered what Annabelle had said about spending the day in the nude. The effect was immediate. I had to take my nightie off to wash anyway, but doing so made me feel incredibly vulnerable because I knew I wasn't going to be putting it back on, or anything else. Sophie got back into her uniform, which made it even worse.

Annabelle and Marcus were downstairs, both in their khaki dress uniforms. They took no notice of my nudity, just ordering us to make breakfast. That didn't stop me being aware of the state I was in and, whatever Annabelle might think, it was impossible not to feel sexually humiliated. After all, Sophie might have been in a subordinate uniform, but at least she had her clothes on!

Some people don't care; I do. By the time we'd cleared breakfast away my fingers were trembling. The military fantasy was obviously continuing and I was worried that it might still include me, with thoughts of being made to do the assault course in the nude and the state it would leave me in. My relief when Annabelle ordered Sophie to attention but told me quietly to sit down was immense.

'Orders for the day,' she announced. 'Cherwell, drill, cleaning duty, kitchen. Birch, day pass.'

'We're going shopping in Milton Keynes,' Marcus supplied. 'Well, I'm going shopping. You're going flashing.'

I froze, with all my fear of exposure and nudity welling up inside me. He meant it, I knew he did, and the relief I'd felt just vanished. I was going to be made to show off my body in front of total strangers, the thing that used to get to me even before I realised how badly I needed to be spanked. Immediately I wished I'd kept my mouth shut, although it was impossible to deny my sexual response.

Sophie made a face, earning herself a mark in Annabelle's book. Flashing was just her thing. She'd

110

been doing it since she was a teenager. So had I, but not of my own choice. I'd always had to be made to do it.

'But I can't just go stark naked,' I protested, once my initial shock had worn off. 'I'll get arrested!'

'Maybe, maybe not, if you stay in the car,' Marcus answered. 'What I aim to do is drive a truck through your fear of being nude. You can wear what you like, but every item of clothing is going to cost you a dozen strokes with a birch rod when we get back.'

'What about my shoes?' I asked, already frantically trying to work out how to get away without showing too much and still avoid a really bad birching.

'As you please,' he answered, shrugging. 'Still, lots of girls go barefoot in the summer. Why pay twenty-four cuts of the birch just to keep your feet covered?'

'Run along now,' Annabelle added, 'you won't gain anything by dawdling.'

I'd have gained precious time before having to show off to the population of Milton Keynes. I'd never been there but I'd seen it from the motorway and I knew its reputation: big and busy, undoubtedly with a huge shopping mall. Also undoubtedly full of bored men who'd just love to watch a girl in an embarrassing predicament, not to mention plenty of youth to laugh at me and older women to make disapproving noises.

My first thought was to dress properly and take my birching. That would have been bra, panties, top, jeans, socks and shoes, eight items. Eight items meant ninety-six strokes of the birch, which was far, far more than I could possibly take. Birch stings like crazy, and it pricks the skin. Ninety-six strokes would leave me with my bottom flayed and, although I knew they would go that far, they'd probably make me take what my bottom couldn't across my back, my legs, even my belly and breasts. I just couldn't face it.

So I was going to have to show off. Barefoot I could handle without a fuss, which saved me forty-eight strokes, half the total. It was still too many. My boobs are small enough and firm enough for a bra not to matter all that much, although I knew my nipples would be perky, which was going to be embarrassing. Embarrassing, yes, but worth avoiding twelve birch strokes for, so no bra. I could lose my panties as well, so long as my skirt was long enough, even though the feeling of not having them on was going to get to me in any case.

What I did have was a summer dress, knee length and very light. It would be obvious I was nude underneath, but I wouldn't actually be showing anything. I was still blushing as I pulled it out of my bag, thinking how easily Marcus would be able to lift it up and flash my bare bum. For that matter he might just yank it over my head and leave everything showing.

I was about to put it on when I had a better idea. Marcus was in uniform, but the week before he'd been in overalls, one piece, thick green cloth. It took me less than a minute of hunting through their room to find them. Putting them on was another matter. They were large, absurdly large. I had to turn the legs and sleeves back and they still looked slack. In the mirror I looked pretty silly, a bit like a girl I'd seen in a one of those baggy clown outfits, only without the pompoms down the front. Silly, yes, but dressed, and at the expense of only twelve birch strokes, which I'd taken before.

Going back downstairs I was feeling pretty smug, if also worried about getting an impromptu spanking for being clever. Marcus just laughed and told me to get into the car.

The mall was everything I'd expected, vast and full of exactly the sort of people I'd have been most embarrassed to have see me naked. I got some funny looks, in my bare feet and paint-soiled overalls while all the other girls were in pretty summer clothes, but it was nothing to what it might have been.

I'd also expected Marcus to make things as bad as possible for me, but he contented himself with pulling my zip down to show off my cleavage, or as much of a cleavage as I've got anyway. It was so hot that I didn't mind that anyway, too much, and there were plenty of girls showing a lot more. I was sent into Waitrose while Marcus disappeared in search of a DIY store for purposes he refused to explain but which I felt sure involved my continued training.

It felt odd being nude under my overalls, vulnerable, but not frightening, so that I was gradually turning myself on. I also felt special because Milton Keynes is a pretty soul-destroying place, which really brought my sense of being naughty and secretive into contrast. I was also thinking of Sophie being put through Annabelle's sadistic military fantasy and feeling very lucky to have escaped.

Back with Marcus, we wheeled our trolleys out into a vast car park. He'd parked in a remote corner, well away from other cars, presumably so as not to risk his paintwork. We'd come out of a different entrance, so I was slightly disoriented, but before too long I realised that we were going the wrong way.

'The car's that way,' I told him as we reached the edge of the car park, a grass slope with some bedraggled bushes at the top.

'I know,' he answered. 'OK, off with them.'

'What, my clothes?'

'What else? You're going to streak.'

'Here!?'

'Here. You didn't think I'd let you get away without even showing a bit of tit, did you?'

'Well, no, but look, I won't just be showing my boobs. I'll be showing everything!'

'You've got no panties?'

'No! I didn't want the extra birching!'

He just laughed, clicked his fingers and pointed at the ground.

'Come on, Marcus,' I babbled, 'I'll get seen. Some-one'll see which car I run to. We'll get reported.'

'Not if you're clever. Stay down among the cars, or find a man and let him fuck you in return for a lift over to my car. If you're lucky he might do it for a blow-job. Now strip, or it's straight to the station.'

I hesitated, but began to strip, crouched down between two big cars. It took seconds, just shrugging the overalls down off my shoulders and kicking them off my feet. Marcus walked away and I was left, nude, squatting down with my arms crossed over my chest and my heart absolutely hammering.

It was a good four hundred yards to the car and there were people all over the place. I was sure to be seen and it was bound to be by some old busybody who'd be straight on the phone to the police. Then there would be the humiliation of being taken down to the station, questioned and whatever else they did to girls caught outraging public decency.

What I wanted to do was crawl under a car and hide, but I knew it would only postpone the inevitable. Marcus's suggestion of dodging from car to car was stupid because I'd have to cross several open lanes to get to his car. The idea of begging help from some kind-hearted man was better, even if he did demand sex from me. Asking a young woman was an even better idea, as I could explain it was just a sadistic prank my boyfriend had played on me.

Unfortunately I couldn't see anyone suitable, but people were coming towards me, two women, both about sixty, in neat, fussy clothes. I could just imagine their reaction on catching me naked and I scurried round to the front of the bigger car, an old Granada, to hide myself.

Crouched low, praying that nobody came over the grass bank, I waited, only to see the indicators flash on a BMW just three cars away as the alarm was deactivated. I felt the panic rising up and forced it back, willing myself not to run. I heard the doors open, the women's voices, then the doors shut once more. The car moved off and I let my breath out.

I couldn't cross the car park, I just didn't dare. I didn't dare ask for help either, I no longer had the nerve. My only chance was the bushes at the top of the slope and after one quick check to make sure nobody was looking I ran up the bank and in among them, hiding myself and only then realising that they were spiky. That was almost the last straw. Not only were the leaves tipped with nasty little thorns, but the ground was spread with rough bark chippings.

My skin was already covered in scratches and little pinpricks, but I didn't dare come out. All I could do was try to reach the car, which meant following the bank, an L-shape some six hundred yards long. I had to stay on my knees or be seen, which meant crawling through the chippings with the plants jabbing into my bare flesh. It hurt so much, and with that and the constant fear of discovery I was quickly in tears, as pathetic as ever.

I made it in the end, scratched and bleeding, sweaty and tear-stained, trembling with reaction, but unseen. Marcus was lounging by the car, with the back door open. I dived in, burrowing in among the shopping bags, which was all I had to cover myself.

'Very cute,' Marcus remarked, looking down at me as he came to shut the back door. 'If we weren't so public, I'd fuck you right here.'

He slammed the back door before I could answer and I was left to try to cover my naked body with two full Waitrose bags as he drove out of the car park. Various hard things were digging into my flesh, but I didn't care, and stayed right down until we were clear and he could speed up.

'You bastard, Marcus!' I managed when I finally found the courage to pull myself up on to one elbow.

'Is that any way to talk to your master?' he answered, but there was laughter in his voice. 'I ought to punish you for that really, you know. In fact I might. You've turned me on and it'll make a good prelude to getting my cock back up that tight little cunt.'

I didn't answer. The overalls were on the back seat and I reached for them, quickly, because we were still in traffic and anyone in a lorry cab was going to be able to see right down on to me. I was still shaking, and it was hard to dress while my pussy was wet and if I'd had the guts I'd have masturbated then and there and let them all see.

We were in Bletchley by the time I was decent, but Marcus didn't turn off on our road. I'd expected punishment, and fucking, but I'd thought it would be back at the farm. Now I realised I wasn't going to be so lucky.

He parked by a canal, in a wide space on the road. It was lonely enough, or would have been at night, and to judge by the number of Durex littering the ground it was popular with the locals. I know the sort of place, where young couples come for sex and the dirty old men hang around in the bushes, wanking while they watch. There's nowhere better to give a girl a spanking, as it's sure to be appreciated, while the nature of her audience makes it all the more humiliating, but again, that sort of thing tends to happen at night.

I thought he'd fuck me in the car, stripped and probably spanked first, so that he could show me off to passing motorists and maybe the odd canal boat. Instead he bundled me out of the back and led me down to the canal. No sooner were we out of sight of the road than I was ordered to drop my overalls around my ankles. I did it, shivering as my body came on show once more, scared and vulnerable in the bright sunlight, but very, very excited.

With everything showing I was made to touch my toes and was spanked, bum to the canal, hairy pussy stuck out, listening for the sound of a boat and

116

squeaking to Marcus's firm swats as they fell. He gave me twenty, hard, leaving me warm and ready. Only when he'd finished did I hear the sound I'd been dreading, the soft chug of an engine. I tried to jump up, but Marcus caught me around the waist, holding me tight with my spanked bottom to the canal. I was really struggling, but he wouldn't let go, and as I heard a shout I realised we'd been seen.

It couldn't have been worse, it really couldn't, not from the point of view of humiliation anyway. The boat was a hired launch, with a party of lads in it, all thoroughly drunk. They began to cheer as they saw us, laughing and telling Marcus to fuck me in front of them. He answered, cheerfully, telling them that I'd been naughty and that he'd had to spank me. That really got them going, catcalling and whistling, some calling him a pervert, others congratulating him and saying he should have beaten me harder. One of them threw a can as they passed, which hit my bum and bounced off, leaving a trail of sticky beer running down between my cheeks.

Marcus called out again, telling them he was going to fuck me. He took me by the hair, dragging me into the bushes with them still watching. Out of sight, I was thrown down on a bed of long grass and cow parsley and my legs were kicked apart as he fumbled with his fly. His cock sprang out and I sat up to suck it, eagerly, utterly humiliated and absolutely desperate for cock. I'd been spanked in public, bare, with my titties swinging as well. It was so rude, and so me.

He got down on me as soon as his cock was hard. I wanted to roll over and show him my bum but he held me by the ankles, pulling my legs high and wide so that he could watch as he fucked me. His cock touched my pussy and went up, really easily, into the creamy, gaping hole. My overalls were still on, stretched taut between my ankles, which felt perfect, the final rude touch as I was fucked in the grass.

I let my thoughts run as he did it, building myself up to the point at which I'd be unable to resist putting my finger to my pussy. I thought about my streak, the way I'd been allowed to lull myself into a false sense of security and then made to do it anyway. I thought about my public spanking and the boys who'd seen it, and the wet, cold feeling of spilt beer trickling down between my bum cheeks. I thought of being thrown in the grass and just fucked were I lay . . .

Marcus came, jerking his cock out of my pussy at the last instant and doing it all over my pubic hair. I reached down immediately, intent on rubbing his come over my pussy as I frigged, only to stop short at the sound of voices, rough, male voices. It had to be the lads we'd seen, who obviously weren't content with just a flash of a spanked bum and a pair of boobs. They were laughing and calling out for us.

'Come on, mate, we know you're around!' one yelled.

'All we want to do is borrow your tart!' another added.

Lads make me feel uneasy at the best of times, but this was awful. Being shown off was one thing, just adding to my humiliation. Actually facing them was quite another. I was cursing Marcus as I tried to struggle into my overalls, and myself, for being such a slut. After all, I could perfectly well have stopped it.

'Into the field!' he hissed, desperately trying to stuff his still erect cock back into his fly. 'Quick!'

There was a cornfield behind us, across a nettle-filled ditch and a barbed wire fence. If it hadn't been for my bare feet we might have made it. As it was I was still hesitating when a row of eager faces appeared in the gap between two elders through which we'd gone for our sex.

We just stood there, looking at each other. There were eight of them and they knew what they wanted, but they really didn't know how to go about getting it.

I hadn't realised how young they were, and if they had plenty of lust then there wasn't a lot of confidence. I was blushing anyway and trying to cover myself. I'd pulled my overalls up, but I hadn't had time to close the zip, so I had to hold the front closed to stop them seeing my chest. At last the biggest of them, a red-haired boy running to fat, stepped forward, taking a long drink from his beer can before speaking.

'How about it then, mate?' he asked, addressing Marcus but with his eyes firmly locked on me.

'How about what?' Marcus answered.

'Your missis, your girlfriend, whatever. Likes to flash it about a bit, does she?'

'I think you've got the wrong idea . . .' he began.

It was his accent that was the problem, pure public school, with all the arrogance that goes with it. They took against it immediately, one of them imitating him and several others laughing in response. That got him angry.

They started to argue and I could see where it was going. Marcus had a lot of courage, but ex-guards or not, he'd spent too long behind a desk and keeping fit by playing squash. Most of them looked as if they worked in factories or on farms, with real muscle from constant hard work. Besides, eight to one was hardly fair odds. I didn't want Marcus getting beaten up, let alone what might happen to me afterwards.

'Look, I'll do it,' I said suddenly. 'I'll pose for you.'

That shut them up, although Marcus was going to say something until he caught my eye.

'Pose?' one of them asked. 'What, like in a porn mag?'

'Exactly. Any pose you like.'

'While we jerk off? I'm no wanker, lady. I want to fuck you.'

'Yeah, right up your posh little twat!'

'Up her arse!'

'Yeah, see how stuck up she looks like that.'

I realised that my accent wasn't doing me any good either, while what inhibitions they'd had were fading fast. Marcus tried to say something and it quickly started to get nasty again, until I was forced to speak up.

'OK, OK, I'll suck your cocks,' I promised, 'and I hope you're proud of yourselves.'

The biggest one answered with a leer.

'Let them, Marcus,' I said. 'It's not going to hurt me.'

'Yeah,' one drawled. 'You sit down over there and watch. We'll show you how it's done.'

'I'm going to spunk in her face!' one said. 'I fucking love that!'

'Yeah, in her face! Let's give her a Bukake bath, like in that Jap video.'

The biggest of them had already freed his cock and was standing over me. Marcus stood back, glowering, but probably grateful underneath. I knelt up, wondering how I was going to feel with eight loads of spunk in my face. The boy pushed his cock up close, so that I could smell the mixture of man and dirt.

'Tits out for the lads, love,' he said, 'then get sucking.'

I shrugged the overalls off my shoulders, letting them fall down off my breasts. Because they were so big on me they went right down, so that I was sitting nude in a puddle of green cloth, with my smacked bottom showing behind. Having been spanked felt very appropriate for what I was about to do, exactly what ought to happen to a girl who lets herself get into a situation where she has to suck more than one cock. With the feeling that it was my own stupid fault, I leant forward and took him in. The others cheered.

He was quite big, with a thick, fleshy foreskin. It tasted disgusting when that started to peel back, but I soon got over it, sucking my cheeks in to make saliva. I gagged a bit as I gulped down the taste, which made them laugh. He'd pulled his balls out, so that as he grew erect it was all sprouting from his fly, a great thick cock and two fat balls in a wrinkled scrotum. His flesh was the palest white, with a ruff of coarse ginger hair sticking out to all sides. I took him in my hands, stroking his balls and masturbating him into my mouth, which brought fresh calls of encouragement from his mates.

There really is nothing quite so sexually obscene as a set of male genitals, especially when the cock is erect and stuffed in a pretty girl's mouth. It's the contrast, of a delicate, sensitive face set against the bloated, ugly penis and swollen, fleshy ball sac. Now I had to do it, eight of them, one after another, and they were going to deliberately spunk in my face.

I wanted to masturbate, but I didn't dare, sure that they'd end up fucking me if I showed I was turned on. Normally I'd have done it, or at least if they'd been just a bit less crude, a bit less basic. I wanted my face spunked in too, just to know how it felt with so many doing it, and to feel the senses of erotic humiliation and disgust I knew it would bring.

The big lad was rock hard in my mouth and he seemed happy just letting me suck on his shaft and stroke his balls. I couldn't have that, in case the others got restless and fucked me anyway, so I drew back, pursed my lips and sucked hard on the head on his cock. He gasped, his cock jerked and suddenly my mouth was full of spunk. Grunting aloud, he jerked it out of my hand, wrenching at the shaft to send the second spurt high up into my hair, the third over one eye, the fourth across my lips before he wiped the last of it across my cheek and stood back.

It felt revolting, slimy and wet, and I had my face screwed up in disgust. One of my eyes was closed and some had actually gone in it, while a heavy blob was dangling from my fringe, until it broke to fall on to my chest. They were laughing at me and cheering their mate for making such a mess, while another was already coming forward, his trousers opened to reveal a pair of purple underpants.

As I opened my mouth he flopped his cock out and straight in. I began to suck, firmly, feeling the first boy's come running slowly down my face as the second came to erection in my mouth. Like his friend he was soon hard, but unlike his friend he wasn't going to take any nonsense about letting me take the first spurt in my mouth.

When he was ready he pulled it out and took a grip in my hair, pulling my head back and jerking his erection frantically, right over my face. I shut my eyes, screwing my face up, listening to their laughter and then warm, sticky fluid splashed over my face, across my nose, into my open mouth, on to my chin and lower, on my neck and breasts as he milked himself over me and his friends clapped and jeered.

The third one was already hard when he got to me, jamming his erection into my mouth and holding me by the ears so that he could fuck my head. I had no control at all and he was deep in my throat, his cock head jammed into my gullet to make me gag. Men love that, those who know the trick, and he came almost immediately, mostly down my throat but over my boobs too, while he wiped his cock in my hair.

Number four made me put on a show, licking his balls and cock shaft as he preened his erection in front of me. I was still doing that when he came, really unexpectedly, a fountain of spunk just erupting from his cock, into my hair and down my forehead and nose.

By then the remaining four all had their cocks out and were jostling for who was going to be next. I decided for them, taking hold of the smallest cock, belonging to the guy who'd first suggested spunking all over my face. He was eager and came in no time, mostly across my boobs, but making me suck what was left out of his cock. The next was a real bastard, making me take it in my open mouth, mix it up with my saliva, then spit my whole filthy mouthful into his hand so that he could smear it in my face and over my breasts. He had a good feel too, until number seven pushed in to get his turn.

Both my eyes were closed, the lids smeared with spunk, screwed up in disgust as yet another stiff cock was thrust between my lips. I began to suck, but he had no patience, and did it all in my mouth, and almost immediately. The eighth took over, another one who liked to hold me still and fuck my head, and as he was doing it there was fresh laughter, then a burst of light from beyond my closed eyelids and I realised they were photographing me.

That was the final humiliation and, as I opened my mouth to let the last man take his cock out and spunk up in my face, I could no longer hold myself back from masturbating. My hand went down my overalls and I found my pussy, wet with Marcus's spunk. I opened my eyes as I began to rub, heedless of the mess, and for my trouble caught the boy's full load right in one. I struggled to blink it out, only to have him wrench my head around by the hair and fill the other with his second spurt. The camera flash went again, and there was more laughter.

It hurt in my eyes, but I didn't care, I was too desperate, too excited. Nine men had come over me, eight in my face, and I was utterly, utterly soiled. My hair was caked with it, may face slimy and wet, my mouth so full it was bubbling out of the sides and trickling down my chin. It was even coming out of my nose, and my boobs were filthy with it, even my pussy was soiled, and I was masturbating in it.

They were laughing at me in my excitement, calling me a tart and a slapper as I rubbed at myself and smeared their mess over my breasts and face. I didn't care, in fact I wanted to be insulted, to be utterly humiliated, and my only regret by then was that their come wasn't dribbling from my pussy and bumhole as well.

I was nearly coming; I knelt back on my legs to show them all my pussy, rubbing frantically, pausing to smear more filth up over my breasts and down on to my belly, then rubbing again as I was called a bitch, a whore, a filthy, fucking pig and worse, as if it was fine for them to spunk all over me but totally utterly, unacceptable for me to actually like it.

I came on that thought, of how they expected me to react with disgust and shame, and there I was masturbating in front of them, totally blatant, as rude as can be, a real slut, and all the time my head filled with exactly the thoughts of chagrin and revulsion they expected me to feel, wanted me to feel. It was glorious, long and slow and wonderful, with every nerve in me alive to the sensations of my body and my head swimming with all the dirty, humiliating things I like best, and learning to accept my nudity be damned.

It was actually quite funny, because once I'd come they were so embarrassed themselves that they left with hardly a word. Marcus wasn't best pleased and we drove back in silence. What had happened had made him feel weak, out of control, which he hated. I didn't mind so much and would have tried to cheer him up if I'd had any energy left.

What he did do was help me clean myself up and make me promise not to tell Annabelle. I wasn't sure why, but he explained that she'd get in a real state over it so I agreed. With her ego I could imagine she might be jealous, even though what I got up to was really nothing to do with her. It seemed best to keep quiet anyway, so I agreed, contenting myself with the prospect of describing the experience to Sophie.

Back at the farm they were still indulging their fetish for military goings on, with Sophie on her knees in her string vest and khaki panties, scrubbing the kitchen floor. I was told to strip, which I did without any real trouble. After all, after what had happened just being nude in front of friends was hardly a problem, and the fact that it was obligatory didn't seem to matter any more.

Of course that was what they were trying to achieve, to shock me out of my hang-up, but I knew perfectly well that given a week or two in a less sexual environment I'd be just the same as ever, getting in a tizzy if the wind caught my skirt.

Annabelle had eaten lunch, pheasant pâté and hot buttered toast, also Sophie, corned beef and mash made up with water and lard. Marcus and I hadn't, so I served him while the others went out to play on the lawn, with more drill, of which Annabelle never seemed to tire.

Lunch restored Marcus's good humour, more or less, and by the end he had me standing still with my hands on my head while he fondled my bottom and sipped a glass of cold beer. I'd eaten the same muck Sophie had, and could have done with the beer, but I was glad he wasn't the moody sort who'd sulk all afternoon over their injured pride.

I spent the rest of the day in the nude, doing menial tasks around the house and thinking about my birching that evening. It's the way they used to whip the boys at Eton, right up to the sixties. Before cane became widely available it was the standard thing in schools, both for girls and boys I imagine. It was given up because of being too cruel, and now I was going to get it.

Annabelle had studied her technique and she did have compassion, some at least. Both are very important qualities for a dominant woman, or man for that matter. Too many think that just having the right attitude makes them an expert. What Annabelle didn't have was her own experience of being on the receiving end, and really, every responsible dominant should know how it feels for their playthings.

She loved to make us watch the clock, and we'd been told it would happen at six o'clock. I'd been washing up tea, while Sophie had been polishing boots. She had no top on, nor her own boots, just her green army trousers, and her face and breasts were covered in smears of boot polish, while her skin was glossy with sweat and her hair in rats' tails. We were called out like that, on to the lawn, and stood together.

Annabelle came over to us, looking Sophie up and down. She liked us in a mess and a smile was creeping on to her face despite her best efforts to look stern.

'Punishments then,' she said happily, pulling her little book from her pocket. 'Cherwell, you are improving, but you're hardly fit. I think we need to get a bit of weight off you. Pull down your trousers.'

Sophie responded immediately and I watched from the corner of my eye as she lowered her trousers to her knees, revealing the standard khaki panties.

'Knickers down,' Annabelle snapped.

Sophie's knickers came down to order and she was left standing naked from the knees up. Annabelle walked once around her, squeezing her bottom, then mine. Back in front of us, she cupped my breasts, running her thumbs across my nipples until they came out. Stepping to Sophie, she gave her the same treatment, weighing them thoughtfully in her hands.

'Fat,' Annabelle said, stepping back. 'Very well, you are both on regimes. Sophie, to get rid of some of that puppy fat. Penny, to shed herself of the ridiculous idea that it is somehow inappropriate for her to be naked. Sophie, what do you weigh?'

'Eight stone ten,' Sophie answered.

'Eight stone would seem a healthy weight for a girl of your height. So, every day, at six o'clock, you will receive a stroke of the cane for every pound over eight stone. You will also receive whatever other punishment you may have earned.'

'Yes, Miss.'

She sounded pretty miserable, and I knew Annabelle had touched a weak spot. Sophie is sensitive about the size of her bottom and boobs, but everyone loves her figure, which puts her in a dilemma. Annabelle's motive was clear. If Sophie's weight was being controlled by someone else then the dilemma went away, and it was one more step towards total submission to her mistress.

'Sophie has decided to stay with us for while,' Annabelle informed me. 'You will do the same, I hope?'

The implication was not to bother to come back if I didn't, although I doubted she meant it. I really had no choice in any case.

'I'd like to stay,' I answered. 'I'll need to make a couple of calls, but it should be all right.'

'Good,' she answered. 'So, we've already agreed you'll need to pay for every item of clothing you wear with a dozen of the birch. Marcus has told me about your little streak in Milton Keynes. Without even any knickers, apparently?'

'Yes, Miss.'

'How amusing. I would like to have seen that. So you get away with just twelve strokes. Now, it's traditional to send a girl out to make her own birch. If you walk a little way down the drive you'll come to an area of scrub. There's plenty of birch there, so pick enough to make a good switch. It has to be at least three feet long and weigh over three pounds. If it isn't you'll just be sent to make another and given your punishment twice, three times or however long it takes, so get it right the first time. Run along. Sophie, touch your toes.'

I ran, with Sophie's squeals of pain as her whacking began loud in my ears. Annabelle was right about the birch. There was enough of it to keep the most dedicated of floggers happy for years, and all young, tall saplings with plenty of upright shoots. Three foot was easy, as I'm five foot two, so each piece had to come over three-fifths the height of my body. Three pounds was harder, as I had no idea how much fresh birch weighs. The result was that I ended up with a huge bunch of twigs that came up to my shoulder.

Running back, I found Sophie still bent over on the lawn, clutching her ankles and with a good fifteen fresh cane welts decorating her bottom. Both Annabelle and Marcus were standing behind her, admiring the view of well-beaten bottom and pouting, wet sex.

'Stand up and cover yourself,' Annabelle ordered Sophie as I approached. 'Right, Penny, up in the cherry orchard, I think. We'll string her up from a tree by her hands, don't you think, dear?'

'Better still, by her ankles, upside down,' Marcus replied. 'Twelve strokes, so let's go for four across her bottom, four across her titties and four across her belly, that should do it.'

I couldn't help wincing. I'd imagined they'd just do my bum, which may hurt, but is undoubtedly the part of a woman's body that responds to beating with the most sexual reaction and the least pain. Well, a few prefer their breasts whipped, but not many. Being strung upside down wasn't much fun either, and I'd be totally helpless.

Sophie was sent for rope and towels, while I was frogmarched to the orchard, Annabelle holding me by one ear and Marcus swishing the birch through the air. They hadn't bothered to measure it, nor to weigh it, but then it was pretty obvious that it passed the test.

The cherry orchard was overgrown, with long grass between quite tall trees. It took a while to find one with a branch at the right height, by which time Sophie had caught up. She had two hanks of thick white rope and a towel. I was told to get on the ground, which I did, my heart getting gradually faster as Marcus tied my ankles together with the towel. The rope went over it, padding my skin, which I was grateful for. My hands were tied behind my back for good measure and to stop me struggling.

That done, they hauled me up, Annabelle and Sophie lifting my body as Marcus hauled on the rope. My legs went up, then my body until I was upside down and clear of the ground, completely helpless, unable to protect myself in any way whatsoever. To make it worse, the blood started to go to my head immediately, and I was dizzy even before Marcus had measured up his swing against my buttocks.

I tensed, the birch swished through the air and my bum exploded in prickling, stinging pain, all over, and also on my thighs and back. I screamed, really loudly, at which Annabelle laughed and called for a halt. She walked off, but not far, coming back with an unripe apple, which was jammed in my mouth, effectively shutting me up.

With me swinging silent and helpless on the rope I was thrashed, three more across my bottom, three on my chest and three over my belly and upper thighs. Each one was like fire, the little crooked twigs cutting into me to leave my skin flushed red and covered with thousands of tiny red marks. It hurt so much, and I was writhing about on the rope, with my teeth locked on the apple, until with the second-last stroke I bit through it. It fell out, leaving me to express my pain with a last scream before it was over.

I was hanging there, panting, looking up at the beads of blood on my breasts and belly. My whole body felt warm, tingling. I hadn't even cried; it had been too sudden, too much of a shock. I felt punished though, beaten and humiliated and ready to accept whatever sexual act was expected of me.

What they did was make Sophie lick me as I hung there, holding my burning bottom with her face pressed to my pussy. That left my face against her crotch, with the green material pulled tight over her pussy, right in front of my face. I could smell her sex, but I couldn't help her, only let her do it to me.

Annabelle and Marcus watched, arms around each other, smiling as I was brought up to orgasm under Sophie's tongue. I nearly passed out when I came, and the pain and stress of hanging from my ankles spoiled the climax, leaving me feeling cheated.

The rope had been tied to the tree trunk and Marcus undid it as soon as I'd finished wriggling. I was lowered to the ground, where I lay, letting the blood flow back into my legs and waiting for the awful dizzy feeling to go away. It had been hard, and a lot less sexual than most punishments, a real lesson, and I was very, very glad that I'd worn only one garment. If they wanted me nude, they could have me nude.

# Five

I slept naked, in Sophie's arms. She been told to wear clothes in bed, to emphasise my nudity. All she had on was an army shirt and her khaki panties, but it made me feel submissive to her, something I'm not sure Annabelle would have wanted, which left me feeling naughty as well, and I ended up masturbating with her panty-clad bottom sat on my face, which gave me a much better orgasm than the one in the orchard.

It wasn't clear what was supposed to happen in the morning, for her anyway. Her uniforms were a mess, so she went downstairs in the same inadequate string vest and tiny khaki panties she had worn the day before. I went naked, feeling very self-conscious, but not about to put myself in line for another birching. Downstairs, Marcus and Annabelle were still in their night things, very relaxed, with no hint of anything military. We made their breakfast, more or less by force of habit, then our own, Sophie taking a small bowl of bran and black coffee.

'Good girl,' Annabelle addressed her, 'keep up the good work and we'll soon have that little tummy off you.'

She reached out to pinch the strip of soft flesh between Sophie's vest and panties, smiling as she did it.

'What are we up to today?' I asked.

'Something to help solve your little problem,' Annabelle answered me. 'First, you said you'd stay?'

'I'd like to,' I answered, 'of course. May I make a phone call?'

I went out into the hall, wondering what I should say to Amber. The truth certainly, as she knew what was going on and any excesses on my part could always be bought at the tip of her riding crop and by my tongue. The problem was that I couldn't say it in their hearing, so I contented myself with a very casual statement about my comings and goings, pretending I was speaking to a flatmate. She answered with a detailed description of what she was going to do to me when I finally got home. That left me trying to hide a grin as I returned to the kitchen, but nobody seemed to notice.

'You're staying?' Annabelle asked.

'For as long as I like,' I answered, 'or at least for as long as you'll put up with me. Quite a while, I hope.'

'Good,' she answered. 'Upstairs then. Today we work on your sense of modesty.'

'Modesty?'

'Get upstairs, you'll see.'

I went, thoroughly puzzled, as short of the bathroom, the bedroom has to be the place in which nudity feels most normal. We'd made the bed, just one of those things we'd learnt to do to avoid on-the-spot spankings, so I lay on the covers, staring at the ceiling and feeling slightly uneasy, if not actually frightened.

Nothing happened for quite a while, although I could hear them moving around downstairs. Finally it was Marcus who appeared, dressed in a thing like a lab coat, only pale green, and carrying a big plastic container. He began to take things out, pulleys, cord, a long metal bar, shiny metal hooks, bits of thick leather. Those I recognised, bondage gear from the collection I'd seen in London.

'Am I going in bondage then?' I asked.

'No,' he answered. 'You're going in traction.'

'Traction?'

'That's right, traction.'

He pulled out the last items from the bag, a huge roll of bandage, plastic sheeting and plaster of Paris. I just lay there staring, not quite believing what they were going to do to me. Bondage is one thing, and I'd already figured out that the pole was a leg-spreader so that I'd constantly have my pussy open and not be able to do anything about it. Having legs put in plaster was something else.

Marcus set to work, ignoring me as he fixed the pulleys and cleats to the beams and threaded the cord into place. There were two pulleys, both double, and as he started to screw one in directly above my head I realised that he was going to do my arms too.

With the fittings in place, he made me get up and spread the plastic sheet on the bed, then went for a bucket. He was still whistling as he began to bandage me, first one leg, then the other, then my arms. I just lay there, taking it, unable to protest. It seemed so extreme as a way to keep me helpless and exposed, yet there was obviously more to it, some medical fantasy and, after all, where does modesty have to be so completely sacrificed as in a hospital?

As he bound my limbs I felt my self-control slip slowly away. With all four done, I was told to hold out a leg, perfectly straight. He began to paint on the plaster. I felt the heat of reaction as it set, and the gradual stiffening, bit by bit until I could no longer move my knee. The second followed, then my arms, with me feeling more open and more helpless until at last I had all four limbs stuck out, stiff and heavy, plastered from my upper thighs to my ankles and from my shoulder to my wrists.

With my limbs rigid, he began to manipulate me like a doll, lifting me into the exact centre of the bed without thought for where he was putting his hands, then having a good feel of my boobs and pussy. I thought he was

133

going to fuck me, and he could have done, without me having the slightest choice in the matter. He contented himself with a feel, before putting the straps around my ankles and wrists and tying each to the dangling end of a piece of cord. Ready, my rigid limbs were hoisted up, one by one, and tied off on the cleats to leave me spread wide on the bed, unable to do more than wriggle my torso. Only then did he pull out his cock.

He knelt on the bed to make me suck him hard, feeling my boobs while he did it. As soon as he was stiff he got down between my legs, held me around my waist and just fucked me, like one of those revolting blow-up dolls, manipulating my helpless body on his cock until he came, deep inside me. With that he tidied up his things and went, leaving me with warm spunk trickling down between my bum cheeks to wet the sheet beneath me.

I lay there for what seemed like ages, completely overwhelmed by my feelings. Nobody who hasn't been tied up tight at somebody else's mercy knows how strong heavy bondage is, even when it's just a game. It's always worse with men, who can do as they like, and fingers and cocks tend to go into holes without much thought for whether they're invited. Not that the girl needs to feel guilty, or even responsible, not when she can't even move. This was worse. I wasn't just tied; all four of my limbs were completely rigid, so that I couldn't even kick and struggle, which I always feel I need to do.

My next visitor was Sophie, who grinned as she saw my open pussy and slid a finger straight up my hole, which shows that women can be as a bad as men. She was in a nurse's uniform, which I'd guessed she would be, and it was a genuine one, which was typical Annabelle. Not that I minded, because it's a lot sexier seeing a genuine nurse's uniform pulled up so that she can be spanked than if it's a tarty fake version you can buy in sex shops.

It was pale blue, tightly belted at the waist and snug on her hips and chest rather than tight, with a pinny at the front. Her hair was pinned up, with a little hat to match the uniform, along with sensible shoes and what were probably tights underneath.

She was also carrying something, which put a lump in my throat the instant I realised what it was: a shaving kit. I am hairy, very hairy, not just around my pussy, but down between my bum cheeks. Being that hairy adds to the humiliation when I'm made to show it off, so I seldom shave. Now it didn't look like I had much choice.

Sophie didn't even bother to ask, but told me to be a good girl and not wriggle as she sat down on the end of the bed. I was told to lift my bum and a towel was slid underneath and, just like Marcus, she used it as an excuse for a feel. She inspected me too, spreading my bum cheeks with her thumbs and tutting as she saw the spunk smeared around my pussy hole and over my anus. I was told off for that, then for being so hairy and making extra work for her.

I felt the sting of humiliation at her words, biting my lip and telling myself that I really couldn't be so pathetic as to start crying before they'd even got to work on me properly. Because they hadn't, I was sure of that. Being put in traction was just a preliminary. There are all sorts of awful medical things a pervert can do to a helpless patient, and I was sure Annabelle had thought of most of them.

Sophie had begun to work a lather up in the white enamel kidney dish she'd brought the shaving things in. She had a brush and a safety razor, but also a wicked-looking cut-throat, which she had put on the bed beside her. All I could do was lie there and wait to be shaved, staring at the ceiling as I felt cold soap touch my lower belly. She worked it well in, all over my pussy, even between the lips. The brush tickled my clit rather

135

nicely, but the soap quickly started to sting and I was soon gasping in reaction.

I was told not to be a baby and had the tuck of my bottom slapped for my trouble, just once. She went back to soaping me, stuffing the brush up my pussy to make sure I got plenty of stingy soap inside me, then going down between my bum cheeks and on to my anus, which stung nearly as much.

Only then did she decide that I wasn't spread open enough for her to get at my bottom crease. She thought about it for a while, made another remark about how inconvenient and unhygienic it was of me to be so hairy, then took hold of the bed and pulled, dragging it along the floor. My arms were immediately wrenched up above my head and my legs pulled high, leaving my bum stuck out and slightly off the bed, with the cheeks wide apart.

Sophie ignored my squeak of protest and gave a satisfied nod. Taking up the razor, she flicked open the blade, deliberately holding it up so that I could see it before lowering it slowly on to my pubic mound. I felt the cold metal press to my flesh and froze, trying desperately not to move as she began to scrape away my pubic hair.

She did it slowly, bit my bit, washing the razor between strokes. I felt my mound denuded, first the bulge so that I had a little hump of bare flesh like a monk's tonsure, then the top, the sides and my lips. All the while my pussy was throbbing with the pain of the soap. I knew I would be red and swollen and I could feel how open I was, and not just because Marcus had fucked me.

With my pussy bald, she showed me how I looked in a mirror, with my hairless mound shiny and pink and my lips puffy and fat. Not that she was finished, quickly going back to work on the hair between my bum cheeks and finishing with my anus stretched between finger and thumb as she did the little nest of fur which surrounds the hole. Only then did she clean me up, washing away the soap and bits of hair with a sponge. Again she showed me how I looked between my legs, with every detail of my sex spick and span, and also wet and puffy with excitement.

'What a pretty little cunt!' she laughed. 'You should shave more often, Penny.'

'I like being hairy,' I said miserably. 'Now it's going to itch like mad.'

'Maybe Annabelle'll make you stay shaved,' she answered. 'Now, a little powder and I'll see about making your lunch.'

'Don't I get a lick?'

'What a disgusting suggestion! Honestly, how dare you? I've a good mind to report that remark to sister!'

'Play fair, Sophie, you can see the state I'm in.'

'Uh, uh, no orgasms, Annabelle's orders. We can't have you getting excited, can we? Anyway, think of the authenticity angle. I know it's nice to think of real nurses providing oral sex to girls who can't help themselves, but I'm sure they don't, not really.'

'Fine, but orderlies don't really fuck the patients!'

'True, but then Marcus isn't in traction; you are.'

With that she left, flouncing out of the room with a deliberate wiggle of her bottom, leaving me feeling helpless, frustrated and close to tears. I really could do nothing, not physically, but only think. Some girls claim they can come just by fantasising. I can't.

Nor could I do anything to keep my mind off the state I was in, but only wait, thinking about my aching pussy and wondering what was in store for me. To make matters worse, she'd left the door open and I could hear them downstairs, if not clearly. At one point Sophie was punished, probably with a spanking, and it was impossible not to imagine her uniform skirt being pulled up while she was held wriggling across Annabelle's knee. I was sure she'd have had tights on, and her bum would have looked gorgeous, encased in tight, see-through nylon, probably with a pair of big white panties on underneath, maybe navy blue. It would have all come down, leaving her glorious bum bare and round and spankable, before she got it.

I heard the squeals, then other, more passionate noises, and I wondered if they'd made her come, or even if she'd been allowed to make Annabelle come, which made me seethe with jealousy. It was always me who got the worst of it, always me who was made to really suffer. It was just so unfair!

Only it wasn't. It was exactly what I needed to bring me properly to heel, and Annabelle knew it. She'd said I had a problem with my modesty and, the way I was, I was being allowed none whatsoever. Sophie hadn't even pulled the bed back, so whoever came in got a prime view of my body, every detail showing, my pussy and bumhole right in their face and, worse, shaved. It was going to get worse too, I just knew it.

I hadn't seen Annabelle all day and I kept expecting her to appear with some medically inspired torture device, maybe to catheterise me or to give me an injection in my bottom. I'd had a thing about that for a long time, since some bastard at school had spread a rumour that we had had to take our BCG jabs in our bums and not our arms. I'd had no reason not to believe him and had spent a week in ghastly anticipation of the moment I'd have to pull my panties down in front of the school doctor.

Thinking about that made my frustration even worse. Fantasies kept building up in my head: of me with my panties down in front of the doctor and about fifty girls and boys; of being in the same helpless state in a real hospital, being used for sex, with the men fucking me or sodomising me and the women queuing up to sit on my face. I imagined the curtains being pulled around me and the staff coming in, one by one, male students to spunk in my face like the boys by the canal, a huge fat matron to sit on my face and make me lick her, a wrinkled old cleaner, with his oversized cock up my bum.

I was wriggling on the bed, wishing there was some way to get enough friction to my clit to make me come. My eyes were shut and my thoughts were getting dirtier and dirtier. The fat matron was back, only demanding her bottom licked clean, laughing at my protests, posing her vast white buttocks over my face, spreading them with her hands and my tongue poking out in helpless submission . . .

Annabelle's cough made me jerk in surprise, tugging my limbs against their plaster cases. That hurt, and it took me a moment to settle back. She was standing over me at the end of the bed, giving her a prime view of my spread pussy. Like Sophie, she was in a nurse's uniform, but dark blue, with a more elaborate hat. Her face was set in disapproval, and I knew I'd been caught.

'We'll have none of that dirty stuff,' she snapped, then stepped around the bed and slapped me, full in the face.

'I'm sorry!' I whimpered. 'I can't help it!'

Again her palm smacked into my face, on the other cheek, then again on the first. I protested, squealing, with the tears already welling in my eyes, at the sheer helplessness of my predicament more than the pain.

'Can't help it indeed!' she sneered. 'Revolting!'

'I'm sorry,' I repeated, 'please don't slap me again.'

She did, once more, a real stinger, right across my left cheek to leave me with both sides of my face smarting and flushed.

'You deserved that, you dirty little tart,' she said. 'Now, where was I? Ah yes, you're suffering from modesty. Well, we shall soon see about that.'

She went back to the end of the bed, bending to pick something up. It was a kidney dish, the same or another, with a pair of plastic gloves lying over something lumpy. She put it down on the bed and removed the gloves. I craned my head up to see what was in it, then wished I hadn't. There were speculums, two of them, and a pot of skin cream.

I knew full well where they were going, and I sank back on to the bed with a hollow groan. She pulled the gloves on, all the while looking down at me with her face set in haughty contempt. Twisting the lid from the cream, she dipped two fingers in, bringing them out coated with the sticky white paste. They went straight to my cunt and up me, without preamble. I groaned as I felt my hole fill, wishing she'd put her thumb to my clit while she did it. She was fingering me and smearing the cream around the mouth of my pussy, so close but never there. I began to push myself against her, praying she'd take pity on me. All I got was a slap on my hairless pussy mound. Her fingers came out and my hole closed with a long farting sound, which earned me another slap.

'Disgusting! Can't you control yourself?' she snapped.

I just burst into tears. It was so unfair, to treat me so rudely and not to acknowledge my desperation, to smack me and insult me when I couldn't even move my limbs, and not even bring me off when they'd got me in a state. Being told I was disgusting because I'd made a rude noise when she'd opened my pussy was just the last straw.

'An absolute baby!' she remarked, and put her creamy fingers to my bumhole.

One went in, then the second, both pushed right up, fast, stretching my hole wide. I gasped in shock at the sudden, firm penetration of my body, arching my back as she began to finger my arse. She slapped my pussy again, but I was too far gone to feel anything but pleasure and the awful shame of being so utterly exposed.

'Rub me off!' I begged. 'Smack me off if you have to. Anything!'

She slapped my pussy again, hard, and I pushed my belly up, moaning at the thought of having my clit smacked until I came.

'Revolting . . . filthy . . . vulgar . . . little . . . whore!' she said, punctuating each word with a smack, right on my sex.

'Please, yes!' I begged. 'Like that, harder, spank my pussy, Annabelle, really hard. Keep your fingers in, yes, harder, make me come, Annabelle, slap me hard, ow! Annabelle, no!'

She'd stopped, leaving me right on the edge, and at the same time she'd pulled her fingers out of my bottom. I lay there, panting, mumbling brokenly to myself, the tears running down my face. She clicked her tongue in disapproval, or maybe amusement, nothing more, and I felt the speculum press to my pussy. It went up, so easily that I barely felt it, at least until she started to open the screw.

I felt that all right, my poor pussy stretched wide, opened, slowly but surely, until I was gaping far wider than I'd have needed for an examination, far wider than any cock had ever stretched me. I felt so open, and I was gasping in reaction, my toes wriggling and my hands clutching the rope that supported my plastered arms. I thought I'd split, and began to whimper, begging her to stop.

She did, but before I could even get my breathing under control I felt the cold, hard plastic of the second speculum press to my anus. It went in, spreading my greasy bumhole like a small but impossibly hard cock, easing up my rectum with my ring stretching wider as it went. Unlike the one up my pussy, I felt every inch of it go in, straining my hole like a good-sized cock even before she started to twist the screw.

When she did begin to spread me it hurt, and I gasped in pain. She stopped, waiting for me to get control of myself, then started again, only to stop the instant my squeaks once more became pained. I was panting in reaction, the sweat prickling on my skin, as slowly, inexorably, my bumhole was stretched to the point where I was sure my ring was going to split at any moment.

She stopped, leaving me moaning on the bed, spread out like a star with my rigid limbs stuck out, my pussy and bumhole agape to the air. I'd shut my eyes, and I opened them to find her holding a mirror and a torch.

'What does this do for your precious modesty?' she asked, and shone the torch up my pussy, moving the mirror until I could see.

My pussy hole was stretched a good four inches wide, pink and moist inside. Deep down I could see the head of my cervix, like a little pink bumhole or a sea-anemone with the tentacles drawn in. It was moving, pulsing in my excitement, trying to lap up a sperm pool that wasn't there. Above the gaping hole my pussy lips had been splayed out, with my clit a little pearly nub, peeping out from under her hood. Lower down, my bumhole was stretched only slightly less than my pussy, maybe three inches across, pink at the mouth, deep red further in, a tube of puffy, wet flesh closing in darkness beyond the end of the speculum.

'Answer me!' Annabelle demanded. 'How does it feel with your cunt stretched and your bumhole held open?'

'Rude,' I answered weakly, 'so dirty.'

'Do you want to come?'

'Yes, Annabelle, please!'

'Because you feel exposed and humiliated?'

'Yes! How else could it be? Please, Annabelle!'

'No.'

'Please, I beg you. You can do anything with me, anything!'

'I know I can, and make you beg me to do it.'

'I know. I'm yours, Annabelle, totally, your slut, your plaything. Just make me come, please!'

'No. You have a lesson to learn. How dare you feel humiliation because I can see the intimate details of your body? You say you're mine, but you're not. If you were, being naked in front of me would be natural to you, even being exposed the way you are now.'

I didn't have an answer, so I tried to plead with my eyes, the way I had after my caning. She'd relented, allowing me to nuzzle her bottom. Now she just smiled and gave the screw of my anal speculum a final twist.

'You'll learn,' she said confidently as she turned to leave, 'because you stay like this until you do.'

'Annabelle, no! Please, Annabelle!'

'Shut up, or I'll have your head shaved and we can put that in plaster too.'

I knew she would do it, so I shut up.

Lunch came at noon, on a tray brought by Sophie, who put it down near my head after having a good giggle at the state Annabelle had left me in. It was spam fritters, more disgusting lardy mashed potatoes and over-cooked Brussels sprouts, all piled high on a serving plate, far more than I wanted.

'Now you're going to be a good girl and eat this all up, aren't you, Penny?' she asked as she sat down on the bed.

'How can I?' I demanded.

'Easily enough,' she answered, reaching for the pillows to prop by head up.

'A little then,' I agreed, 'not much, it looks disgusting.'

'It's good for you, lovely spam, greens and mash, your favourite.'

'No it's not!'

'Well you're going to eat it up anyway, all of it.'

'I won't!'

'Yes you will, because Nursie knows best. Besides, if you don't eat it all, Sister is going to smack Nursie's bottom.'

'Good.'

'Do you want it up your pussy instead, Penny Birch?'

'No, Sophie, not that, no.'

'That's better, now open wide.'

I obeyed, reluctantly, but thinking how it would feel, and what I would look like with a load of spam and mash packed up my pussy. She spooned some up and put it in my mouth. It was as nasty as I'd expected, but I swallowed.

Spoonful by spoonful it was fed to me, until I began to feel full, then bloated. When I tried to rebel I got my breasts smacked for my trouble, and again for not swallowing fast enough. By the time the plate was finally empty my tummy was a hard, swollen ball, almost as bad as it had been after the army breakfast. Unfortunately there was gooseberry fool and cold, lumpy custard to follow.

Again I tried to refuse, and again I got my boobs slapped and the threat of having my pussy loaded full of it. In the end I ate it, but not before both my breasts were red and smarting, with the nipples standing up, rock hard. On the last mouthful I tried to hold it in my mouth, but she was wise to the trick and held my nose, stroking my neck until I was finally forced to swallow it down.

I now felt worse than I had after the army breakfast, bloated and fat, also slightly sick. The only consolation was that in my condition I couldn't very well be made to do the assault course.

'Medicine time,' Sophie announced as she dabbed the smears of food away from around my lips.

'I'm not ill,' I answered sulkily.

'Sister says you're to have your medicine and –'

'– and Nursie will get her bottom smacked if I don't,' I finished for her. 'I wish she'd do it. I'd do it myself if I wasn't stuck like this.'

'No,' she laughed, 'that wasn't what I was going to say at all. I was going to say that if you won't take your medicine we're going to have to put a tube down your throat and force feed you.'

'I'll take it!'

'I thought you'd see sense.'

She left, with the tray, returning almost immediately with a huge jug of some mauve fluid and a cup.

'Take your time,' she said, holding the brimming cup to my lips. 'The dose is two litres, and you're going to take it all, whether you like it or not.'

It was disgusting, which I'd expected, bitter and sticky.

'It's dilute sloeberry juice,' she said as she poured the second cup. 'They've had me picking them most of the morning.'

'I thought you were playing nurses. Didn't I hear you getting a spanking?'

'That was earlier.'

'Tell me.'

'No, drink up. You know you're not supposed to get excited.'

'I'll drink it all without any fuss if you promise to frig me off afterwards, and you can tell me about your spanking while you do it.'

'You'll drink it without any fuss anyway, Penny, it's that or the stomach tube.'

'Please, Sophie. I need to come so badly.'

'Tough.'

'Please.'

'Oh all right, but you mustn't tell Annabelle.'

I drank after that, as fast as I could, thinking of the moment when Sophie would put her hand to my clit. In between pouring the glasses she began to touch me, stroking my tummy and the hairless bulge of my pussy mound, until by the time I'd finished the last of it I was as urgent as before. Sophie put the cup down, stood and stretched, pushing her breasts out against the fabric of the uniform.

'Tell me then,' I said, trying to think sex and ignore the bloated feeling in my tummy. 'What did she do to you?'

'She spanked me, like I said,' Sophie answered. 'Now, I'd better hurry, or I'll get another dose.'

'You said . . .'

She just wagged a finger at me, bent and picked up the jug and cup, walking from the room without another word. I was left seething, once again near to tears. Nobody came after that, and I was left to lie there with my pussy and bumhole stretched wide and nothing better to do than wallow in my misery and watch the dust motes dance in the beams of sunlight coming in at the windows.

The discomfort of my huge lunch faded slowly, and so did my desperation. Eventually I slept, only to wake stiff, thirsty and with my bladder uncomfortably full. The pattern of light and shade on the floor and one plastered leg had shifted, quite a bit, and I judged it to be late afternoon.

I needed water, and a bedpan, so I yelled for Sophie. There was no answer. In fact I could hear nothing in the house, only birdsong and the distant sound of a tractor outside it. Nobody was in and I began to feel a trace of panic. Wondering if it was deliberate or if they'd simply forgotten that I needed my bodily functions taken care of, I called out again, trying to yell at the open window. All I managed to do was frighten a bird in the garden.

I was going to have to wet myself, it was as simple as that. There was only so long I could hold on, especially with the speculum pushing out to increase the strain on my bladder. The sensible thing was just to let go, but that's easier said than done. I hadn't been potty trained for nothing and I couldn't bring myself to do it unless I really had to.

Eventually I did. I was starting to get cramps and it just hurt too much. I let go a little, sighing in relief as the warm pee bubbled up from my pussy in a little yellow fountain and trickled down around my sex lips. Some went up my pussy, and I realised that was what was going to happen.

That was awful, but I couldn't help it, with the plaster so high up my legs that I could barely twist my body. I tried anyway, hoping to spray it out on the floor. Twisted as far as I possibly could, until that too hurt, I pushed out my belly and strained. The pee spurted out, some pattering on to the floor but mainly over my left leg, dripping back on to the bed. It was too late to be fussy and I let go, a high arch of golden piddle rising and falling back as I let out a long, blissful sigh of relief. It was pattering down on my tummy and soaking the bed cover, but most of it was going on the floor and that was what mattered; anything as long as I didn't get my pussy filled.

I let it all go, squeezing out the last of it over my tummy in a series of little spurts. Afterwards I felt a lot better, despite my lower body being wet with my own piddle, while my bum was in a soggy patch. I tried calling again, but with no response, and eventually I went back to daydreaming, occasionally shifting my body in the rapidly cooling pool of pee.

A little later I heard the clock in the parlour strike five and not long after that the sound of a car engine. It was them, Marcus's voice clear as he ordered Sophie to unload something, then Annabelle's saying she was going to check on the patient. I'd been hoping Sophie would come up first, so that she could clear up for me, and I was frantically rehearsing what I should say to Annabelle even as the door came open and she stepped into the room.

She saw immediately the pool of piddle on the floor, the wet patch on the bed and the stains drying on my leg and tummy. Her hands went to her hips and she shook her head in resignation.

'Can't you control yourself for five minutes?' she demanded.

'Sorry, I couldn't wait,' I answered. 'I did try!'

'Pathetic,' she responded. 'Well, we shall see what happens to incontinent little brats, shall we? Right.'

She went to the window, yelling for Sophie, before returning to me.

'You'll need to be douched,' she said, 'and given a bed bath. Next time, do try to hold on.'

'I couldn't!'

'Well it's just as well we've got a bedpan for you then. Now, I suppose these had better come out, for the time being.'

She started to loosen the speculums, which actually really hurt as my strained flesh slowly regained its proper shape. Even then I was left feeling sore and open, but it was still an extraordinary relief. I felt grateful too, at least until I realised why she'd done it.

My bottom was already well stuck out, but with a few quick adjustments she pulled my legs higher still, up over my body so that my bum was off the bed and pushed up higher still. I thought it was to let Sophie get the wet bedclothes out from underneath me, but as soon as she had fixed the last piece of cord back to its cleat she went to the chest of drawers and picked up my long-handled hairbrush.

I got whacked. Twelve hard strokes were applied to my bottom as I jerked and writhed on the bed. I think more people have disciplined me with that hairbrush than any other implement, and it always hurts. The handle is a tempting shape, which was why I'd bought it in the first pace, and as often as not it gets pushed up my pussy when the spanking is over, that or my bumhole. Annabelle chose my pussy, sliding the brush handle up just as Sophie came hurrying into the room.

'Clean her up and change the bed,' Annabelle ordered. 'The little baby's wet herself.'

'I couldn't help it!' I mewled.

I was feeling thoroughly sorry for myself because the spanking had been so unfair. Annabelle ignored me, Sophie throwing me a dirty look as she started to work. I was given my sponge bath then hauled up by Annabelle, so that I was actually hanging from the beams while the bedding was changed. All the time the hairbrush was left in my pussy.

'In future,' Annabelle instructed me as she lowered my legs back into a relatively comfortable position, 'call for a bedpan when you need the loo. If you wet the bed again I'm going to cane you.'

'Yes, Sister,' I managed.

'Good, I'm glad we understand each other. Now, for the night, I think we'd better put you in a nappy.'

It was pitch black when I woke up from a scary dream in which I was being held down by four medical orderlies while a doctor stood between my thighs, his erection in one hand, prodding my belly with the other and telling me I needed regular fucking in order to destroy my sense of modesty.

It still took me a moment to figure out where I was and why I couldn't move, before I remembered being put in plaster and systematically humiliated. Possibly their efforts were working because I felt even more ashamed of myself now than I had with the speculums up me.

I was in a nappy. Sophie had put it on me, folding a piece of thick towelling double and sliding it under my bum. The front had been the pulled up tight between my open legs and the sides pinned in place with two huge blue safety pins. Even Annabelle had laughed at the sight of me in it and sent Sophie to fetch Marcus so that he could see it too.

It felt soft and heavy around my middle and I was covered, but that didn't stop me feeling more humiliated

149

than ever. Whatever it hid, however comfortable it was, the fact remained that I was wearing a nappy. They'd liked the sight so much they'd even photographed me, which was something they hadn't done much of.

Since then I'd listened to Sophie get her six o'clock caning, twelve strokes, and been spoon-fed a dinner of stew and dumplings. After that had come my medicine, another two litres of sloe juice. I'd lain awake for hours after the light had been switched out, praying I'd make the morning so that I'd be able to avoid the final agonising shame of actually using the nappy. Sophie was sleeping in another room and I was sure they'd play with her, adding jealousy to my woes, but finally I'd gone to sleep.

Now I was awake again, but it wasn't morning. What had woken me was the pressure in my bladder and I knew immediately I was not going to make the morning. Worse still was the uncomfortable feeling in my tummy. I wasn't going to make it.

I lay there half asleep, feeling the tension in my body grow slowly and trying to cope with it by turning myself on. It was all I could do. I had no choice about filling my nappy, but it would be a lot easier for me if I could feel rude about it. It wasn't hard, not after what had been done to me. Just being put in nappies would have been enough, never mind the agonising helplessness of being put in traction, the shame of my exposure, the helpless, vulnerable feeling when Marcus had fucked me, being shaved, having both holes spread open with speculums, being force-fed, wetting myself, getting my spanking . . .

It felt so helpless, so wonderfully helpless, totally out of control. I was going to fill my nappy and I couldn't stop myself, there was no choice, no guilt because I'd decided to do something filthy. I'd had it done to me, all of it, and now I was going to get what I deserved, the final humiliation.

I was half asleep, my mind hazy and full of dirty thoughts. I was even wondering if I'd be able to come. The nappy was quite tight, and if I could only get a fold of the towelling on to my clit it might just be possible to work up enough friction to get there, perhaps if I could press my pussy to the edge of the plaster cast on one leg.

The pressure was growing, my bladder starting to sting, my bottom hole beginning to pout to the pressure in my gut. I wanted to hold it, only to let go when I really couldn't stop myself. It wasn't going to be long. Already my breathing was getting deeper. I began to wriggle my toes, holding myself back, feeling the pain rise, then die, rise and die again, each peak less easy to endure than the last.

I was moaning, softly, in response to the growing pain, with a helpless, panicky feeling, the feeling of knowing that I was going to do something improper, something unpardonably rude. The tears were starting in my eyes, my moans turning to sobs of pure shame, my belly tensing in pain, the strain rising, until I was gritting my teeth against it.

It died, fading, leaving me panting in relief, only to rise again, and this time I knew I wasn't going to be able to hold back. My mouth came open in a little, broken cry of pain and despair as I gave in. My bumhole was opening, the head pushing out, and there was nothing, nothing whatsoever I could do as I began to fill my nappy with dung, then pee as well as my bladder exploded and I screamed out loud.

I was crying as I did it, piece after piece squeezing out into my nappy, squashing against the material, down between my cheeks and up over my pussy. I was shaking my head too, in an ecstasy not that far from orgasm, and panting really hard. There was so much, far more than I'd normally do, from the huge lunch I'd been forced to eat. Every time I thought I'd stopped there seemed to be more, stretching out the pouch of my nappy until it was really bulging. There was plenty of pee too, soaking into the towelling to make a squashy, sodden mess, all over my bottom and right up on to my belly.

At the end I had to push, just to squeeze the last of it out. By then I was smiling, feeling dirty and wanton and just praying I could get that little bit of friction I needed for my clit. The weight of my load was pulling the nappy taut over my pussy and I was sure that if I could only twist my hips around far enough I could press myself to the hard edge of the plaster and use the soft, pee-soaked nappy to rub off on.

I turned, and felt my load shift in my nappy. My face screwed up in automatic disgust at the sensation, but I was still grinning, thinking just how filthy I was being. I pressed, trying to get the pressure, only to stop in sudden shock at the creak of the door.

A wave of utter, mind-blowing shame hit me as the light went on and then I was staring at Sophie and she was staring back, her mouth opening as her gaze settled between my legs. It was obvious what I'd done and, as it sank in, she shook her head.

'You are a dirty bitch, Penny Birch,' she said quietly.

I couldn't answer, the lump of embarrassment in my throat was too big to let me speak. She was in panties, white and too tight, not a stitch else, her boobs quivering as she stepped forward.

'You couldn't help it, could you?' she asked softly.

I shook my head.

'How does it feel?'

'Dirty, so dirty,' I managed.

She was looking at me, her mouth slightly open, her eyes wide and moist. Her tongue darted out, licking her top lip, running along the lower. She was trembling and, as I watched, her hand came forward, to cup the obscene bulge in my nappy.

'I'm going to make you come, Penny,' she breathed. 'I'm going to make you come now, in your own mess.'

She pushed, and my load squashed up against my pussy as she put her knuckles to the front of my nappy.

'There, yes, please, Sophie,' I moaned, throwing my head back and abandoning myself to what she was about to do.

Sophie began to rub, pressing her knuckles on to my pussy through the nappy, on to my clit, and all the time squashing the mess up over my bottom. I could feel the weight and the sticky feeling as she slapped the full load of dung against my bottom over and over and I started to moan, my back arching in unbearable ecstasy, starting to come, whimpering, thrashing my head from side to side and writhing my crotch against her fist and then, at the last moment, she slapped me hard between my legs. I felt my pussy fill at the very peak of my orgasm and I just screamed in mindless, filthy bliss.

# Six

They kept me in plaster for the rest of the week, bare during the day and in my nappy at night. Sophie changed me, powdered me and generally took care of me, even giving me the occasional sneaky orgasm when Annabelle wasn't about. Marcus fucked me a couple of times, but seemed to prefer either Sophie, who could respond properly, or coming over my food and watching me eat it. Annabelle kept order, punishing Sophie at six o'clock every evening, always in the parlour, and giving me the occasional dose of the strap or my hairbrush just to keep me in trim. She also made me spend an hour each day with both my holes stretched wide to the speculums.

She was right too. As things settled into a routine I could feel my sense of modesty being gradually eroded. After a while being naked became familiar, normal. Even having to wear my nappy didn't seem so bad. I actually felt that I was losing something, especially as none of my orgasms came close to the extraordinary intensity of the first, and at the end of the day that had been focused on my sense of humiliation.

When my casts finally came off I was so weak that I could barely stand. They let me recover in my own time and Annabelle was really sweet to me, letting me kneel at her feet and even kiss them. I'd stayed nude, except for my army boots when I went outside, and it did feel right.

Other than routine punishments and tasks, nothing special was done, until one morning we came downstairs to find Marcus and Annabelle already up, sitting at the kitchen table with mugs of coffee and a large-scale map spread out in front of them. They just nodded to us and carried on talking, so I sorted out the coffee while Sophie made toast and we joined the others at the table.

The map showed the area, with the farm boundaries marked in red and the roads in blue. I leant over, finding the house, then the wood in which they'd built the assault course. Both were well away from the road, which ran along the northern margin of their land and cut through it to the west.

'We can't really use these fields at all,' Marcus was saying, pointing to that part of the land beyond the road, 'and we'll need to screen the road here and along here.'

'What are you doing?' I asked.

'Keeping the land safe from prying eyes,' he answered. 'That way we can have more space to play with, and we've got some really good ideas.'

I nodded, feeling my normal response of mingled pleasure and fear at the thought of what this was going to mean for me.

'Today you work,' Annabelle added, 'in the nude of course, but you can wear your army boots. Sophie, what are you doing?'

'Making my toast ... Miss. Sorry, shouldn't I?'

'Jam, Sophie. What did I say about your weight? Come here.'

'But ...'

Annabelle pushed her chair back and snatched out for Sophie's wrist, catching it and taking the slice of toast and jam from her fingers. I was already giggling at the sudden look of panic on Sophie's face, then really laughing as Annabelle pulled her close. She was given an instant to see what was going to happen to her before the toast was pushed in her face. It stuck there for an instant, then fell off as Sophie was pulled forward, leaving her face covered in sticky red mess and a bit of half-melted butter. She went down, over Annabelle's knee, bum up, squealing in shock and protest as her panties were jerked down.

It's always funny to see a girl get a spanking, and I was smiling behind one hand as Sophie was given hers. She hadn't expected it at all and there were bits of jam flying everywhere as she shook her head about in shock. Annabelle did it hard, making Sophie kick and buck to show off her pussy and bumhole, which was even better, and by the time it was over I was wondering about sneaking a crafty frig.

What I didn't expect was to be caught by the hand and pulled down on top of Sophie, with my thighs spread open across the small of her back. Annabelle set to work on her little pile of female bottoms and I was soon squeaking and kicking just as much as Sophie, and showing even more. I was told it was for laughing. Afterwards we were both sent to stand in the corner with our red bums showing to the room, until Annabelle and Marcus had finished their breakfast.

The spanking put us in our place, keeping us ready and obedient despite the fact that we were working. Actually, there wasn't much difference between being Annabelle's plaything and actually doing work for her. She was just as bossy and just as picky, expecting everything to done perfectly and done fast as well. There was still six o'clock restitution time anyway, at least for Sophie. I was safe as long as I stayed nude, but that didn't stop me feeling as if I was going to get a spanking at any moment.

What they wanted to do was screen the farm completely and she had us making hurdles to block the few places from which anything might have been seen. Not that there were many, with the place so overgrown, but quite enough to keep us busy. I had imagined I was going to be made to work naked on the farm, and now I was, but they kept me away from the boundaries, leaving Marcus to put the hurdles in place.

For once Annabelle condescended to actually do something, teaching us how to make the hurdles and even bringing out bread and cheese for our lunch. It was hard work, and repetitive, but quite exciting. After all, they were creating a great place to play. I was looking forward to the possibilities it offered, and not just for the immediate future. The only problem was Annabelle.

One advantage of going in for corporal punishment as sex play is that a lot of things can be resolved with a good spanking for the offender. Not really serious things, but often things that would create serious problems in other circumstances. If Anderson and Bart's bet had involved Vicky or Amber, even Melody, I could have admitted to what I'd done afterwards. I'd have been punished, hard, but that would have been that. The trouble was, I couldn't see Annabelle taking the same attitude.

Basically she took herself too seriously. She'd also read too many books where couples create a full time dominant/submissive lifestyle, with the dominant partner actually the centre of the submissive's existence. That was how she felt it ought to work, and she and Marcus had put an immense amount of time and money into creating a situation where it could, at least technically.

What we were now doing was setting up an environment in which the normal rules of society didn't apply. Others have done the same, for reasons of religion more often than the desire to create a sado-masochistic paradise, but the principle is always the same. To really work, those involved have to do more than just accept the rules. They have to be brought to the point where the rules become normal, and society outside is abnormal. That was Annabelle's ideal.

All she needed now were her slaves, and she seemed to have a pretty good idea about how to get them. She was also going to be pretty determined to win her bet with Anderson and Bart, for the sake of her ego; Marcus too. I was sure she genuinely wanted me dependent on her, otherwise I could have told her, had a temporary tattoo so that she won, then taken the consequences when Anderson and Bart found out.

For me, the trouble was that my pleasure in kinky sex has always been more mental than physical. I like to break taboos, to be naughty, to be perverse. The less acceptable to outside society the better, so long as it suits my conscience, and the three basic limits of safety, sanity and consent. Take spanking, which used to be regarded as a good and perfectly fair way of punishing a woman. Now, with the arrival of feminism, it is seen as a gross affront to female dignity. It is, and that's why I like it so much. Annabelle didn't want that; she wanted the kinky things to be normal, which was in exact contradiction of my own needs, for all the pleasure she had brought me.

She was strong though, and I didn't feel quite so secure in my beliefs as I'd been at first, especially after spending a week in plaster. During that time I'd been totally dependent, and if it was Sophie who'd done the work, then it was Annabelle who was ultimately in control. I wasn't broken yet, but I could see that it was possible to accept her as a rightful mistress, and that scared me.

I knew that I needed to feel safe again. Even in her rare moments of compassion, Annabelle's dominance was completely unyielding. What I wanted was for her to lighten up, to stop being Mistress Perfection, maybe even to explore the submissive side of her character. After all, whatever she said to the contrary, I was sure she had one. Why else was she scared of Melody Rathwell?

Actually, what she needed was a bloody good spanking, and Mel was just the person to do it. She was physically capable and she wouldn't listen to any nonsense from Annabelle. Her attitude was that if you liked to punish other people you ought to be able to take it yourself, and I'd seen her punished by Morris or her sister often enough to know that she meant what she said.

She wouldn't actually spank Annabelle against her will, but she might if she thought Annabelle wanted it but needed to be forced to make the fantasy work. It was a pretty wicked thought and it left me feeling guilty, but not that guilty. After all, Annabelle expected me to accept my punishments, all or nothing, with no stop word. She also expected to change my attitude to nudity. Given that, it didn't seem so wrong to try to change hers, both to nudity and to getting her bottom smacked. The question was, how to go about it?

That kept my mind occupied as I worked on my knees in the yard, making hurdle after hurdle with Sophie, while Annabelle brought us the wood and Marcus set them up.

It took the rest of the day, and the next. Each evening, at six exactly, Sophie was given her caning, seven strokes, then six. Her bottom was a mess, so much so that Annabelle had to do her thighs, which really made her squeal. However, nobody could deny that the weight loss regime was working. I got away with it, never having put on a stitch, and on both occasions Annabelle contented herself with putting me across her knee, just to remind me of my place.

Marcus fucked us both each night, being very careful to keep his favours even. Annabelle kept to her routine of masturbating over the sight of us being punished. By

159

the Thursday morning I was settling into the routine of work under their authority. Being naked had completely lost its sting, at least around the farm, and the regular six o'clock punishments seemed normal and perfectly reasonable.

Only twice had our little world been disturbed, both times by local farmers asking what Marcus was planning to do with the land and whether they could rent any. He had rather assumed that physically remote was going to mean socially remote and had assumed that stout fences would be enough to deter nosy neighbours. To put them off he said that he was intending to use the farm as a base for paintballing games and that he was sealing the boundaries so tightly to prevent over enthusiastic players from crossing on to other people's land. It was a good cover story, and if neither of them was particularly happy about it, at least they believed him. On both occasions Sophie and I hid in the stables until the visitor had gone.

It was at lunch on the Thursday that Marcus declared the farm to be ready. None of it was visible from public land, and very little from private, other than a couple of places overlooked by higher ground. Even those were so heavily overgrown that it made little difference.

'No more hurdle-making then,' Sophie said with relief.

'Don't worry, there's plenty of work for you,' Annabelle told her. 'For a start, you're going to be doing the housework alone.'

'Alone, why?'

'Because,' Marcus answered, jerking a thumb at me, 'as soon as that has finished its food, it goes out.'

I looked up in surprise, wondering what he was talking about.

'Actually,' he continued, 'I really don't know why we let it in the house in the first place.'

'She's pretty,' Annabelle answered. 'I like pretty things.'

'Pretty, yes; housetrained, no,' Marcus answered. 'Come on you, out.'

I still had no idea what he was talking about, but his intentions were obvious. Rising, he took hold of me by the ear and jerked me to my feet, still with my mouth full of sausage and mash. I was dragged to the back door without another word, thrown out and given a boot up my bottom to help me on my way. The door slammed behind me and I was left standing in the yard, rubbing my bottom and wondering what they were doing.

Suddenly, and without the slightest explanation, they had started treating me like a stray cat. I'd been kicked out, literally, but there was no implication that I was supposed to leave the farm. Instead it seemed they wanted me to live like a wild animal, or at least a feral animal.

As always, I tried to fathom their logic and decided that it represented yet one more step in my debasement. I'd been made a servant, a soldier and a patient, all roles with limited freedom, but all human roles. Now I was to be an animal, less than human. They'd got me wrong. They might see being an animal as a low state; I didn't. To me it was simply different.

I now realised why they had gone to so much effort to seal the farm. As before, I was grateful for the effort being made on my behalf, even if it was for basically selfish motives. I was to be a beast, no different to them than the rabbits or foxes living in the woods and fields, except that I had no predators, no competitors and nobody trying to shoot me. I was free, which was a lot more than could be said for any of the human roles.

After a couple of minutes standing in the yard Marcus opened the kitchen window and told me to shoo, so I did. Walking out into the orchard, I thought about how I should react, and behave, and also how they were going to react to me. I was still in my boots and I considered taking them off, only to abandon the idea as impractical.

Food was not going to be a problem. For one thing the blackberries were starting to ripen in the hedges, while there were plenty of other things in the little kitchen garden. From what Annabelle had said, it seemed fairly likely that they'd put scraps out for me as well. In any case, after the amount I'd been forced to eat while my limbs were in plaster, I needed to lose a bit of weight.

Shelter was a more serious consideration, as it was beginning to get cold at night and there had been quite a lot of rain during the week. I didn't want to end up with hypothermia, so it seemed the sensible thing to sort out first.

Basically I was in much the same situation as a pig, without enough fur to keep me properly warm, and about the same mass too. Pigs seem to do well enough in sties, or the little corrugated iron huts I always remember from driving across Salisbury plain. I had no idea if there had ever been pigs on the farm, but it seemed quite likely.

What I'd already decided was not to be seen, or at least not easily. For one thing, it just seemed right. For another, I'd learnt enough about Marcus and Annabelle's fantasies to be fairly sure I wasn't going to be left in peace. They obviously weren't going to shoot me, put out traps or anything dangerous, but both of them had plenty of imagination and more than enough cruelty.

The outhouses were all too close to the farm and I'd seen enough of the orchards to know there was nowhere suitable in them. The same was true of the wood with the assault course in it. It seemed best to look further afield, and before long I had found what I was looking for. At the bottom of the valley, and only a hundred yards from the road, was an old pill box, no more than a square of red brick with a flat concrete roof, a door and three gun slits. It was perfect, and exactly where they would look first.

Using ferns and grass, I made a comfortable nest, spent a quarter of an hour curled up in it, just thinking, and left. Security felt the most important thing, but that was largely instinctive. Really it was warmth. What I needed was a den, somewhere snug enough for my body heat to count, and dry. Other things, like insect bites, I would worry about later.

I chose a holly bush, on the grounds that it was somewhere they'd assume I'd avoid. It was right at the edge of the farm, by the stream, but could be approached with no risk whatsoever of being seen from the woods outside. As there usually is with holly, there was a curtain of foliage with a hollow space inside. Using twigs, I constructed a framework, building a nest completely invisible from outside. This I lined with long grass from the orchards, working carefully to leave as few signs as possible of my presence.

By the time I'd finished the sun was close to the horizon, throwing the wood into shadows. I like to think I'm immune to superstition, but as dusk gathered it was impossible to deny that there was an eerie atmosphere and, with the temperature dropping, I quickly began to feel cold and, with that, also lonely, vulnerable and hungry.

I'd been eating blackberries as I worked, so I wasn't going to starve, but for some reason I badly needed to be near human beings, if no more than that. Not feeling quite so wild and free as I had earlier, I decided that it was time to see if Annabelle had been kind and put some scraps out for me.

After dark it was going to be pitch black, so I ran back up the slope quickly, wondering if I should crawl into the stable or the barn after all. Approaching the house, I found that the lights were already on, with the kitchen windows bright rectangles of yellow light. Inside it looked warm and pleasant, with Marcus and Annabelle seated at the table while Sophie washed up.

Staying back in the rapidly gathering shadows, I made my way to the back door. Sure enough, I'd guessed right. An old plate had been put out, piled high with food, bacon rinds, bits of cabbage, potato peelings and what looked like the scrapings from their plates. It was hardly appetising, but very appropriate. I still made a quick inspection to make sure no slugs had arrived first. There are limits, and anyway, it wouldn't have been very fair on the slugs. Besides, some species are poisonous.

It was clean, so I got down on all fours and stuck my face in it, munching away happily. The taste and texture were revolting, but it felt good to be doing it, showing that I was coming to accept the condition I'd been put in.

What I didn't do was eat it all, not because it was slops, or because I was full, but because I could. One thing Annabelle was fanatic about was us eating up our food, even though she was trying to get Sophie to lose weight. Now, for the first time in nearly two weeks I didn't have to eat everything on my plate.

It was nearly dark by the time I'd had enough, so I left, across the lawn, which was a mistake. I heard Marcus's yell and turned just in time to avoid an army boot, flung at me from the window. I ran all the way to my den, where I curled up in the soft grass with my hands between my legs, stroking myself for comfort until I at last fell asleep.

Friday passed quietly. I found myself feeling increasingly detached, with the way I looked at things changing to suit my situation. Not all of this was fanciful, as I wasn't at all sure what would happen to me if I went near the house. Annabelle's intention in making me an animal had to be to get rid of the last vestiges of my modesty, but they were sure to want to have their fun with me as well. They were cruel enough to put a girl in plaster for a week, and if I didn't expect to find Marcus doing the rounds with a shotgun, he had plenty of other choices. If he was going to subject me to them, he was going to have to catch me first.

Strangers were also a problem. I knew the farm was sealed, but the hurdles weren't enough to stop a determined trespasser. Even then, I was naked out-doors, and it wasn't at all the same thing as being naked in the house and around the farm buildings. I'd always been near shelter and seldom alone for more than a few minutes. For me, naked is vulnerable, and I'd have felt the same way if the farm had been surrounded by a fifty-foot wall with razor wire on the top.

So I skulked around in the overgrown area, avoiding both the farm and the boundary fences, also the assault course, where Annabelle spent much of the day exercising Sophie. That left me an irregular ring of land with plenty of cover and only two little fields as open ground. I explored and ate blackberries and tried to enjoy the feel of sun and air on my bare skin without feeling scared all the time.

I did a lot of listening too, for voices or mechanical noises mainly, but also for alarm calls from other animals and anything else that might indicate a human presence. Twice Marcus came out, presumably to look for me, but I avoided him. Once a group of people walked along the road when I was within earshot, talking loudly, which was eerie, making me feel more detached than ever.

At some point in the afternoon I masturbated, using my fantasy to allay my fears of what could happen to me. I imagined a farmer coming to see Marcus and taking a short cut across the land. I thought of him as big, especially his hands, which would be rough and dirty with soil, with huge, thick fingers and skin like leather. He'd be fat too, not flabby, but really fleshy, with a big, red face and white hair.

He'd see me and chase me through the dappled sunlight of the wood. He'd catch me and throw me on the ground, where I'd lie panting and wide eyed, watching as he freed an enormous cock from his trousers. It would already be hard, a great, thick, dirty shaft of red-brown meat, which he'd push up me, fucking me in the leaves until he came up my pussy. I felt better for the orgasm, but I stayed cautious. Fantasy is one thing, reality another.

Nobody came, and the afternoon blended towards evening, with shrill squeals from the house indicating six o'clock as Sophie got her caning. There were only five, and it was clear that her regime was working. After dinner I had my scraps, this time approaching through the yard to avoid Marcus's boots.

On the Saturday morning I realised that something was going on. I'd woken to a chilly dawn and ran to warm up, which left me both hungry and thirsty. I was in one of the orchards, trying to find any fruit that was ripe enough to eat, when I heard a car and then a voice from the direction of the gate. I assumed it was another farmer and hid, only for a second car to arrive, and a third.

With the fourth car my curiosity got the better of me. Creeping carefully through the long grass, I approached the farm; until I could see them: two Mercedes, a BMW and another Range Rover. It seemed unlikely that four well-off landowners had decided to visit Marcus at the same time, so I stayed where I was, watching as a another BMW and finally one of the new style Volkswagen Beetles appeared. That I recognised: it belonged to Bart Pelham.

I watched him park and get out, along with two men who had arrived in the BMW. They greeted each other, shaking hands and talking in loud, confident voices. Marcus emerged from the house and was given the same effusive, even excited greeting. Bart went to his car, taking a heavy-looking black case from the boot and showing it to the others, amidst more laughter. Other people started to come out, including Annabelle and Sophie. None of the others were familiar to me. I had no idea what was going on, but it was making me nervous.

For one thing there was something conspiratorial in the way they were acting, also smutty, like a group of boys about to peep on a girls' shower room. Another was that, while Annabelle and Marcus were in battle dress, Sophie was in jeans and a T-shirt. Lastly was the fact that all the visitors were men.

Some were in khaki or camouflage gear, which made me think that Marcus and Annabelle might have extended their army fantasy in some way, perhaps playing to Sophie's exhibitionism by making her do things in front of a large group of men, even giving her to them. Bart was just the person for that sort of game, but if the others had been experienced enough in dominance and submission games to handle it, I was sure I'd have at least recognised a few. Also they'd have sniggered less.

What was clear was that they all knew each other, and that they were all fairly well off. They also seemed to be somewhat in awe of Annabelle, some even a bit shy of Sophie, which was ridiculous. Several had cases, much like Bart's, many with stickers and some marked with splashes of brilliant colour. That was when I realised what was happening. Marcus had told the farmers the truth. He was going to do some paintballing, and I didn't imagine they'd be going about it the conventional way. I'd thought I had no predators. That had been stupid. Even lions have predators, even blue whales. One predator anyway: man. I was going to be hunted, and shot.

My instincts were telling me to run for it, but I stayed put, determined to find out as much as possible. There were eleven of them in all, including Marcus and Annabelle, twelve with Sophie. She was the only one who did not have a gun, all the other's did, and they seemed to be a major topic of conversation. I managed to pick out words such as 'pump-action' and 'semi-automatic', all of which were not only terrifying, but hardly sounded sporting.

Little coloured boxes where distributed, one colour to each person, which Marcus wrote down on his clipboard. Evidently they had made it some sort of competition, with the colours showing who had scored a hit, presumably on my tender flesh. I was still clinging to the faint hope that it might not be me they were hunting when Marcus gave Sophie a pair of goggles. I heard him tell her to go and find me and my worst fears were confirmed.

I'd seen enough and retreated carefully back through the orchard, my heart already hammering in my chest. What I wanted to do was run for cover, but first I needed to find Sophie, quickly. Marcus had found my false den and I guessed that was where Sophie would go first. Sure enough, I managed to catch up with her as she reached it.

'Hi, Penny, all right?' she greeted me. 'Look, you've got to put these on. I can't tell you much . . .'

'I already know,' I answered, 'I was watching. They're having a hunt, aren't they?'

'Yes,' she admitted.

'Who are they?'

'A bunch of city friends. They don't know much, only that they're hunting a naked girl. Marcus has told them he's hired you for the day, for . . . well, you know.'

'No. What?'

'Well he can't really tell the truth, can he? He said you're a call girl. He's charged them two hundred each to help with the cost.'

'A prostitute?'

'A very expensive one.'

'The bastard! So what are they allowed to do?'

'They've all got different coloured paintballs, nets and stuff too. Whoever catches you gets to have you. You're supposed to give in when you're hit.'

'How much does it hurt?'

'I don't know. Annabelle says it's like being poked with a stick. I don't suppose it's any worse than a cane stroke, but it does leave a bruise.'

'Ow!'

'If you can't handle it, go AWOL. They won't go off Marcus's land. I'll say I couldn't find you. But if you do, they're going to put me out instead.'

'Don't worry, I can take it. Anyway, who says they're going to catch me?'

'They know what they're doing. The way they talk, you'd think they were all big game hunters.'

'They're just boys with toys. Anyway, give me the goggles, but walk back slowly. Say it took a while to find me and that I'm . . . let's see, up in the top orchard. Walk back that way.'

'OK, but it won't do any good. They're going to make two lines of five, leading out from the farm to the boundary, then sweep round so that you get herded between them. Annabelle is what they call a maverick, on her own in the middle. If she hits you, they all get to take turns.'

'With her, I hope.'

'No, Penny, not with her.'

'Oh dear. Look, I'm going to hide in the pipe on the assault course. They won't expect me to be there. I'll see you later.'

She nodded, wished me luck and walked away through the trees. I ran immediately towards the assault course, changing direction as soon as I was sure she couldn't see or hear me. I'd lied to her about my hiding

169

place because I was fairly sure she'd tell Annabelle. I'd also exaggerated my confidence, but I wasn't going over the wall. I wanted to speak to Bart and I wanted him to be the one to catch me. He knows what he's doing. The others I wasn't so happy about. I knew the type, brash, confident but hardly sexually skilled. More importantly, I didn't expect them to have any respect for me, especially when they thought I was a prostitute.

Unfortunately it was impossible to know where he would be in the line, so my best bet seemed to be to try to avoid the initial sweep and hope they'd break up, then seek him out just as he was seeking me. In fact, as he knew more than he was supposed to, it was probably what he would expect.

Hiding was my immediate problem. They would work out all the obvious choices, like concealing myself in the actual house or the outbuildings. Not that I was supposed to know what was happening, but if I wasn't found easily they'd soon start searching. Another choice was to climb a tree, but again it seemed likely that anything I thought of, they would too. The best choice was to go outside the boundaries as, while they might well guess, they couldn't follow, at least not far. Then again, it risked running into a complete stranger, while I could be absolutely certain that Annabelle would make me pay if she found out.

It was a dilemma, but as a whistle blew in the distance I realised the sensible choice. It was not an easy one and fear and panic were already threatening to overtake me, making me want to run blindly through the under-growth, just from the knowledge that I was being hunted. I didn't, forcing myself to think logically and do what was ultimately for the best.

Annabelle was likely to investigate my false den first and wait for the jaws of the pincer movement to close, hoping I'd try to go to ground. I wanted to avoid her, so I ran around the boundary of the farm, not really worrying about concealment. Sure enough, as I reached the edge of one of the little fields a man emerged from the far side.

Unfortunately it wasn't Bart, but he was as good as the next best thing: late thirties, slim, tawny haired, with an aquiline face and a very assertive expression. I stayed down, watching him as he scanned the field, then loped quickly to one of the boundary hedges, following it and searching as he went. He was about to enter my side of the wood when I took my heart in my mouth and broke cover.

I just ran, full tilt across the field, stumbling over the rough grass, expecting the pain of the ball in my back at any second. He didn't shout, but it was impossible not to look back, and there he was, standing with his legs set apart, aiming the gun right at me. I heard the snap of the gun and felt a jolt of real fear, but no pain. He cursed. I realised he had missed and I was running, just as fast as I possibly could. Again the gun snapped, a jolt of pain shot through my leg and I was down, rolling on the grass and clutching at my thigh.

'My kill!' he yelled.

He sounded incredibly pleased with himself, and was already walking over towards me. There was a big smear of brilliant pink paint on the back of my thigh and it hurt so much that all I could do was sit there, rubbing at myself and saying ouch over and over again. He came up to me, grinning.

'You know the deal?' he demanded.

I nodded.

'In the bushes then,' he ordered. 'I like it from behind.'

He actually helped me up and held my hand as we walked over to the nearest piece of cover, which surprised me. Once there, it was a different matter, with the sudden burst of gallantry evaporating as fast as it had come. He kissed me first, really hard, bruising my lips and forcing me to open my mouth under his. Before he'd had his fill of snogging me his hand was already down between my thighs, with two fingers fumbling for my pussy. I was opened, really roughly, and finger-fucked as I clung on to him, still kissing.

With his cock out of his trousers I was pushed down and made to suck it, all the while with him looking around and telling me to take it deeper. Obviously he didn't want his mates to get there before he'd had his fun. I did my best but he was big and already half stiff, so I kept gagging on his knob. He pushed me down on my knees in the leaf mould before he was fully stiff. I went, turning to stick my bum up for rear entry, as he had asked.

'Hard in the mouth and fuck them doggie-style,' he said with satisfaction and I felt his cock press to my pussy.

After a couple of pushes it went up and he began to stiffen inside me. He took my bottom in his hands, spreading my cheeks with his thumbs as he began to fuck me, deeper and faster. I knew his eyes would be on my bum, they always are when a man takes the trouble to spread a girl's cheeks. They like to see our bumholes and the way their cocks make our pussies pull in and out because it's rude, and because it makes them feel in control for us to have everything showing.

It was exciting because he'd hunted me down and now he was in me, which appeals to my submissive fantasies. I was even getting to the point of wanting to bring myself off when he came, quite unexpectedly, whipping it out and spraying spunk all over my bottom.

He'd barely put his cock away when he was calling for his mates, ignoring the fact that I was not only stark naked but had his come spattered across my bottom. Two where already walking across the field and a third appeared from beyond the hedge as we stepped out, with him leading me by the arm. The fifth in his group took a moment more, coming from the other direction, and to my relief it was Bart.

The others took longer, Annabelle, then Marcus and the other team. They were talking and making jokes, very excited, and pretty well ignoring me, except for Bart, which was exactly as I'd planned it. The one who'd shot me, Gavin, was really full of himself, boasting about his shot at a moving target and pointing out my messy bottom as evidence of his virility.

They were impressed and eager for another go, if rather shy of me. I'd have rather they'd been friendly, but shrugged the feeling off, contenting myself with telling Bart to follow the stream to the edge of the farm and look for a holly bush.

I was sent off again, without even being given a chance to clear up and, as I ran for the bushes, I heard Annabelle announce that the next hunt would start in ten minutes and that it was a free for all. Ten minutes wasn't much time, but it was enough, and when I heard the whistle once more I was hidden in my den. It took Bart maybe half an hour to get to me, and he arrived full of apologies, explaining that one of the other hunters had latched on to him, trying to persuade him to work together.

'As long as you're here,' I answered as he pulled himself into my hiding place.

He kissed me and put his gun down.

'Safe, I think,' he declared after a moment of listening. 'So how's it going with Miss Dominant?'

'She's good; so's he. At the moment they're trying to break my nudity taboo.'

'And they're succeeding?'

'Maybe. They certainly give me other things to think about. My thigh really stings!'

'I can imagine. It's bad enough through clothes, and girls generally wear chest protectors. I see they gave you goggles though.'

'Yes, they're not completely demented, but they do take it right to the edge of consent. When we've got more time, I'll tell you about being in traction. For now, I want you to get Mel Rathwell up here.'

'Melody? Why?'

'Because if you don't, Sophie Cherwell's likely to end up with a pussy tattoo, even me.'

'Shit.'

'Annabelle's so aloof, so untouchable. She genuinely believes that her dominance places her above us, and she's got us under a lot of pressure. You know how it works.'

'I was rather counting on the fact that it doesn't, not for you anyway. Come on, Penny, where's the girl who let some French tramp piss all over her?'

'Sitting next to you. Annabelle's different. She's just as cruel and just as perverted, but she's compassionate too, when it matters. It would be too easy to fall in love with her.'

'You won't, though?'

'I fell in love with Amber.'

'Amber's Amber. I don't believe I'm hearing this. Look, we'll throw in four bottles of the La Tâche. How's that?'

'I'm going to try, Bart, don't worry about that. For now, I need to see Annabelle unbend, and I'm sure she's got a thing about Mel. Ideally I'd like to see Annabelle spanked, tell Mel that, but anything would do.'

'OK, I'll try.'

'Thanks, and I'll be following the stream up towards the assault course if you want to shoot me.'

'I'll catch you there.'

He winked at me as he left, checking for other people before ducking out and jumping across the stream. I waited, counting to one hundred, then followed. Nobody was around and I made my way slowly along the stream. I could see why Bart had chosen the assault course. He'd presumably seen it and knew that it offered enough quiet nooks where we could enjoy ourselves at leisure. Knowing him, he'd want to bugger me, but I didn't mind because I knew he'd do it slowly, and well, and make me come while his cock was up my bottom.

My dirty thoughts were my undoing because I never heard Annabelle, only the snap of her gun and the pop as a burst of vivid scarlet paint exploded across the bark of a tree. Even then I didn't see her, but I heard the tone of command in her voice as she ordered me to stop.

I nearly did, but not quite, and her second shot went past me, somewhere off into the woods. I was already running, scrambling up the side of the stream and away, as a third exploded against the ground, just inches from my foot.

Unlike Gavin, she called out, yelling to the others that I was headed up the slope. They answered, the calls seeming to come from all sides, screams of delight. I ran, really panicking, not even sure where I was going. Annabelle kept firing, but I was dodging between trees and she was just too far away to hit me. For one moment of hope I thought I might get clear before the others caught up, only to see a green ball burst on the ground and hear a yell of disappointment.

I kept going, my legs already burning with the strain, dodging as Marcus stepped from behind a tree and fired, missing me. Annabelle fired again, hitting Marcus, and for just a moment I felt an exquisite satisfaction before a ball caught me in the shoulder and a puff of yellow paint splashed into my face. The new hunter called out in triumph and I reeled, but I kept my balance, hurling myself past Marcus as he struggled with his gun. The assault course was ahead of me and I saw Bart step out from the cover of the climbing wall.

Never trust a sadist. His arm came up, the gun snapped and the purple paint of his ball exploded across my chest, hitting me exactly between my breasts. It was like being punched and I nearly went down, but caught myself, darting to the side and the guns began to snap, one after another.

A ball caught my leg, another my arm and I was running in desperation, up the track, towards the house, the only place I knew I'd be safe. Another ball hit me, right between my bum cheeks, and I really screamed, only to get another in my chest and new hunters closed in on me.

I ran, staggering, stumbling on the tractor ruts, dizzy with pain and terror. Again and again I was hit, on my back, on my legs, in my hair, but mainly on my bum, which I suppose they thought made the most amusing target. Every one hurt and I was squealing crazily and running in blind, mindless panic to the tune of their laughter, the snap of the guns and the smack of the balls on my flesh. Many missed too, and time and again I saw the little splash of colour on a nearby tree, driving me to yet greater panic.

Then I was on the lawn, with three hunters in front of me, bringing up their guns. One was Gavin, who fired, pink paint splashing across my belly as I doubled up to the impact. Another ball got me in the side and I jumped up, going into a demented, ridiculous dance as ball after ball hit me, all over my body, my limbs jerking and thrashing in a hopeless effort to avoid the hits, with the crazy laughter and the endless snap of the guns and pop of balls on my skin singing in my ears, until at last I collapsed.

It stopped then, Annabelle calling on the hunters to cease fire, which brought me so much gratitude. I couldn't move, but only lie inert on the lawn with the sky spinning slowly over my head. I hurt all over and I could feel the paint trickling down my skin, wet and cool. It didn't matter that I was nude, or spread out for the first man to stuff his cock up me; I was just too far gone to care.

I saw Annabelle, her beautiful face alien behind the protective goggles. She was standing over me, her gun held up, her finger on the trigger. Other faces appeared, surrounding me as Annabelle brought her weapon slowly down, pointed it directly between my breasts and depressed the trigger.

Why I didn't stop the first time I was hit I don't know. It would have been so much easier, and so much less painful. On the other hand, I wouldn't have experienced the full effect, the real experience of being hunted and brought down, and at bottom that was what I had wanted. At least, it was what was going to be best to look back on because, at the time, I was far too scared to make any rational decision.

After Annabelle had given me my mercy shot, I was taken into the yard for a victory photograph, then put under the pump. Marcus washed me down while the others gleefully compared notes and tried to count the marks on my body. It was impossible, with so many overlapping and the colours so mixed together, but fifty seemed to be a conservative estimate. There was no doubt that every one of them had got a shot in, probably more than one, as they managed to identify traces of all eleven colours on my paint-splattered body before Marcus had cleaned my hair and taken my goggles off for me.

They were absolute bastards, all demanding the right to fuck me and arguing over who should go first, despite the state I was in. They wanted their fill of the hunting game too, suggesting that I should be put in a net or a game bag with just my head sticking out. One, a really thin man with slicked back hair, even suggested that I be hung on a gibbet by my ankles.

Bart told him he was psychotic and promptly suggested that I ought to be put in the game bag, but hog-tied and with the sacking split so they could get at my sex.

That met with all-round approval, but for once Annabelle insisted on asking me if I could handle it before I was used. They'd pushed my submissive button and my endorphins were running as high as they ever had, so I just nodded, knowing full well that if I backed out I would regret it in the long run. Marcus went to fetch the sack.

Bart volunteered to hog-tie me, claiming to have worked with pigs, which caused another round of laughter. Now washed down, I was made to lie on my back in the yard, with my legs tucked up and my hands gripping my ankles. A few deft twists and a single knot immobilised me, leaving me helpless and with my pussy and bumhole on show to all eleven of them.

They had a good stare too, although not that openly, until Marcus came back with an ancient hemp sack which looked as if it had been used to store grain. I was picked up and bundled into it, before the opening was pulled close to leave me with just my head sticking out and my body in the sack, sat upright in the centre of the yard for another photograph and more jokes at my expense.

It was Annabelle who slit the sack, feeling to locate my bum and cutting a long slice in the hemp. I'd imagined they'd want to watch, like the lads on the canal bank, but Marcus picked me up, carrying me with my bare bottom stuck out through the hole, to an empty stall, where I was dumped on a pile of rotting straw. No sooner was I down than he began to undo his army trousers, and I realised that he'd decided to have first go.

Out came his cock, and into my mouth as he knelt and put a hand down to explore my bum. I sucked, letting the pleasure of being so thoroughly abused build in my head as his cock stiffened in my mouth. With eleven men in the queue behind him I didn't think he'd take long and, sure enough, as soon as he was stiff he rolled me on to my knees and stuck his cock into me from behind.

As he fucked me, I could hear the others outside, drawing lots for the order they would use me in. Then came a new voice, Sophie's, offering beer and sandwiches. Most accepted and I wondered if they'd be drunk by the time they came to take their turns with me. If so, it would make them ruder, less inhibited, more likely to do really dirty things to me. They had earned it, even though I doubted any but Bart would have understood, and as Marcus pulled his cock free of my pussy to jet spunk across my naked, bruised bottom I was hoping they would.

Gavin was right about making a girl suck then taking her from behind. If a girl has been tied up, or has to do as she's told, it's the choice most men will take. The second guy who visited me gave me the same treatment, almost stroke for stroke, differing only in that he kept calling me a dirty bitch while he did it. The third was much the same, except for having a bit of a rub between my bum cheeks before he went up me. Fortunately there's always the odd pervert.

Both came up my pussy, which was getting really soppy by the time the fourth guy appeared. I was lying on my side, with my bare bum sticking out of the hole in the sack, everything on show. He took one look at the other men's come dribbling from my gaping vagina and called me a filthy slut. That didn't stop him having a feel, pawing my bottom while he stroked at the bulge in his trousers.

Most men love to make girls show everything, especially the really rude details many like to keep hidden, and most of all, their bumholes. He was inspecting me, but it wasn't until he began to tickle my anus with a finger that I realised he was going to sodomise me. I looked down to find his cock out, a fat, pale one, not all that long, but very thick, with a round, bulbous head.

He was wanking it, slowly, his eyes fixed on my bumhole. I relaxed my ring, trying to show willing, although I was pretty sure I was going to get buggered anyway. In response he pushed the tip of his finger suddenly up my hole, which made me gasp.

'This'll be a lot tighter than your sloppy cunt,' he remarked. 'Had a prick up the shitter before?'

'No,' I lied, sure that he'd take a lot more pleasure if he thought he was taking my anal virginity, and maybe give me more pleasure in return.

'Good,' he answered, 'nothing I like better than a virgin arsehole.'

He'd been pushing his finger in while he spoke and it was well up me. I was a bit dry after being washed, and because I'd been fucked on my knees, no spunk had run down from my pussy.

'Ow!' I protested as he tried to push a second finger into my ring. 'If you really must do that, loosen me up a little.'

'What with?'

'The other boys' spunk. Just dip in my pussy for a bit.'

'Don't be disgusting!'

'Spit on my bum then, anything.'

'No, I've got a better idea.'

He was wearing a one-piece camouflage suit, with no shortage of pockets. I looked down, wondering what he was up to, to find him opening a box of paintballs. They were yellow, and I wondered if he was the one who'd shot me first in the woods.

'Paint?' I queried.

'Gelatine and food colouring,' he answered, 'harmless, but it should grease your box well enough.'

I nodded, pushing my bum out to make it easier for him. His hand went between my cheeks and I felt the smooth round ball, pressed to my bum, then a sudden release of pressure and a wet feeling as it burst over my hole. Again he did it, and a third time, all the while nursing his cock. I could feel it running down my bottom and there was plenty up the hole when he finally decided I was ready and put his knob to it.

'Relax, it won't hurt that way,' he said, and pushed.

He caught me a bit by surprise and it did hurt a bit as the fat cock head was jammed into my ring. I gasped, then began to pant as he fed it up my bum, pushing, easing back and pushing again to slowly fill my bumhole with cock. With it all up he took hold of the sack, rocking my helpless body on to his cock and pushing at the same time. I could feel my bumhole pulling in and out and hear the squashy, squelching sound as I was buggered.

I do love that, lying at ease on my side while a cock is fed back and forth up my bottom, slowly, with no rush, just in and out until I'm dizzy with pleasure. When sex is casual, or spontaneous, I much prefer my pussy, but when I've been spanked, or anything that involves painful attention to my bottom, then there's nothing better than to finish by masturbating with a cock up my bumhole.

Unfortunately I couldn't masturbate, not hog-tied in a sack, and while he certainly wanted to take his time with me, the others began to get impatient, demanding their turns and asking if he was having trouble getting it up. At that he gave me a resounding slap across my bottom, took a firmer grip of the sack and jammed his cock hard into me. I gasped as my insides were shoved up, then again, and he was hammering his cock into me, his teeth set in effort, ignoring my cries of shock and pain, buggering me deeper, harder, and stopping with it pushed right up to the hilt as he came up my bottom.

He'd been really rough and it left me sore, also wet. I could picture my bumhole, wet and spongy, bright yellow with paint, surely a tempting target for their cocks. The fifth man was shy and said nothing as he made quick use of my pussy, with me on my back. He held the sack, which tore a little, riding up my back and thighs until a lot more than just my bottom was sticking out of the hole.

The sixth was another mouth and doggy-style man, and another who liked to talk, describing to me how I looked in my sack and with spunk and paint smeared all over my pussy and bottom. The seventh was a joker and stuffed my pussy with paintballs. A whole handful went up, bright blue ones, until I could feel my pussy bulging with them. I thought he'd fuck me to make them burst, but he used my mouth instead, masturbating with just his head between my lips and deliberately coming in my face.

The eighth got the paintballs. He must have seen them wedged in the mouth of my pussy, but he was already hard and just didn't care. Rolling me on to my back, he took my thighs and just pulled me on to his cock. I felt the balls explode inside me and the wet gelatine burst from my hole, spurting out to trickle down between my bumcheeks. He began to fuck me, each push sending a new spurt of gelatine out, until he came and added his spunk to the mess. When he stood up, his balls and cock were brilliant blue, and for all the state I was in it was impossible not to laugh.

I wanted to come by then, really badly, but I was waiting for Bart. What I got was number nine, who cursed his mates for making a mess of my mouth, pussy and bumhole, then promptly made use of all three. He was a bastard too, doing it in my pussy first, then forcing it up my bum, and only then going to my mouth. His cock was absolutely filthy, but in it went and I was made to suck him with my mouth full of the revolting taste and the blue paint trickling out around my lips. When he came it was in my face, the second one, and he deliberately did it over my eyelids, leaving me unable to open them, blind as well as helpless.

Bart was last. I was getting in a bit of a state and he soothed me for a while, stroking my hair and whispering to me, before he buggered me. I'd known he would, and I wasn't surprised when I felt the firm head of his cock press to my bumhole. It stung as it went up, stretching me out until I once more had that blissful, stuffed feeling, with the sense that the cock inside me is filling my whole body. He began to rock me on his erection, slowly, his hands stroking my bottom and legs.

I let myself go, knowing he'd do it for me as I thought of the state I was in and what had been done to me. They used me so hard, making me their plaything, their sex toy, nothing but a little fuck dolly, naked and ready for their amusement. I'd been hunted down like an animal, made to run naked through the woods, chased, brought down and fucked on the ground.

Bart was pushing harder, long, even strokes so that I could feel my ring pulling in and out and the straining, bloating feel of his stiff cock each time it filled my hole. His hands had found my sex, stroking my pussy mound, smearing come and paint over my skin, which was rough with the little hairs that had begun to poke through.

My mind went to the blind terror of my second run, the pain and the sense of panic as they'd shot me again and again, fifty times, covering my whole body in paint, bruising me, abusing me until I was dizzy and out of control. Then it had been under the pump in front of all of them and into the sack, tied at the neck, slit to let them get at my sex. Their cocks had gone up, one by one, in my mouth, up my pussy, up my bottom.

His hand reached my pussy, rubbing in between my lips and at last on to my clit as he pushed his cock right to the hilt up my bottom. As he began to masturbate me he changed the way he was moving in me, to short, jerking motions, keeping my bumhole moving as I was frigged.

It really all came together then; all my fear, helplessness and pain turned to pure sexual pleasure as I started to come. My pussy closed, oozing out bits of paintball and spunk, my bumhole squeezed tight on his cock and I was screaming, clutching at my bonds, straining in the tight ropes, begging to be used and hurt and spunked up even as he obliged, landing a stinging slap on my aching bottom as his cock jerked inside me and suddenly my bottom was full of hot slimy come.

I really writhed as he did it in me, coming again and again, to peak after peak, wriggling on his cock and screaming out my ecstasy. I could feel it all, the rope on my wrists and ankles, every bruise, every blemish, the come and the paint on my face, and over my pussy, but best of all, most wonderful of all, the thick, meaty cock jammed so, so deep up my bottom.

# Seven

After the paintballing I could feel myself going down. The world outside the farm hardly seemed real, and there was no sense of resentment at the way Annabelle and Marcus had treated me, only gratitude for having made so much effort.

I'd been sent back into the woods after they had finished with me, in the same way an angler might throw a carp back after weighing and measuring it. I hadn't even been allowed under the pump for a wash.

The stream has served well enough, but I'd had to dry off by standing in the sun in one of the little fields. It was there, standing naked in the warm afternoon sun, that it really sank in. Some of the cars were leaving, I could hear the engines, men's voices too. All of it seemed so remote, so inaccessible, and so frightening. I remembered the sound of my parents' car the day they had dropped me off at university, leaving me to fend for myself, and how for just a moment I'd felt more dependent on them than since I was a child.

I just stood there, stock still, listening, wondering if my feelings were like those of a fox listening to the sound of a meet disbanding in the evening. Each voice was distinct. There was Annabelle, her voice friendly, easy as she said goodbye, to Marcus, firm and in control, to a braying laugh from one of the men, a man who had just shot me and fucked me as I lay tied up in a sack. There was vulnerability, and fear, but each voice sent a new shiver down my spine at the thought of what they'd done, filling me with the urge to touch myself, which was definitely not the reaction of a hunted animal.

Only when I heard the sound of Bart's voice did I leave, moving back into the shelter of the wood. I was exhausted, enough to want to retreat to my den without bothering about my scraps. Once there, curled up on my bed of grass and leaves, I was asleep in no time.

It was next day that I was caught in the net. In the morning I was cold and hungry. Assuming that every-one would still be asleep, I started for the house, intending to sneak into the kitchen and pinch something from the fridge. I was thinking of strawberry yoghurt, which Annabelle always had in but which I'd never been allowed, and I simply wasn't looking where I was going. One moment I was walking, and the next the vegetation had closed in around me and I had been whisked off my feet, into the air, along with grass and ferns and bits of twig.

I very quickly realised that I was in a net because both my feet had gone through holes so that my legs were sticking out of the mesh. That was bad enough, but it had closed over my head and all I could see was greenery and a tiny bit of sky. I couldn't see properly and I couldn't touch the ground, which brought me to the edge of panic before I managed to get myself under control and stop thrashing about uselessly.

Getting out was not going to be easy, but it was not impossible. First I had to get my legs free of the holes, which was really difficult because it was so hard to get any purchase and the net kept swinging to and fro with my movements. I was aware that I would be making a frankly ridiculous display of myself, especially as I had to keep pushing my bottom against the mesh, but I at least had the consolation that nobody was looking.

At least, that was what I thought, until I finally managed to get my face to an opening and found Marcus standing there, still in his dressing gown, grinning at me with his morning erection in his hand.

He fucked me through the net, pulling the mesh taut against my bottom and entering me as I hung there, contorted into the most awkward position with my legs bent back at the knees and my rear end stuck out into his lap. There was nothing I could do about it and he just used me, really taking his time, because at the end of the day he was only what they call piss-proud and it took ages for him to get properly excited. In the end he came up me and left it dripping out of my pussy to the ground beneath.

Instead of letting me down, he went to one of the trees, an overgrown apple, to break off three of the long suckers that had come up around the base. I watched as he plaited them into a long, whippy switch, tying off the ends with twine. Ready, it was applied once to my bum, where my flesh was poking through the net, making me twitch and squeak at the sudden sharp pain.

I watched him disassemble the trap, which had been triggered electronically, cursing myself for not paying attention. With the power off, he undid a knot and I was dropped to the ground, landing on my bum with a squeak. I tried to escape, but he had quickly pulled the top together and bound it with twine, leaving me helpless.

He threw me over his shoulder and walked back to the farm, whistling happily to himself but never addressing a single word to me. As I'd guessed, nobody else was about, and I wondered if the trap had been alarmed in some way. He didn't seem inclined to explain, merely dumping me on the pantry floor and starting to make coffee, still whistling.

With his coffee ready, he sat down, put his feet up on me and began to read a book, *Thornton on Outdoor Pig*

*Production.* Sophie was the next one down, in her maid's uniform. She gave me a look of surprise and a little amused smile, but said nothing, evidently having been forbidden to do so. Annabelle came last.

'I caught it,' Marcus announced, prodding me with his foot.

'So I see, well done,' she answered, bending and pulling a piece of fern aside to expose my sex. 'A female, I see. Shall we breed her, or stock up on bacon?'

'There's not enough meat on her for bacon,' Marcus answered. 'We'll breed her. We need a new sow.'

'Fair enough. Well get her out then, before she messes the floor.'

'Sure, I'll chain her in the end stall.'

That was it, cruel, casual and abrupt. They were going to make me a farm animal, a pig.

I nearly laughed aloud. After everything she'd put me through, every gradual debasement, and she had finally reached my favourite fantasy. I adore being a piggy-girl, rude, messy and irresponsible, far easier to handle than the military fantasy, except for one thing.

They were joking about the bacon, but I wasn't so sure they were joking about the breeding. As Marcus once more slung me across his shoulder I was having panicky visions of being put out for a real pig, some great, lust-driven boar to whom one pink and naked female was much like the next. They are bad tempered, massive, vicious, and do not easily take no for an answer. I'd get fucked.

What I couldn't do was ask, just in case they were joking but decided it would be funny if I revealed my feelings. All I could do was hope that they were no more likely to have me covered by a boar than to use me to stock up on bacon.

I was dumped in the stall, on the usual mouldy straw, while Marcus went to the back. Rolling over, I saw him take hold of a great rusty ring, which must have been original. What was attached to it wasn't – a shiny new chain, in steel. He gave it a good tug, checking it was secure, before kneeling down by my head.

'Good girl, don't struggle, come on now,' he said, and began to feed the chain into the opening of the net.

It was put around my neck, not tight, but so that I could not possibly get it off. He kept on talking, soothing me with words as he held the links together and clipped a heavy padlock into place. I was caught, with a vengeance, as reliant on them as I had been while in plaster, only without the consideration due to a human patient.

With me chained, Marcus undid the twine and rolled me out of the net. I stayed on all fours, silent, knowing full well that any unpiglike behaviour would earn me a thrashing with the switch, and it looked painful. I got it anyway, two swift cuts across the width of my bare bottom, presumably just to make sure I knew exactly what it felt like.

He left. That was one thing with them. Whatever they did, they always made sure they gave me plenty of time alone, to really let the state I was in come home to me. It does work, like making a girl wait with her panties down before she's spanked or caned, and then putting her in the corner with them still pulled down afterwards. Having to think about it always adds to the experience, and that's just as true for a piggy-girl.

They'd given me something to think about as well. Rationally, I was sure they wouldn't do anything as dangerous as have me covered by a boar. It wasn't too perverted for them though, not if I was on the receiving end, and there was a nagging doubt that they might not realise how aggressive boars can be, or that they might do it but with protection, perhaps with his trotters bound and with a muzzle on to stop him nipping me.

If they did, I knew it would be too much. It would break me and I'd cry off, which might or might not be the end. That didn't stop me thinking about it, especially with nothing to do but lie on the straw in the warm, still air and think pig.

I just had to do it; it was impossible not to. With a sigh of despair for my own filthy mind, I got into pig-mounting position, on all fours, with my knees set wide and my bottom lowered to leave my pussy gaping. I was at the end of my tether, so I could feel the strain of the chain against my neck and imagine I'd tried to get away before being caught by my mate.

My hand went to my breasts, stroking the weight of each as they hung from my chest, wishing I had twelve instead of two. For a while I just stroked my nipples, breathing gently as my excitement rose to the point where I could really let myself go. It came surprisingly fast and, as my hand went back to my pussy, there I was, small and pink and female, a little sow, barely more than a piglet, put out to be bred.

I'd be one of the slender, modern breeds, Landrace, I think they're called. They'd be making a cross though, and the boar would be another breed, something huge and hairy, a good old-fashioned pig, like the ones in story books, enormously fat, black perhaps, but unlike the ones in story books, he would have the most colossal, corkscrew-shaped cock hanging under his great, wobbling belly.

He'd come up behind me, sniffing my pussy to get me excited, female scent. No, not pussy, that was for girls, better what Marcus called it: cunt. I'd be down, my rear-end stuck out in helpless response to his sheer maleness, scared, trembling, but eager for him to mount me, eager for his cock to twist up into my ready hole. He'd grunt and I'd feel his weight on me as he started to climb up, on to my back, his rough hair scratching my tender skin. His huge belly would spread out over my back, pressing me down into the straw, his flesh hot against mine, his breath hotter still on my neck.

My neck would be taken in his jaws, really gently, but hard enough to make absolutely sure I didn't try to struggle, to make absolutely sure that I knew who was boss. Then it would go up, his great, fat cock, stuffed rudely up my cunt, right up.

I'd be fucked, rough and hard on the ground, squealing in tune to his frenzied grunts as he humped me, in and out, pumping crazily in my hole, a great, fat black pig mounted on my back, humping my poor, aching cunt as I squealed and screamed in burning, mindless ecstasy . . .

Which was exactly what I was doing, with my bum wiggling in the air and my fingers working between my sex lips, pressed painfully hard to my clit. It was a great orgasm, really long, rising slowly to a peak with my filthy fantasy running over and over in the mind, just imagining the feel of the great fat belly crushing me down into the straw and the huge cock pumping frantically into my body.

The spell broke when I suddenly remembered the most irritating fact, which is that pigs actually have rather small cocks. Fortunately it came too late to spoil my climax and I slumped happily into the straw, feeling very dirty and rather pleased with myself.

It wasn't until lunch that I saw anybody; Sophie, now dressed as a farm girl, complete with green wellies and an iron pail. She came to the front of my sty, leaning on the gate and looking down on me, smiling.

'Have they got your number, Penny Birch,' she said happily. 'You make a great pig, the best. Here, I've got some lunch for you.'

I wanted to tell her that with her fat bottom and heavy boobs she'd have looked better still, but I contented myself with an inquisitive oink. She put the pail down in the sty. I caught the scent immediately.

'Tomatoes,' she said, 'very good for fattening pigs, or at least that's what Marcus's book says. Apparently it improves the flavour of the meat.'

The pail was full of them, mostly overripe, rich red with the skins bursting in places. I put my face in among them, gobbling one up, then a second, as Sophie watched, smiling happily. I wanted to ask what they were doing to her, and if she knew what they had planned for me. Especially I wanted reassurance about the breeding, but I knew better than to speak, or to do anything that Annabelle or Marcus might judge as inappropriate.

It was just as well because, before I'd even managed to nuzzle the next tomato up into my mouth, Annabelle appeared beside Sophie. She had a stick, which she used to poke me in the soft flesh of my hip.

'Do you think she'd like to be loose?' Sophie queried.

'Oh, I'm sure she would,' Annabelle replied. 'The question is, can we trust her not to stick her snout in where it doesn't belong?'

'Well, no, I don't suppose so.'

'No, but I'll tell you what we could do. Let's give her a nose ring. Then she can be led easily but we can let her run free. You can get them at Tame Valley Farmers, they only cost a few pence.'

'Great, we can have her pierced at the same time I get my tummy button done.'

'Don't be silly, we can't bring a pig into the jewellers. I'll do it myself. After all, if everything's properly sterilised, what problem could there be? It's easy.'

'I suppose so.'

'The problem is getting her to stay still. If she doesn't want it she'll struggle, and we won't be able to do it. If that happens, she'll just have to go to market.'

'That would be a pity.'

'True. Now come on, you've work to do.'

They walked away, leaving me in no doubt as to the choice I'd been given, and why I'd been given it. Annabelle wanted us pierced, and it was quite obviously a test run for the tattoo. From the sound of it Sophie had already agreed to a navel piercing, presumably to be decorated by dog tags with Annabelle's name or something. I was a pig, so I needed a nose ring.

I could choose to struggle when they came to put it in, in which case they'd back off. That would be that. I'd be sent away. Alternatively I could submit, have my nose ring fitted, presumably along with something to mark me as Annabelle's property. With us pierced, we would both be nicely set up for the tattoo. Whatever happened, whatever it took, I had to stay. I was going to let them do it to me.

Shortly afterwards the three of them went off in the car, leaving me to my overripe tomatoes and thoughts of making myself Annabelle's slave. I was a bit worried too because there had to be a chance of some local farmer coming to visit, or maybe an official of some sort. The gate stayed shut unless it was released from the house, but that didn't stop anyone climbing over. If they did, and chanced to look in the yard, there was a good chance they'd catch me and, as I was chained to the wall by my neck, there was absolutely nothing I could do about it.

All afternoon I was starting at noises, but nobody came, until what must have been close to tea time and then I recognised first the sound of the Range Rover's engine and then Marcus's voice as he opened the gate. They came to me almost immediately, looking thoroughly pleased with themselves, especially Sophie. She was in a crop top, with her tummy bare and the new piercing showing. It was a little gold ring, with two tiny dog tags hanging from it, engraved dog tags.

'Kiss my tummy, piggy,' she said, 'and read these.'

I nuzzled her tummy and kissed the gentle swell as I read the tags. Both were the same, with just 'Sophie' on one side, and 'I belong to Annabelle' on the other. Just seeing them sent a shiver right through me, with both jealousy and need welling up inside me. I kissed her again, then put my lips to the tags and kissed again.

'Down, girl, don't get too excited,' she said.

'Don't worry, we've got a present for you too,' Marcus added, burrowing his hand into his pocket.

He pulled out a little transparent bag with a red and blue cardboard seal marked 'Tame Valley Farmers'. Inside was my ring.

It was quite obviously no girlie piece of fashion jewellery, but the real thing, a nose ring designed for a fully grown pig. It was pure copper, perhaps a tenth of an inch thick and a good two inches across, a huge thing by the standards of most body jewellery. There was also no doubt about what it was. Sophie would get away with her little gold dog tags, unless somebody actually read them. Everyone was going to know I had a pig ring through my nose.

'We'll have to have it engraved, of course,' Annabelle said to Marcus.

'Naturally,' Marcus replied. 'That's if she'll take it.'

'Oh she'll take it. She'd beg for it if she could speak.'

'Let's see then. Sophie, help me hold her down.'

They grabbed me, Marcus rolling me quickly over on to my back as Sophie grappled for a hold. I went with the pressure, providing no resistance whatsoever, allowing myself to be pinned down on my back, with Marcus sitting on one arm and Sophie on the other.

'There's no fight in her at all,' Annabelle said. 'I told you so.'

She had a bag, marked with the name of a jewellers in Bletchley, presumably where Sophie had had her piercing done. She set it down, pulling out a pair of the rubber gloves she's used for the medical fantasy, a tube of antiseptic cream and a tiny spray can.

'A numbing agent,' she said, 'that way she won't kick up a fuss when the needle goes through.'

A hard knot was forming in my tummy. It was worse than being prepared for a spanking because my craving always keeps my anxiety down. I actually felt slightly sick as she took out a sterile needle and laid it carefully on the plastic bag. It was more than I could do to look and I shut my eyes, telling myself to be a brave girl and that it was silly to make a fuss over a little thing like a piercing.

It was easy to say, not so easy to do. I heard the hiss of the canister and felt the cold, wet sensation on my nose. It began to numb and, as Annabelle's rubbery fingers found my nose, smearing antiseptic into my nostrils, I could barely feel it. That didn't stop me thinking about it and, as she let go, I gritted my teeth, waiting for the sharp stab of the needle.

Again she touched me, pulling my septum out. I felt the needle touch and there was a sudden sharp stab, that was all. I was breathing hard, but holding on, one hand held securely in Sophie's and the other clutching at the straw. I felt the actual ring touch my nose, pressure, and the most extraordinary sensation as the copper ring slid into the hole.

'Through it goes,' Annabelle said, 'gently does it . . . and we're there.'

It was done. I had a pig ring through my nose, and it was hers.

'There we are, piggy,' she said. 'That wasn't so bad at all, was it now?'

It was, my eyes were watering, not from the pain, and only partly from physical reaction, but mainly because of the significance of what had been done to me, the ring marking me both as a farm animal and, more importantly, as her farm animal.

She slid it through a little further and I opened my eyes. Her face was inches in front of mine, set in a frown as she studied the catch.

'How do you close it, Marcus?' she demanded. 'There's a hole, but nothing to put through it. Look at the packet.'

'Use this widget,' he answered. 'You screw it in, I suppose.'

He passed it to her, a tiny brass bolt with a nick at the centre and a bent head. I could see it, inches in front of my eye, as she twisted it into the hole, sealing my captivity. She tightened it, her face set in concentration, changing suddenly to annoyance.

'Shit!' she swore. 'It's snapped off!'

'Oh,' Marcus said, 'no, hang on, it's supposed to.'

'How do we get it out then?'

'We don't. It's not supposed to come out.'

For one moment Annabelle continued to look cross, before bursting out laughing even as what Marcus had said sank in and my own expression changed to serious consternation.

'Oh will you look at piggy!' Annabelle laughed. 'What a face!'

I had every right to make a face. I had a pig ring through my nose and there was no way of getting it out, save for taking a hacksaw to it.

'Show her in a mirror!' Annabelle went on. 'Sophie, run and get a mirror.'

I know it's vain, but I am pretty, or at least I'm always told I'm pretty, and not just by people trying to get into my knickers. At least I can look in the mirror or at a photograph without immediately wanting to pick faults. When Sophie brought the mirror back and showed me my face with the big copper ring through my nose it was like looking back at a stranger, more than a stranger in fact, a girl from a strange culture, even a strange creature. For a start my hair was mussed up and full of bits of straw, while my skin was streaked with dirt and tomato juice. There were pips and pieces of the bright red skin smeared around my mouth and on my nose and cheeks as well. That made me look like a dirty little brat whose face had been pushed in a load of old tomatoes, but no more. It was the ring that really did it, the big, copper pig ring, something no girl would ever choose to wear unless she wanted to be brought down, brought down right to the level of being a farm animal, a pig. Yet despite all that I was still pretty, a pretty piggy-girl, yes, but pretty.

It was a wonderfully submissive image and I could only stare, watching my face as the tears rolled down my cheeks, tracing trails through the dirt and tomato stains. I was crying because my emotions were too powerful not to. There was strong humiliation – and frustration – for what had been done to me. There was a sense of relief, of irresponsibility, of release. There was submission, glorious, overwhelming submission to the people who had brought me so far. There was also arousal, because the whole thing tapped straight into my sexuality.

They let me watch myself, Annabelle with a knowing, proprietorial smile, Marcus cool and amused, Sophie hiding her giggles behind her hand. Eventually it was just too much. I shut my eyes, my head swimming, wanting to masturbate, badly, but wanting to be told to do it.

'Look at her,' Annabelle remarked. 'She's wants to come.'

I stuck my bottom out, responding to her understanding of my needs. My hand went back, finding my pussy absolutely sopping with juice. I began to masturbate.

'Sophie, get your face in piggy's bum,' Annabelle ordered. 'Put the mirror where she can see herself.'

Sophie obeyed immediately, resting the mirror against the wall of my sty and scrabbling round behind me on all fours. Something cold and wet squashed against my bum, right between the cheeks, tomatoes, and then Sophie had buried her face in my bottom and I was in heaven. She was licking up the tomato pulp, off the inner curve of my bum cheeks and in the crease, where the skin is so sensitive. It is such a dirty thing to do, for a girl even to kiss another girl's bottom, let alone lick, let alone lap up messy, overripe tomato pulp right from her bumhole, which was what Sophie had begun to do.

I opened my eyes, watching my piggy face as I was licked, still rubbing at my pussy. I felt the soft, round shape of a tomato pushed against my fingers. It burst, right in the hole of my pussy, pulp spraying over my thighs and trickling down my fingers. Sophie's tongue was up my bottom, right in the dirty little hole, and my mouth had fallen open in helpless ecstasy. Another tomato was pushed to my pussy, a firmer one, stretching my hole wide before it too burst and my hole filled with squashy, cool tomato pulp. I could barely see, my eyes hazy with tears and half closed in my ecstasy. What I could see was my nose, with the ring hanging down over my open mouth, swinging to the rhythm of my masturbation. I could feel it too, through the hole Annabelle had made, puncturing my flesh, taking control of me, marking me as her own . . .

My pussy started to contract and I felt the mess of tomato flesh squash out against Sophie's chin. She was probing my bumhole with her tongue, so deep, right up the little ring, opening me wide into her face. I was rubbing, my clit bumping under my fingers, to one side, then the other as my orgasm rose in my head and I stared open mouthed at the image of myself as a dirty, soiled girl pig, filthy with muck and marked with her owner's ring, Annabelle's ring.

I came on that thought, my ecstasy mixed with an overpowering gratitude to Annabelle, almost worship. It might have been Sophie's whose tongue was up my bottom, but it was Annabelle who had ordered her to do it, our mistress, who kept us in our place and kept us so, so high on sex.

I was left alone for the rest of the day, just lazing in my sty and enjoying being a pig. When I needed to pee I just squatted down and let it all spurt out, which gave me the best of the wonderful irresponsibility that goes with the role.

Six o'clock was marked by Sophie's screams, four of them as she took her daily dose of the cane, probably across her thighs judging by the fuss she made. The air had began to cool and I began to make a nest of straw to sleep in, wondering if the pail of squashy tomatoes was all I was going to get to eat.

It was. Sophie came out after dinner to deal with Mabel, but there was nothing for me. Nor was there anything to do, except eat rotten tomatoes and play with myself, both of which I did before curling up in the straw and falling asleep, before it was even fully dark.

I woke to an irritating tickling sensation and absolute blackness. For a while I lay with my eyes shut, trying to get back to sleep, but it was impossible. The straw was a lot less comfortable than the grass in my den and I seemed to be sharing it with an assortment of the local fauna, spiders mainly.

Eventually I sat up, feeling rather irritable. I thought about masturbating, but it didn't feel right and the night was also quite chilly. As my eyes adapted to the night I became able to make out the shape of the barn roof against a sky sprinkled with stars. A fox barked somewhere in the distance, filling me with a sudden sense of space and loneliness.

I wanted to be in a warm bed, snuggled up to Amber, or Sophie, or anyone really, as long as they would give me a cuddle. With that came the understanding of what it was actually going to be like to be Annabelle's slave. I would have to submit my will to hers totally, without reserve. She was right, I wouldn't suffer nudity, or bondage, or punishment and derive my pleasure from that suffering. I would accept those conditions as natural, as normal, as my appointed place.

She'd already nose-ringed me and when I came over the experience I had felt that it was right, that I could only experience true happiness as her owned slave. That had been at orgasm. Now, in the cold loneliness of the night, chained by the neck in a country pig sty, I wasn't so sure. After all, my previous orgasm had been over being caught and effectively raped by a boar pig, and I certainly don't really want that!

Amber always made me feel protected. Annabelle made me feel protected, but also insecure, and never more than now. I didn't mind what she'd done to me, at all, but at that moment I needed to be able to speak to someone, and as my hands went to the chain around my neck I was fighting down a bubble of rising panic.

It was secure, absolutely secure, thick steel links joined by a heavy-duty padlock, strong enough to hold a horse, never mind a seven-stone girl. The links were shut tight, but they weren't welded; I could feel the thin gaps with my nails. I was padlocked at the neck, but I knew there was no padlock at the other end.

Sure enough, Marcus had fixed the chain to the old ring by opening a link and closing it on another. The link he had opened was off centre, with a gap, too small to pull the chain through, but not too small for the lip of the pail my food had come in. I crawled over to get it, with my melancholy feelings turning rapidly to mischief as I fumbled in the darkness. With the pail resting on my lap I managed to get the opened link on to the edge, jamming it down, twisting with all my strength and praying that I had enough leverage.

I did. By the time it came open far enough to disengage I was running sweat and my hands where in agony. It didn't matter. I was free. Naked, nose-ringed, but free.

For a good minute I just wallowed in my sense of triumph, before trying to decide what to do with my freedom. For one thing it was temporary because by morning I needed to be back in my sty, securely fixed to the wall. Even then I was sure I'd damaged the pail and there seemed to be every chance of a heavy session under the pig switch in the morning. If I was going to be whipped, I wanted to earn it.

The first thing I needed was Sophie, for a cuddle. That meant getting into the house, which was both locked and alarmed. My only chance was to throw gravel up at Sophie's windows and hope I could wake her, and that they hadn't put her in bondage for the night.

Annabelle and Marcus's bedroom faced the front of the house, so I went on to the lawn, feeling my way in the darkness. I could see the gable ends of the dormitory windows, little else, but it was enough. Five minutes later Sophie was leaning out of her window, with her light on, frantically signalling me to be quiet.

I got my cuddle, and more. She was in her maid's nightie and big white knickers, but stripped off to hold me and very soon decided she wanted to play with my chain. We wrapped it around our bodies, head to toe, lying on top of the bed and pretending to be chained together while we licked each other to climax. She needed comfort too and afterwards I spent a lot of time kissing and stroking her cane welts to make her feel better.

It was good, and it felt naughty as well, because we both knew we'd be in serious trouble if Annabelle caught us, not just me, but Sophie, for failing to report my escape. She explained that to me as we talked after sex, that Annabelle wanted us loyal to her, not to each other. She also told me her feelings, that she was enjoying the experience, but still felt out in the cold because Annabelle would never unbend. I agreed and in the end, cuddled together and feeling secure in each other's arms, I told her about the bet and the pussy tattoo.

I had to. It would have been wrong to let her make the decision without knowing everything. She was my friend anyway and, for all Annabelle's efforts, I felt close to her and didn't want to lie. I thought she'd be furious, and she did feign outrage, but as much at Bart

201

and Anderson as at Annabelle and Marcus. She also threatened to spank me for not telling her before, but held back, contenting herself with assuring me that she was quite capable of looking after herself and that there was no way she was going to get the tattoo. As she explained, the dog tags were one thing, and could be removed easily, but a tattoo was permanent.

It would have been nice to sleep with her, but I didn't dare. After a last kiss and cuddle I left, sure that if I lay in her arms much longer I would just doze off. I asked if she knew what time it was and to my surprise she guessed that it wasn't that long after midnight, which meant I'd woken up at perhaps a quarter past eleven.

I left the way I'd come, down the servants' stairs towards the back door. On the way up, the corridor had been in absolute blackness. Now it wasn't. A thin line of golden light showed beneath the bathroom door. It was a fair way from me, but I still froze, not daring to move. Several of the stairs down to the kitchen creaked and, with no carpet to muffle them, I was sure I would be heard.

I was equally sure that to whoever was in the bathroom my end of the passage would appear totally black. So I stood still, on the bottom step, peering down the passage, with a lump of apprehension in my throat for what was going to happen to me if I was caught. Moments later came the sound of a tap and then the bathroom door opened.

It was Annabelle, in a black silk negligee and matching panties, only she didn't actually have the panties on. It looked so good, with her little bare behind showing under the hem of her negligee and the panties trailing in her hand. I could only stare, enchanted by the way her bottom moved as she walked, the sweetly rounded little cheeks rising and falling. She has never let me see it, not bare, and now there it was, and so pretty, so kissable.

I just wanted to lick her bottom for her, but I knew that if I offered I was more likely to get the pig switch than what I wanted, so I waited, following the gentle movement of her cheeks as she walked to the far end of the passage and in at their bedroom door.

It was obvious what was going on. They'd either just had sex or they were about to have it. I'd often wondered how they made love together, if Annabelle was still prissy about showing her body, if she went sub to him, or he to her, or neither. Now I had a chance to find out and I just had to take it, even if it meant getting caught. I didn't care if they thrashed me until I passed out. I didn't care if they made me eat my own dirt. I had to know.

I counted to twenty and began to creep along the corridor, very slowly, planting one bare foot in front of the other. The chain was coiled in my hand and I made sure to keep it still and not to knock it against anything. I kept expecting one or other of them to step out into the corridor, catching me red handed. Neither did, and I made it, freezing outside their bedroom door with my heart hammering and a lump the size of a football in my throat. I heard a creak and I nearly wet myself, but nothing happened and when it sounded again I realised it was the wooden frame of their bed. Then came Annabelle's voice, very soft, little more than a whisper.

'Talk to me while I do it.'

The muscles around my mouth twitched into a smile, then a manic grin as I heard a wet, smacking sound. She was going to suck his cock, which might not seem all that submissive, but for her . . .! I could just picture it, with her pretty face full of the same fat cock that had been in my mouth, my pussy. It had been up my bum and now she was going to suck it, with her cheeks sucked in and her lips wide around the shaft of his cock. He was going to talk as she sucked as well, and it was sure to be dirty.

'What do you fancy?' Marcus said.

'Oh, I don't know,' Annabelle said, 'to see Penny with that ring through her nose, and when the bolt snapped! Sophie was good too. I love it when they cry. I can't wait until they're ready.'

'Nor me,' Marcus agreed. 'Just a few more days, I think. You're very wet.'

'I know, and you're very hard. Shall I climb on?'

'Yes.'

She wasn't going to suck him, which was a shame, but they were masturbating each other, which was something, and they were going to fuck. There was a pause, presumably as she mounted him, then a lovely wet noise and a sigh, which I took to mean she had slid herself down on his erection.

'When they're ready,' Marcus went on, 'I want to watch you use your strap-on, up their little cunts, with the tattoos showing. Up their bumholes too.'

'Yes,' Annabelle answered, 'perfect, and make them suck it clean. That's what I want. It was so hard when Penny wanted to kiss my bum. I just wanted to pull my knickers aside, to stuff her sweet little face in there, to come while she licked my bottom. She needed it so badly.'

'She'll get it, sweetheart. When she's tattooed you can make her your toilet slave. Chain her to the lavatory, nude, and make her only job in life to lick your bottom clean.'

'Yes, perfect. Carry on like that. Just keep talking.'

I could actually hear Annabelle masturbating as she rode him, a wet, fleshy sound, along with her breathing, and his too. As for their fantasy, it was so dirty, and I was having trouble keeping my fingers away from my own pussy.

'Yes,' Marcus said, 'perfect. Chain her to the lavatory, by the neck, kneeling, nude, stark naked, with her hands tied behind her back. Keep her there, as your toilet slave. She'd have to keep her knees open so her tattoo showed. You could make her drink from the lavatory bowl. You could make her clean it with her tongue. You could stick her head down it and piss on her. You could dab your pussy dry with lavatory paper and make her eat it. No, you wouldn't need paper, because she'd be there, to lick you clean, to stick her face in and put her tongue right up your dirty bottom . . .'

'No, the tattoo,' Annabelle broke in.

It was said in a gasp, the sound of a girl right on the edge of orgasm.

'She'd be tattooed all right,' Marcus went on. 'Tattooed right on her sweet little cunt. Shaved bare and tattooed on her cunt, tattooed with our names, tattooed as our property, tattooed for everyone to see, on her sweet little cunt . . .'

He stopped abruptly, with a choking sound, and I knew he'd come. Annabelle's orgasm followed immediately, a long sigh of bliss, then a jumble of words.

'Penny, Penny, do it for me, you little filthy, dirty, brown-nosed little dirt-bag slut!'

She finished with a gasp, after which I could only hear her breathing, slow and even as she came down from her orgasm. I had my eyes closed, trying to block out the image they had created, of me kneeling nude by the lavatory with my sole purpose in life to keep Annabelle's pussy and bottom clean. I wanted to masturbate over it, so badly, and I was turning away with exactly that in mind when Marcus spoke again.

'So you really think they'll do it, both of them?'

'Yes. Like I hoped, they're both natural submissives. It's just a question of getting them to truly recognise their natures. Penny's closest, I think, and I can get her there, I'm sure of it. I've got her figured out. Whatever we do to her, we've got to make her come over it. That fixes it in her mind as acceptable. I just need to plant the idea of a pussy tattoo in her empty little head, give her the promise of sex with me if she'll do it and we'll be there.'

'And Sophie?'

'Not far behind. She's different, less repressed, and she doesn't have such a strong urge to be mothered. It's her need to shed responsibility that I'm counting on.'

'I can't wait to see Bart and Anderson's faces when they see the tattoos.'

'Especially that bastard Anderson. He's so smug. Imagine telling me I ought to be spanked myself before I did it to anyone else! Bastard!'

'We'll have to invite them to dinner of course, and serve the La Tâche, to really rub it in. We could even let them fuck Sophie and Penny, that would be ironic.'

'No way, but you can do it in front of them. They'll be spitting jealous.'

Marcus chuckled and the bed creaked. I began to back away, worrying that they'd want the bathroom after sex. I was feeling pretty confused as I crept slowly down the passage. Listening to Annabelle climax had left me feeling very dirty indeed. What had come afterwards I was less happy about, especially her opinion of my intelligence. I knew it wasn't true, after all – women with 'empty little heads' don't get made university lecturers – but it still hurt.

Inexperienced dominants often make the same mistake, assuming that submissives are stupid just because we're obedient and docile. Annabelle and Marcus had never seen me as anything other than a submissive, so I could see why. Besides that, I had let myself be led, very easily.

On the other hand, it was comforting to think that they'd completely failed to realise I'd been planted on them, and that made me feel better about having my intelligence insulted. I also knew why she was holding back. Intimate sex was the carrot to the stick of her cruelty, the one thing to be held back until we had our tattoos. If I didn't get my tattoo, I wasn't going to get Annabelle, a thought that left a queasy feeling in my stomach. I wanted her, badly, and worse after seeing her bare bottom and hearing what she wanted me to do to her.

I remembered what she'd called me – a little filthy, dirty, brown-nosed little dirt-bag slut. It was hardly flattering, but it was just the sort of thing that runs through my head when I'm coming, especially when I've been really dirty. It had been like that when I'd done it on the assault course, and when I'd filled my nappy. We did work together, very well, and if she'd only been prepared to relax, just a little, I might even have done it, had the rotten tattoo, just so that I could get what I needed so badly. After all, my pubic hair's really thick and bushy, and there's always laser treatment.

I didn't masturbate in the end. I wanted to, but when I got back to my sty my head was still full of confusing thoughts and I decided to fix my chain back to the ring first. By the time I'd done that my hands hurt and I'd just lost the moment. It was cold too and I had to completely cover myself with straw to stop my shivering. Even then I didn't think I was going to sleep, but I did.

In the morning I was a piggy-girl again, at least once I'd drunk the mug of hot coffee Sophie sneaked out to me. It had rained in the early hours and the air was still fresh and wet, with a heavy blanket of cloud overhead. It was a lot warmer though and by the time I'd finished the coffee and had a chat with Sophie I felt able to face the day, if not exactly ready for it.

My escape seemed like a dream, but their conversation was clear in my head, and my reaction to it. Annabelle had shown no hint of submission during sex, which I'd been hoping for. She'd gone on top and not even given him a token suck, so far as I knew. Possibly she was the pure dominant woman she claimed to be. Certainly she had been outraged by Anderson having suggested she learn how it felt to be spanked before dishing it out to others. That is actually a really sensible suggestion and if it hadn't been for the bet I wouldn't have let her punish me exactly because she didn't know how it felt. It also seemed likely that Anderson would have volunteered to do the spanking himself, and imagining her reaction really put a smile on my face.

Marcus came out not long after Sophie had left, carrying a box of tools. He ignored me, other than a quick glance into the sty before going into the barn. I knew he was using it as a workshop and wondered what he was up to. After a while I heard hammering, not steady, but occasional sudden flurries of blows. Silence would follow, and then more blows.

Eventually he emerged, holding a bundle of thick straps, brown leather and fitted with heavy-duty brass buckles. It was too small to be anything for Mabel and there was only one other animal on the farm. It was clearly no piece of purpose-made SM gear, but a genuine horse harness, cut to size and refitted for a human body, for a pony-girl.

He hung it on the door of my sty and went back to the barn, leaving me to think about what was coming. Like being a pig, I could handle being a pony. It's Amber's favourite thing, and what brought us together. It was easy to imagine Annabelle as a pony-girl mistress, exercising me, putting me through dressage routines, maybe even jumps, all at the tip of a whip. I didn't suppose they'd actually made a cart for me to pull, as Annabelle's fantasies were not really as highly evolved as Amber's. After all, when I was a piggy-girl for Amber I had a little rubber snout and a curly rubber tail stuck on my face and bottom to complete the image.

There was no cart, but there was something else a lot more worrying. It was a yoke, a great padded thing of wood and leather, made to fit around my shoulders. I could see the purpose of it, as with it on I would be able to pull with the full weight of my body, for what that was worth. The question was, what would I be pulling?

The answer was a plough. It was a huge rusty thing, really ancient with a single share and a massive wooden frame. Marcus had difficulty moving it and there was absolutely no way I was going to be able to pull it, let alone through the heavy, soft soil of the fields. I was wondering what he was hoping to achieve, until he produced another harness, much larger, and went to Mabel's stall.

Half an hour later I was off my chain and in harness, crawling along behind the carthorse on a pair of thick knee pads. I'd been put in first, kneeling in the yard as Mabel watched me with her great placid eyes. She had then been led out and harnessed in front of me, so that I was well clear of her hooves but firmly fixed to the plough as the rear animal of a two-in-hand formation. That was bad enough, but Marcus had fixed two wooden prods to the plough so that if I held back I got poked in the bottom and legs.

It was so cruel. I had to crawl, and I had to pull. If I slacked, the pricks stabbed against my bottom. I had to stay directly behind Mabel, which meant going through the occasional pile of horse dung as well as mud. I discovered this as Marcus led us down to one of the small fields, Mabel dropping a huge, steaming load of dung on the grassy track, which I just couldn't avoid. I went in it, feeling it squash up around one leg as I stumbled in my effort to avoid the main pile. Marcus laughed and gave me a flick across my bottom with the pig switch.

I was close to tears by the time we reached the field and my body was already wet with sweat. It was hard work, although I was sure that my contribution would make no difference whatsoever to Mabel. After amusing himself by placing a few cuts of the pig switch across my bare bottom, Marcus stamped the plough share down into the wet soil, gave me a last flick across the rump and took hold of Mabel's reins.

She began to pull and I was forced to follow, crawling through the wet grass with my bottom stinging from the pig switch and the soil turning behind me, unable to stand, unable to stop. Before we'd even finished the first furrow my hair was plastered down around my face, my legs were aching and my limbs were filthy with mud. By the end of the second another load of horse dung had been added to the mud, all over one hand and up my arm.

I was filthy, soiled and sweaty, crawling on in blind determination. Occasionally I'd go too slowly, until I felt the stab of the pricks against my buttocks and thighs, forcing me to go faster, and to pull. At each turn Marcus put a few more cuts of the pig switch across my bottom, until my whole rear was throbbing and my pussy felt swollen and ripe. I was praying he'd get bored with ploughing and stop Mabel so that he could fuck me, down on my knees in the wet grass. He didn't, just switching me occasionally and guiding Mabel until I was dizzy with fatigue and barely aware of where I was, with my world limited to the great brown rear of the carthorse, the wet grass and mud, my harness and the stinging pain of the switch.

At some point the sun broke through the clouds, adding heat and thirst to my worries. That was really the last straw. I was trying hard, but I knew I really couldn't go on and at the end of the next furrow I just collapsed on the ground. Marcus gave me a prod with his boot and a flick of the switch across my legs, but when I didn't move he laughed and started back towards the house.

He returned with nosebags and buckets of water, with which he fed and watered us. Mabel was seen to first, as the more valuable animal, I supposed, certainly the more useful when it came to ploughing. Only when she was done was I allowed to drink from my bucket and my bag was tied to my head. It was oats, just that, without even an overripe tomato or a few cabbage leaves to give it flavour. I ate anyway, chewing on the grains and spitting out the husks.

I knew what he was doing, taking me slowly up to the point of exhaustion so that I'd be that much more pliable. That didn't make it any easier, and nor did the knowledge that I'd be made to come over the experience, to fix it in my empty head, as Annabelle had said.

As I ate, so did Marcus. He sat cross-legged on the grass casually eating bread and cheese and washing it down with gulps of beer. After a while his zip came down and he took out his cock. It was such a relief to see it. He could fuck me, even bugger me, anything as long as I didn't have to do any more ploughing, even to postpone it.

He was in no rush, following the bread and cheese with an apple, all the time watching me. By the time he had taken the last bite and thrown the core away into the bushes his cock was rock hard.

First it went in my mouth, sliding it in and out between my lips while he felt my breasts. When he'd had his fill of that, he fucked me, squatting over my bottom to avoid the prods and driving himself down into my pussy. I had to stick it right up to let him in, resting on the yoke, which meant putting my boobs in the wet grass. He'd only pulled my nosebag aside to make me suck him and it was still on, my face in the oats as he humped my bottom.

Before long I was really getting into it, a harnessed pony-girl mounted from the rear, very casually, just so her driver could have a bit of fun during his lunch break. That's the way for a man to fuck a harnessed girl, when he pleases, enjoying the sight of her body and

211

using her pussy as a pot for his spunk when he feels like it, without ever bothering to ask her.

I wanted to masturbate, but at first I couldn't find the energy. When I did I had my thigh slapped for my trouble, but he continued to fuck me, intent on his own pleasure while denying me mine. The denial made me more desperate, more frustrated, and I kept trying, until he got fed up and strapped my wrists up behind my back to stop me doing it.

With me completely helpless and my face pressed into my nosebag, he went back to my bottom. I stuck it up, eager for entry, only to feel his cock press to my bumhole. All I could manage was a little groan of despair as he began to force my little sweaty ring. I tried to relax, but it wouldn't go in, so he dipped himself in my pussy, smearing the juice he pulled out on to my bottom, once, twice, then pushing again. This time when I relaxed, my ring spread, gaping to take his cock head, then the shaft, wedged slowly up my bum until I could feel his balls pressing against my pussy and his pubic hair tickling in between my bum cheeks.

He buggered me slowly, long even strokes, really enjoying me. Slow strokes are always the best, with the bloated, straining feeling as the cock goes in, and the awful, desperate one as it comes out. It feels a lot nicer up my pussy, natural, dizzying pleasure, but it feels a lot dirtier up my bum.

It is a lot dirtier and, being a total bastard, Marcus pulled out and made me take him in my mouth for his orgasm. I sucked willingly enough, with my eyes screwed up to the taste but wishing I could masturbate while I did it, and in due course I got my mouth filled with spunk.

I'd hoped he would let me go once he'd had his fun, but there was no such luck. I was put back to ploughing, only now with both my holes open and wet, my mouth full of the taste of his come and my own bottom, and my head swimming with frustration.

The exhaustion returned quickly, until once more I barely knew what I was doing. Again and again the prods would catch me, jabbing into my bottom and thighs. Again and again I would stumble and go down in the water and mud. Every time I fell Marcus used the switch on me, but I barely felt it, and I couldn't even be bothered to try to avoid the occasional pile of horse shit, just crawling in it.

Eventually he took pity on me. I was taken out of line and my yoke taken off, leaving me to crawl to the edge of the field, where I collapsed, exhausted, indifferent to the mixture of mud and horse dung drying on my body, naked for all the world to see and just not caring. A dozen old maids could have passed by, tutting and making remarks about the way young women behaved and I wouldn't have even moved. I wouldn't have blushed either.

It was only when I became aware of a pair of boots in front of my face that I really realised what was going on at all. They were quite small, not Marcus's, and as I turned my face up I found Annabelle looking at me in sympathy. She squatted down and began to stroke my hair, for once talking to me.

'Ah, you poor little thing. Is Marcus being too rough with you?'

I nodded weakly. She touched my face, very gently, before going on.

'Oh dear, well maybe we should make you a house pet instead.'

Again I nodded.

'You'll have to prove your obedience.'

I nodded once more.

'Come on then, we'll take you back to the house and have Sophie clean you up, shall we?'

She gave me water first, from the bucket, as much as I could drink, then took hold of my harness, helping me up on to all fours. I felt so grateful as she led me away from that awful field. We reached the spot where Mabel had dropped her first load. Annabelle stopped and reached into her pocket, pulling out a hip flask, which she put to my mouth.

It was brandy, and it was so, so welcome, my feelings of gratitude rising once more to the level of worship as the spirit filled my mouth and throat with warm, golden heat. I didn't even suspect why she was giving it to me until she pulled the flask away, stood back and clicked her fingers, pointing right at the pile of horse dung.

'Sit,' she ordered. 'In that.'

I crawled over, feeling betrayed, shaking too. Half of me was hoping she'd stop me, that she was only tormenting me. She wasn't; she made me sit in it, watching as I posed my bum over the great lumpy pile and sat slowly down. I felt it squash over my pussy and up between my bum cheeks and across them as it spread out under my bum.

'Good girl,' she said, 'now take two good handfuls and do your tits.'

I couldn't help the expression on my face as I put my hands down between my thighs, and into the warm, squashy dung. Annabelle was smiling, her eyes sparkling with delight as I put the filthy handfuls to my chest, squashing it on to my breasts, letting her see how dirty they were, then smearing it over my whole chest. The animal reek was thick in my nose and it was squashing slowly up between my bum cheeks and over my pussy as my bottom settled into it. It felt so rude and I just had to wriggle my bum in it, feeling the soggy mess move under me as I caked it on to my breasts.

'Now roll in it,' she said.

There was laughter in her voice and she made a little noise as I turned to present her with my filthy, dung-smeared bottom, expressing both disgust and satisfaction. It was spread on the ground beneath me, with a bum-shaped depression in the middle, even the outline of my pussy lips. I got down, pressing my belly into it, before rolling, making sure I stayed in the pile. At any moment I expected her to order me to masturbate, but she just watched, smiling. I was going to do it anyway, rolling on to my back and spreading my thighs for her.

'No you don't,' she said. 'Not yet. Get up and crawl over to that bit.'

She was pointing to another pile, smaller and still steaming slightly in the warm sun. It was for my face, I just knew it. Sure enough, she came and took me by the hair, holding my head right over the little pile of horse dung.

'Now you get to come,' she said. 'Open wide.'

My face went in the horse shit, shoved down hard, the lumps squashing against my skin. She held me in it, face down, kicking my legs and struggling, hardly able to breathe, my nose full of the heavy smell. I'd shut my eyes in time, but my mouth was full of it, a great fat lump which squashed as I struggled to spit it out. I couldn't, she had my face too well down, holding me by the hair, right in it.

I heard her laugh and her other hand found my pussy, cupping the mound of my sex. Her thumb went up my hole and she began to grind her palm against my lips, spreading them to get at my clit. At the same time she began to rub my face in the dung. I couldn't stop her doing it, and I couldn't stop myself from wanting to come. My head was burning with humiliation, but I found myself pushing my bum up nonetheless, on to her hand, offering myself for masturbation as my face was rubbed in the filth.

She was laughing as she did it, slapping and rubbing at my pussy and all the time with her hand twisted hard into my hair, forcing my face into Mabel's pile. I was gagging on it and really thrashing my legs and writhing my bum against her hand, my breasts wobbling beneath me in the damp grass. It was happening, my pussy responding, the orgasm starting, my hole squeezing on her intruding thumb.

'You're coming, aren't you?' she said. 'Yes, you are. Now get your face in it, you little bitch, right in it, mouth open, you filthy little slut! That's right, eat it!'

I couldn't help it, I really couldn't. My mouth was full of the filthy muck anyway, and I was coming. She was really screaming at me as the orgasm hit me and I just couldn't disobey. I closed my mouth, feeling the thick, foul-tasting paste squash out, back into my throat as my whole sex went into frantic spasms on Annabelle's hand and I was in utter, perfect ecstasy, physically and mentally depraved, coming under my mistress's hand with my face pushed in dung; just beautiful, just perfect.

Annabelle let go the instant my climax broke. I was gagging and I went into a spasm of coughing and retching, trying to get the filthy stuff out of my mouth. My whole body was out of control and I wet myself as I did it, all over Annabelle's hand, which was still clasped to my pussy. I had my bottom slapped for that, but I just let it run out, spraying out behind me and trickling down my legs as I slowly regained my proper senses. Annabelle let me recover, saying nothing and stroking my hair. I was in tears, not surprisingly, and the gentleness of her touch was very welcome. It stopped abruptly and I opened my eyes in surprise at the sound of a new voice, female.

'If you can make her do that, I'm not sure you need me.'

'Melody?' Annabelle replied.

# Eight

I'm not sure what I wanted Melody to do. Certainly I didn't expect her to drag Annabelle kicking and screaming across her lap for a panties down spanking, deserved or not.

What she did do was help me clean up, which involved a scrub down under the pump with carbolic soap and a bath brush. By the end I was bright pink and tingling all over. I was sore from the ploughing too, on my knees despite the pads and where the harness had rubbed. That was taken care of with cream, in the bathroom, followed by some frantic toothbrushing and a large shot of Annabelle's brandy.

By the time Marcus came in from the field Melody and Annabelle were chatting in the parlour, with Sophie on hand to serve and me curled up on the rug, drunk and half-asleep. It was Sophie who had let Melody through the gate, which earned her an impromptu over the knee spanking, bare bottom and all, as soon as Annabelle had got over the initial surprise.

That took a long time, a remarkably long time. Annabelle had even opened a bottle of cold Chablis and poured Melody a glass before she remembered that she had Sophie as a servant. Even then Annabelle seemed flustered and the conversation stayed on the practical subject of cleaning me up until Marcus came back. He was as surprised as Annabelle, if less taken aback.

'Melody? Hi,' he greeted her. 'I didn't know you were coming.'

'Bart Pelham said you wanted my help,' Melody answered. 'With some training?'

'Bart?' Marcus queried, throwing a questioning glance at Annabelle.

'Yes, he said he'd been up here hunting little Penny with those paintball guns and that you wanted my help with something. It sounded fun, so I came. Sorry, have I got it wrong here?'

'No, no,' Marcus assured her. 'Not at all. You're very welcome. It . . . it's just that my remark to Bart was casual, I didn't actually expect you to arrive, especially not so soon.'

'Well here I am. By the look of things you've got these two well in hand without any help. What's the story?'

'Like Bart says, we've been training them. We've decided on Sophie as the maid and Penny as a household pet.'

'Nice. You may fill my glass, Sophie. What sort of pet is Penny then? A puppy?'

'A cat,' Annabelle answered. 'It's more her style.'

'Maybe,' Melody said, 'but you can do more with a dog, liking making her fetch sticks, or beg and do tricks. Cats are too independent to really work as a submissive thing.'

'True,' Marcus admitted. 'Shall we make her a dog then, Annabelle?'

Annabelle gave Marcus a dirty look, but hesitated, sipping her wine to delay her answer.

'It's much better to make her a puppy-girl,' Melody went on. 'Think of what you associate with dogs: obedience, loyalty, trust, all the things you want in a submissive. Sure, cats are prettier, but you want to humiliate her too, don't you?'

'Humiliation is not . . .' Annabelle began and stopped. 'OK, she's a dog, a poodle puppy. Sophie, why isn't there another bottle open? Do I have to spank you again?'

'I don't know, Miss Annabelle. I mean no, Miss Annabelle,' Sophie stammered. 'I'll fetch it immediately.'

'It's never easy to get decent staff,' Melody observed as Sophie scurried for the kitchen. 'Still, at least she's pretty, and obedient. Better than a male anyway; ugly, smelly things, and they're always breaking stuff in the hope of getting punished. Girls are better that way.'

'You're right. Who do you and Morris have?'

'My sister mostly, and other girls. Morris won't let us bring our male subs into the house.'

'Very sensible. After all, it wouldn't do to have them see you or Harmony put across Morris's knee.'

'I don't care. A slave's a slave and they're ten-a-penny. A real mistress does as she pleases, not what her slaves expect her to do, including enjoying the occasional spanking. It can even be a punishment, but ideally, if a mistress has enough self-confidence, she should be able to order a slave to beat her, just for the erotic thrill of it, and still stay in control. You should try it; get Sophie to give you a dozen of the cane.'

Despite my dozy state I nearly laughed. Annabelle knew full well that Melody was submissive to her husband. After all, Mel takes spankings at the club often enough, even the cane. What Annabelle hadn't expected was to have it turned round so neatly. She was blushing, and she didn't have an answer.

Melody didn't press the point, contenting herself with letting Sophie fill her glass. I was enjoying myself just listening to Melody tease Annabelle. She was good at it and had already managed to give Annabelle a way to take attention to her bottom without losing her dignity. It hadn't worked, but from the way Annabelle had blushed it had to have touched a nerve.

They were getting drunk too, on their second bottle of Chablis, without even any lunch. I could just see

Annabelle getting tipsy and randy before ending up across Melody's knee. Once she was over there would be no getting up. I knew that from experience, and I'd seen girls a lot stronger than Annabelle, men too, unable to get up once Mel had got a grip on them. Better still, although Mel wasn't going to spank Annabelle against their will, there would be no nonsense about her precious panties staying up. They'd come down, they always did, and she'd get it bare. With army trousers on there might be a struggle, but that would just make it more fun.

With the level in the second bottle falling rapidly, Sophie was ordered to make lunch. They were getting rude and she was made to do it with her skirt tucked up and her panties rolled down to the top of her thighs. We ate around the kitchen table, Sophie serving, still with her bottom bare, while I was on the floor, begging for scraps, with my hands bent down like a puppy's paws and my tongue lolling out of my mouth.

Melody gave me some ham and a piece of cold chicken, which was the best food I'd had in days, even if I did have to eat it off the floor. Seeing me begging to Melody, Annabelle had to go one better, feeding me from her hand. At that Mel pulled up her skirt, took her knickers down and smeared some pâté on her pussy. I had to lick it off, and she held my head in between her legs until she came, an act Annabelle wasn't prepared to follow.

That was when Mel made her second move, asking Annabelle if she'd ever licked a black girl, and if she'd like to. Annabelle got really flustered, blushing scarlet, but managed to decline gracefully enough and again Mel didn't push. I was sure she'd wanted to do it though, and I wondered if Annabelle had a hang-up about colour, and if Mel knew it.

They got through a third bottle after lunch, and then a fourth. At least the girls did, because Sophie managed to pinch quite a bit and even I was allowed some out of a dog bowl. Marcus was very cool all the time, just sipping his wine and saying very little, but watching us, especially Melody.

It was a beautiful afternoon, warm but still fresh, and at Annabelle's suggestion we went out on to the lawn. I had great fun rolling on the ground to have my tummy tickled and I was really playing my part, hoping to bring things to a head by helping to put everyone in a playful mood.

They loved it, including Sophie, who I kept jumping on, pushing her over so that we could roll on the lawn together. I was pretty excited, especially after licking Melody, and it was impossible to resist pretending to be a boy dog and humping her leg, which had her in fits of giggles as I brought myself off against the flesh of her thigh.

I was switched for that, crouched whimpering on the lawn as Annabelle applied a stick to my bottom. Once I'd been punished, Sophie was held over Annabelle's lap while I was told to sniff her bottom and lick her. I went willingly, spending plenty of time on her lovely bumhole before transferring my attentions to her pussy and making her come in my face.

There was still a call for me to be kept under proper control, so Marcus went to make me a collar out of an old harness. It took him about half an hour, and the finished product was broad enough and thick enough to hold a Rottweiler, with studs and a massive brass buckle. He attached a piece of string to it for a lead and, at the sight of him holding me on it, both girls decided they wanted to take me for a walk.

I knew Melody was going to need to lull Annabelle into a false sense of security before persuading her to take a spanking, but she was certainly taking her time about it. They were getting on really well as I was walked around the farm. For one thing they had stopped playing little dominance games with each other and were concentrating on tormenting me instead, vying to see who could think of the rudest and most puppy-like things to make me do.

Annabelle made me chase a stick, bringing it back to her in my mouth and dropping it at her feet. Melody added an extra touch, by choosing a great thick one I could barely get my jaws around and making me beg before she'd throw it. That had them both laughing, and Annabelle suggested I be made to mark trees as we went along, cocking my leg up to pee against them. I wasn't very good at aiming, and once I'd let go it was hard to stop it coming, so I ended up with more pee running down my thigh than on the tree trunks, which they thought was even funnier.

On the assault course I was made to roll in the mud and go in the stream, but I got my own back by shaking myself all over their legs. That earned me a dose of Annabelle's sergeant's stick, which she'd brought along, applied to my already sore bottom while I knelt with my head clamped between Melody's knees. It really hurt and she was too drunk to aim properly, catching my thighs and hips.

My feet were drumming in the mud and I was I clutching at Mel's legs, both in a desperate effort to dull the pain. My bottom was waggling too, from side to side, trying to catch the strokes on the plump part and not the sides. I admit it must have looked comic and they laughed all the louder, which made Annabelle even less accurate.

I was left sobbing at Mel's feet, my bum up and throbbing with pain. My tears had started and I was feeling really put upon, but I didn't know if I wanted to come or run away and cry in a corner. I wasn't given the choice. Mel held my head firmly between her legs as the round, smooth toe of Annabelle's army boot was pushed to my pussy, and I knew I was going to be brought off.

She began to rub it against me and I began to push back, knowing it was pointless to resist. I could feel the slippery texture of the well-polished leather and knew my pussy would be getting a good coating of boot-black as I was frigged, which brought the thought of the uniform she was in, and in particular the way the camouflage trousers were loose on her legs but hugged her sweet little bottom, emphasising the cheeks.

My mouth was full of the taste of girl, both Melody's and Sophie's, and I was wishing it could be Annabelle as well, both bum and pussy, licked with her trousers and panties pushed down and her rear stuck in my face. I remembered my last time on the assault course, the exhaustion and indignity of my treatment, how useless I'd been.

What they were doing now would have been a great punishment. Making a female soldier into a puppy-girl would have been wonderful, with her crawling about the camp, nude on her sergeant's lead, frequently beaten in front of maybe hundreds of men and other women. She'd have had to pee on the grass, and worse, with so many people watching.

Annabelle had her boot pushed hard against my pussy, low now, with her heel on the ground, so that I could squat and squirm my sex against the hard toecap. I was going to come, with my fantasy building in my head, of a young army girl, made to strip and crawl on a lead in front of everybody, beaten across her bare buttocks, made to piddle on the grass, made to do her dirt in the gutter, squatting down, her eyes closed in furious shame, her face scarlet, her bumhole opening and a piece poking out in front of hundreds and hundreds of people, all staring . . .

I cried aloud as I came, writhing my pussy on Annabelle's boot, imagining the sheer, agonising passion of a girl's shame as she was made to defecate in front of several hundred leering men. It was good, very good indeed, and I'd already forgiven Annabelle for her inaccuracy as my body went slowly limp on the ground. Mel let me go and patted my head, laughing over my excitement and the way they'd brought me on heat.

By the time we got back to the farm I was absolutely filthy, covered with mud and scratches, my bottom a mess of thin red welts and my hair full of dirt where they made me try to crawl down a rabbit hole. I was put under the pump and washed down again before they returned to the lawn.

I lay down at Annabelle's feet, exhausted and still drunk. They were talking and the conversation had started to grow serious, covering their philosophies on dominance and submission. It was interesting, with the contrast of Annabelle's view, which came mostly from books, and Melody's, which came almost entirely from experience. Marcus had Sophie on his lap and was fondling her, occasionally adding an opinion to the conversation.

There was plenty I could have said on the matter, had I been allowed. I was just too tired and before I really knew it I was asleep.

When I woke up it was late afternoon. Sophie was sprawled on the lawn, flat on her back, an empty wine glass still held in her fingers, asleep. There was no sign of the others.

I got up, feeling thirsty and stiff, not really in the mood for being a puppy-girl. There was nobody to give me commands anyway, so I went into the kitchen and helped myself to orange juice. That made me feel a lot better, and some ham and salad left over from lunch better still.

After living on slops for so long it was delicious, and all the more so because I didn't have to grovel to eat it. It seemed likely that the others were asleep and, despite

224

a fair bit of apprehension, I just couldn't resist taking more. I finished the ham and went to see if Annabelle had any chocolate in the dining room sideboard. She did, a whole bar of high-cocoa bitter chocolate, Swiss. I ate it all, reasoning that whatever she did to me it would be worth it.

It was only when I'd finished that I realised the car wasn't in its normal place. Marcus had drunk sparingly and I reasoned that he must have taken the girls into town, perhaps to buy food, perhaps equipment or clothing for some new detail of Sophie's and my training. What mattered was that I had the house to myself.

Immediately I went to the fridge, opening the door with my ears already straining for the sound of the Range Rover's engine or the gate alarm. Neither came, as I took all three flavours of ice-cream available and scooped large measures into a bowl, poured double cream all over it, topped it off with chocolate sauce and ate the lot. It tasted so good, sheer bliss.

The forbidden fruit is always the sweetest, while pleasures can only truly be understood by those deprived. I followed this with another bowl, ending up drinking the rest of the cream with chocolate sauce in it and scraping out the ice-cream tubs.

The only thing I felt guilty about was not waking Sophie. Not that guilty, as I wasn't at all sure she wouldn't have sneaked on me. Besides, as maid I was sure she stole as many goodies as she wanted, even with the threat of her evening canings hanging over her.

I went back to the lawn, curling up where I'd been before, listening for the car and ready to feign sleep. It was just as well because after no more than a few minutes Annabelle and Melody appeared, walking from the house. They were hand-in-hand and I realised they must have been upstairs all the time. My immediate thought was that they had been to bed together.

That put me in an immediate panic. Had they? If so, what had they done? The curiosity was agonising, not to mention the jealousy, thinking of Melody doing things with Annabelle that had been denied to me, for all that I'd effectively asked her to. All I could be sure of was they were getting on very well indeed.

As I lay there I was hoping they would sit down and talk, but Annabelle went straight to Sophie, to give her a gentle kick in the bottom.

'Up, you lazy slut,' she ordered.

Sophie rolled over and pulled herself on to one elbow. I thought Annabelle was going to punish her, but she contented herself with another kick.

'Drinking too,' she went on. 'Come on, Sophie, go and make tea. Penny, wake up. Mel, kick the dog.'

I moved before Melody could apply her foot to me, rolling sleepily on to my front and all fours. Sophie had risen, saying nothing, but walking slightly unsteadily into the house.

As they drank tea I was burning with curiosity. They gave nothing away and it was clear that if they had made love it was to be a secret between them. I knew I could count on Melody to tell me eventually, especially if she'd succeeded in getting Annabelle to accept a spanking. That really didn't help.

I stayed in role for the rest of the day, never once getting a chance to talk to Melody. Marcus returned soon after tea, with shopping, which further reduced my chances of finding out what had happened. One thing became clear though: if they had been to bed, they weren't about to tell him.

We went inside as the day began to cool, by which time it was nearly six o'clock. Annabelle explained about Sophie's weight loss regime, which Mel thought an excellent idea. Nobody seemed to expect me to do anything, one of the advantages of being a puppy-girl, so I curled up in a corner and watched the little ritual.

Sophie was made to strip, stark naked, and sent to fetch the bathroom scales. She weighed in at eight stone four and was told she would therefore be getting four cane strokes. Nothing extra was added, despite her behaviour, and it was just as well because her bottom was a mess. She had been caned every day she had been on the regime, from ten strokes down to four as she struggled to shed her puppy fat. It had worked, but at a cost. Her whole bottom was covered in welts, from old, blue and yellow bruising to the sharp red lines of the previous day's punishment. Her thighs were bad too, back and front, and Annabelle had even put five strokes across her calves.

She stood now, hands on her head as they inspected her. Breasts are too delicate for the cane and the stomach area or anywhere the bone is close to the surface is out of the question. They didn't want to do her hands because it might have spoilt her as a maid, which left them with a bit of a dilemma.

In the end Melody suggested they give her a basti-nado, four strokes of the cane applied across the soles of her bare feet. Melody and Marcus held her still while Annabelle did it. She really howled, but she kissed the cane afterwards, showing genuine gratitude for her punishment.

Sophie's caning brought an end to the rather lethargic mood everybody had been in. She had been told to make three courses and was hard at work as soon as she'd dressed. We were using the dining room too, so she was scurrying back and forth, trying to prepare the room and cook at the same time. I stayed in my corner, just watching and listening to the conversation.

Melody seemed to have forgotten why she was there, and was simply enjoying herself. For all their knowl-edge, it was impossible for them not to defer to her, as for everything they knew about or had done once or twice, she understood it in depth and had done it a dozen times. She even got on to her experiences in California and New Orleans, which had them silent in admiration.

All I could do was hope Mel was being subtle, although that wasn't really her style. When she got on to erotic wrestling, her favourite sport, I thought something might happen. After all, Annabelle fancied herself as fit, and practised various oriental techniques. I was hoping she might be foolish enough to try because I knew she'd lose, and Mel always punishes her defeated opponents. Generally she likes to pee on them, or fuck them with a strap-on, sometimes both. In the parlour it would more likely have been a straightforward spanking, but that would have been good enough for me.

Unfortunately it didn't happen and the conversation moved on. I was getting increasingly frustrated, but I could do nothing. By the time Sophie appeared to announce that the crab salad she had made for a starter was ready, I knew another opportunity had been lost.

With dinner they began to drink again, Alsace with the crab and Volnay with grilled fillets of duck. When Melody proved to know more about the wine than Marcus it impressed Annabelle even more. They were getting drunk again and soon had Sophie's dress turned up to show her panties, then the top pulled down and forward to expose her boobs, which managed to look sexy and ridiculous at the same time.

It was then that things really started to go wrong. Melody suggested that it would be amusing to put ice-cream on Sophie's nipples, both to make them perky and to torture her without having to make any real effort. The idea was taken up enthusiastically and she was sent for the ice-cream. Of course there wasn't any, because I'd eaten it all, and Sophie came back to say she couldn't find it.

'Stupid girl!' Annabelle snapped. 'There are three tubs, in the top compartment. Two are nearly full!'

'I'm sorry, Miss Annabelle, but there aren't!' Sophie answered, already beginning to panic.

Annabelle just grabbed Sophie's arm, wrenching her down across the table. Her head was grabbed and pushed into the plate the duck had been on, coming up smeared with fat and gravy, briefly, before Melody pushed it down again. Using one of the serving spoons, Annabelle applied a flurry of smacks to Sophie's bottom, leaving the already bruised flesh smeared with mashed potato.

They sent her scurrying back into the kitchen, wiping muck off her face and clutching her bum as she went. She went to the fridge, opening every compartment, only to return with her head hung and her hands folded in her lap.

'It's not there, Miss Annabelle, I promise,' she said, really meekly.

'Stupid girl!' Annabelle answered her, got up and slapped Sophie's face.

Annabelle marched into the kitchen. She was showing off to Melody and thought Sophie was doing the same, playing the stupid maid in order to get punished, at least until she'd actually looked herself. When she came back into the room she looked genuinely puzzled.

'There's no ice-cream,' she said. 'Who's eaten the ice-cream?'

'Not me, Miss, I swear!' Sophie blurted out, which was the last thing she should have said.

'No?' Annabelle asked, turning to her. 'Then I suppose Marcus has, or our guest, even me? Are you accusing me?'

'No, Miss,' Sophie stammered. 'I don't know who it was, but I swear it wasn't me, it wasn't!'

In answer, Annabelle took her by the hair, dragging her to the table.

'Greedy, stupid, selfish pig!' Annabelle said, and pushed what was left of the mashed potato into Sophie's face.

The dish came away to reveal Sophie's pretty face completely plastered with rich, yellow mashed potato. There were bits in her hair and, as her mouth came open in shock, some fell on to her breasts.

'It wasn't me!' Sophie howled.

'Rubbish!' Annabelle answered, then reached behind Sophie and pulled out the waistband of her panties. 'Tell me you ate it.'

'I didn't!' Sophie said.

Annabelle took the dish of peas, pouring what remained of them down the back of Sophie's panties.

'Admit it,' she said.

'I can't! I didn't!' Sophie squealed.

The carrots followed the peas.

'Admit it.'

'I didn't, it wasn't, I swear.'

What was left on Annabelle's plate joined the mess in Sophie's panties: gravy, bits of duck skin and more peas. Marcus's plate followed, then Melody's and lastly the butter, almost an entire quarter-pound pat. Annabelle let go of Sophie's waistband and it snapped back on to bare flesh. I could see the bulge in the back of her panties, and a slight stain where the gravy had started to soak through the white cotton. Annabelle slapped it, squashing the mess over Sophie's bottom.

'Beautiful!' Melody laughed. 'What a sight! Make her eat it Annabelle, make her eat it out of her dirty knickers!'

'Yes, do,' Marcus added. 'One should never refuse a guest.'

'Absolutely not,' Annabelle agreed. 'Sophie, knickers off. Eat what's in them.'

The look on Sophie's face was wonderful as she pulled down her panties and stepped carefully out of them. The inside was filthy, with a greenish brown paste clinging to the material and squashed into an impression of her bottom crease and pussy, as if she'd soiled herself.

She couldn't have looked any more crestfallen if she had been guilty, and of course, it was a false accusation in the first place. Not that I could say anything. I was just a puppy.

She knelt down to do it, a little way back from the table so that everyone could see. I watched, as delighted as the others as she held her filthy panties up to her face and began to eat the revolting paste out of them, all the while with her face screwed up in misery. It was the duck skin that really got to her, thick, fatty bits that hadn't cooked properly, and which she had to swallow down, one by one. She did it though, every mouthful, and tried to lick the cotton clean afterwards. When she was finished Annabelle rubbed the dirty panties in her face and told her to go and clean up.

'So, no ice-cream?' Melody asked.

'It's all gone,' Annabelle answered. 'She was serious, and I don't actually think she ate it, and none of us did.'

'Which leaves one culprit,' Marcus said. 'The dog.'

They turned to look at me, all three of them, mainly with sadistic lust, but also with some genuine annoyance.

'So what do we do with her?' Melody asked.

'Oh I know what to do with her,' Annabelle answered. 'Much the same as we did to Sophie. Come into the kitchen.'

I was taken by the collar, slapped and called bad dog as I was pulled after them. They took their glasses, Melody sitting at the table with her chair pushed back as Marcus opened a new bottle. Annabelle went to a cupboard.

'We're going to feed her,' she said. 'Marcus already bought some food, just the cheap brand from some cut price store, but it'll do for her.'

'Sure will,' Melody answered. 'Come on, Penny, you bad girl, din-dins time.'

It was going to be dog food, I just knew it was, the real thing, not a fake. Sure enough, Annabelle took a can from the cupboard, labelled in garish red and green, with a picture of a happy-looking cartoon dog and the price – thirty-nine pence – in big yellow letters.

Melody bent down, taking me by the scruff and pulling me towards her. I didn't know what to do. It had all gone horribly wrong. At that moment I should have been watching Annabelle spanked, not about to be made to eat dog food. Melody was supposed to be my friend and she wasn't following the script!

I was held by the collar as Annabelle opened the tin and scraped the contents out into a plastic bowl. It was put on the floor, right under my nose, and I felt my throat tighten at the smell, a reek like wet, sweaty dog.

'Come on, girl, eat up, nice din-dins,' Melody urged. 'Come on, Penny, be a good dog.'

I held back, pulling against her. My gorge was rising, but so was my sense of submission, and I had a horrible feeling I wouldn't be able to resist.

'Eat up, Penny,' Annabelle said, with a familiar warning tone in her voice. 'It's only fair. Sophie had to eat the contents of her panties and she hadn't even done it.'

It wasn't fair, because what Sophie had eaten was a good duck dinner, even if it had been stuffed down her panties and squashed over her bum. Mine was dog food.

Mercifully Sophie chose that moment to come back into the room, still with her top down but no longer smeared with potato. Unfortunately it only distracted them for a moment before my face was once more being pressed firmly towards the smelly mess in the bowl.

'Eat up, Penny, come on,' Melody said once more. 'Come on, good doggie wants her dinner.'

'Eat it!' Annabelle ordered. 'Come on, Sophie ate hers, didn't she?'

'I know!' Melody laughed. 'Let's see how far we can take the two of them. This can be the first hurdle, and we'll take Penny in the yard and piss on her if she won't do it. The winner gets to lick us out!'

'Lick us out?' Annabelle echoed.

'Sure, why not?'

'No, great idea!' Annabelle laughed.

There was nervousness in her voice, but Mel didn't seem to notice. My heart had jumped at the words. There was just no way Annabelle could back out, not in front of Melody. She was drunk anyway. It was going to happen.

Only if I ate my dog food.

It smelt disgusting and I was sure it would taste as bad, but if I ate it I was going to get to lick Annabelle's pussy, and that counted for so much. Normally, I just couldn't have done it, not unless Mel had forced my head into it and frigged my pussy until I ate. Things weren't normal. I was painfully aroused and badly in need. I found myself opening my mouth, touching my lip to a piece of the meat jelly, licking it to taste salt and dog, and then I was eating it, mouthful after mouthful, biting bits off and swallowing it down, trying to ignore the awful doggy taste and the screaming voices in my head telling me not to be so disgusting.

They were clapping and laughing and cheering, watching me in delight and disgust as I gulped the revolting pap down, bit by bit, until it was finished and I could lick the last few smears from the bottom of the bowl.

'Little slut-puppy!' Melody laughed as I dabbed up the last piece with my tongue. 'Right let's go; first to use the stop word, what shall –'

'They don't have stop words,' Annabelle put in.

'Whatever, it can be red, that's always good. OK, you little sluts, you can cry off anytime. What shall we make them do, Annabelle?'

It was not what I'd wanted. Melody had been supposed to work on Annabelle, not turn on me. She had, and now I was the plaything of not one, but two dominant females, and drunk at that. Annabelle was smiling and not completely steady, with one hand on the table to keep her balance. Melody was no better.

'Wax,' Marcus suggested. 'I'll get candles from the dining room.'

'Wax it is!' Annabelle crowed. 'On the table, girls. Shall we have them tits up or bums up, Mel?'

'Tits up,' Melody said, 'and we'll have to tie their hands. They'll struggle too much otherwise.'

Annabelle went for twine as Melody cleared the table. I crawled on to the top, shaking but determined to take it. The whole thing was falling to pieces, the puppy-girl fantasy, my intentions for Annabelle, everything, but all I could think of was that I had to win the right to lick my mistress's sex. Sophie came up beside me, adjusting her dress to leave her breasts fully exposed.

'Hands,' Annabelle ordered as I lay back on the table.

I put them up obediently, above my head so that she could tie my wrists together and fix them to the table leg, leaving my chest pushed up and with no way to protect my breasts. Sophie was given the same treatment by Melody, finishing as Marcus returned with three of the tall red candles from the dinner table. He turned the lights out, leaving Sophie and I looking up into their faces. It looked demonic, with their eyes glittering with reflections from the flames and orange light dancing across their features. I felt real fear, but I couldn't close my eyes, only push my breasts up and grit my teeth against the coming pain.

Annabelle was over me, smiling, tilting the candle. A bead of wax formed at the edge, grew, fell and I screamed as it spattered over my chest, directly between my breasts. At the same time I heard Sophie's gasp of pain. It had begun, and with the second drip my mouth came open in a soundless gasp, my muscles jerking to the sudden splash of heat on my chest. The third caught my breast, the fourth a nipple and the dizziness was rising in my head, my control slipping as I surrendered myself to the torture.

I felt every splash and all the time I was pulling against my bound wrists, breathing hard, writhing and squirming my body on the table, all the time with part of my brain screaming at me to call out the stop word and my mouth refusing to frame it. Annabelle kept on dripping the wax over my breasts, grinning down at me, a real fiend, the pleasure she was taking in my pain written plainly on her face.

She was giving me a wax bra, aiming carefully, splash after splash on my breasts, until both were covered and at last the pain began to die, fading to a warm, urgent glow as my body responded with sexual need. As I felt that rise I knew I'd got through, and I dared to look into Annabelle's face.

Which was the moment Marcus allowed the first drop of molten wax to fall on to my pussy lips.

I really screamed, twisting my body so that the next drop caught my thighs, only to move back, bracing myself as I presented him with the swell of my sex to enjoy. He nodded and applied the next drip on my mound, where the hair had begun to come through. More followed and I let it happen, hazy with pain and heat but arousal too, and pride, as I held myself still and felt the wax gradually build up into a full bikini, boobs and pussy caked red with wax, my sole regret that Sophie too had failed to break.

They only stopped when the candles had burnt down too far to be safe to hold. By then I was so high that I couldn't stop shaking, or moving either, filled with nervous energy and arousal, really not knowing what I was doing at all. What I did know was that I needed to outlast Sophie and I was trying desperately to think of something I could take but she couldn't.

It was obvious. Not a torture for her body, as she could always take as much as me, but for her mind. I'd remembered something she'd said, and it was just so perfect. The trouble was, I couldn't very well suggest it.

What I did manage to do was whisper it to Mel as she bent to untie our hands. She gave me a look that suggested I was mad, but nodded.

'What now?' Marcus asked as Sophie and I began to peel the wax off our skin.

'Wine enemas and see if they'll drink it!' Annabelle laughed.

'I'm not wasting this Volnay up their bottoms,' Marcus objected. 'They wouldn't appreciate it anyway.'

'Beer then,' Annabelle answered, 'upside down with a bottle plugged up each hole!'

'The beer won't come out; you get an airlock,' Melody said. 'Anyway, guests first, and I've got a better idea.'

'What?'

'You'll see. Just get them spread out on the floor, pussies showing, and get the rest of that wax off.'

She went to the back door and out. Annabelle and Marcus shared a puzzled glance. I lay down as Melody had suggested, flat on the floor with my legs well apart. Marcus moved the table to let Sophie get into the same position beside me. Our eyes met, she smiled and for a moment I felt guilty, but only for a moment. She was still in her dress, but her panties had been pulled off so that they could wax her pussy, and she was bare from tummy to knees. I picked at the wax as we waited for Melody, wincing as my tiny new-grown hairs pulled out with it.

Melody didn't take long and when she came back she was holding a big earthenware flowerpot. She placed it on the table, dipped her hand in and pulled something out, a big, brown-shelled garden snail, its wrinkled grey body already extended. I saw the expression on Sophie's face turn to horror and I knew I'd got it right.

'Hands on your heads,' Melody ordered, 'and if you take them off you've lost.'

She knelt down, holding the snail in front of us, his body and all four tentacles waving as he struggled to find something to stick to. He got it, my left breast, right on the nipple as Melody gently put him down. I felt the wet flesh of his foot, the suction as he gripped and the slimy feeling as he started to crawl, probing at the hard teat with his lower tentacles. Taking the pot, she selected another, holding it right in front of Sophie's face.

'What you've got to ask yourselves,' she said sweetly, 'is which is worse, a little pee-pee, or having a nice, fat, slimy snail crawling over your titties.'

Sophie said nothing, but her eyes were closed and she was breathing hard. My snail was walking down the side of my breast and on to my neck, leaving a trail of cold slime behind him. Melody put the second snail on Sophie, right at the crown of one boob. Her flesh was shaking, her nipples quivering, and they weren't hard.

She took it, even with the snail crawling over her skin. A second one was placed on my other breast, a third on my pussy. Two more were put on Sophie, in the same sensitive places, and Melody stood up. Annabelle was watching us, her face set in mingled disgust and pleasure, Marcus also.

I could feel my snails, all three of them, crawling slowly over my flesh, probing my skin with their tentacles, tasting me with the receptors in the tips. The first was on my neck, nearly at my face, going quite fast. The second was going the other way, off my breasts and down over my tummy. The third had stopped to eat.

I knew it would happen, and as his teeth scraped at the sore skin of my waxed pussy I set my face in an expression of strain. The tickling was enough to drive me insane as he began to feed, but that was all, no horror, no irrational fear, there never had been. Not so Sophie. She began to whimper, then make odd panting noises and clutch at her hair, and finally she broke.

'Stop it!' she screamed. 'Get them off me! Red! Red! Red!'

They stopped it, instantly, Melody pulling the snails off her skin, then mine. I knew I'd done it and, as I returned the creatures to the garden, it was impossible not to grin. Sophie was still gibbering a bit, and I did feel sorry for her, but I promised myself that in due time I would give myself to her, without reserve.

When I came back they were drinking, all four of them, Sophie's hand still trembling as she held her glass. My puppy-girl role seemed to have been abandoned and I poured one for myself, trying not to look too happy.

'Ready?' Annabelle enquired as Sophie drained her glass.

Sophie nodded, turning big, moist eyes to me, then to our mistress.

'In the yard then!' Annabelle ordered. 'Right now!'

Sophie went, looking pretty hangdog about it. Annabelle took her by the ear, drawing out a startled squeak, and she was dragged to the door. Melody followed, and Marcus, with me last. Outside, Annabelle had turned the yard light on, flooding it with brilliant white light. She still had Sophie by the ear, in the very centre of the pool of illumination.

'Pull the dress up high. To your chin!' Annabelle snapped.

The response was immediate, Sophie quickly slipping loose her waist tie and hoisting her maid's dress up, high over her bare middle and braless breasts. She held it there, showing us her body, her boobs quivering with feeling, the nipples standing firmly to attention.

'On the ground,' Annabelle ordered, now soft, but still commanding. 'Kneel, knees wide, leaning back. Keep your dress high and stick those fat titties right out.'

Sophie went down into the position Annabelle wanted, a great position for a girl who is going to be pissed on. Leaning back on one hand, she kept her dress up with the other, with everything exposed, yet still innocent, a country maid, about to be utterly degraded.

'Guests first,' Annabelle said politely, looking at Melody and gesturing to the waiting Sophie.

'Thank you, Annabelle,' Melody replied, 'but why not together?'

Annabelle nodded and, as her hands went to her belt, I found myself staring. She undid it, took hold of her army trousers and pushed them down, exposing high cut, black silk knickers. I found myself licking my lips at the sight and wishing she'd turn around to show me her beautiful bottom.

It took her a moment to get her army boots off, which gave me a nice side view, with her sweetly formed cheeks bulging out of the tiny piece of black silk. Barefoot, her trousers were kicked to the side, she took hold of the waistband of her panties and, with only the slightest hesitation, she pulled them down.

As she straightened I saw her bare pussy for the first time. She was very neat, with little lips and her hair shaved into a precise triangle, thick and dark, but trimmed short. I found myself wetting my lips once more, my whole body trembling at the prospect of what I was to be allowed to do. OK, it was only because she was drunk. OK, it was probably only because she didn't like to look a prude in front of Melody. I didn't care. I was going to lick her pussy, all the way to orgasm. Not yet. First she had something else to do, a treat for Sophie almost as good as what I was going to get myself. Melody had bared herself too, tugging up her skirts and pushing down her panties without hesitation. Her back was to me, the full dark cheeks of her bottom framed between skirt and panties, very pretty, and reminding me that it wasn't only Annabelle I'd be licking. Marcus was ready too, his cock out, held in one hand, pointed right at Sophie's body.

They surrounded her and I moved close to get a better view. Her eyes were closed, her body trembling. Marcus let go, a stream of yellow pee bursting from his cock to splash across her breasts and trickle down over her tummy and the mound of her sex. Some had splashed on Melody, who put a foot out, pushing Sophie back, on to the ground. Both she and Annabelle straddled the prone girl as Marcus stepped to the side, his piss splashing over Sophie's chest and belly.

Melody took one end, Annabelle the other, pussies poised over their victim, knees bent, lips spread, and they let go, one stream, then two, splashing on Sophie's sex and full in her face. They were laughing as they did it, all three of them in abandoned pleasure as they pissed on her, soaking her skin and soiling her dress.

For a moment she took it without reacting, just lying there in the growing pool of piddle, in utter, abject submission. Her knees came up first, and open, pulled between Annabelle's legs so that she could spread herself to the golden stream running from her mistress's pussy. I watched Sophie's pussy fill as Annabelle aimed her stream, the little hole bubbling with yellow fluid, quickly overflowing. Sophie's fingers came down, two pushing up the piss-filled hole to spray it out, the knuckle of her thumb going to her clit.

Sophie began to rub herself, and as she did so she opened her mouth, catching Melody's stream full in it. That too filled and I watched it trickle from the sides as Sophie went into frantic, desperate masturbation. She was soaked in it, her pussy full, her mouth full, her body sodden and dripping. It was still coming too, from all the wine and water they had drunk, and she was lying in a big pool of it, still growing, despite her best efforts to swallow what Melody was doing in her mouth.

Her climax came before they'd finished, her pussy closing to spurt pee out across the cobbles as her back arched. She kept her mouth open, right through it, gaping wide, Melody's pee splashing in the open hole and pouring from one side. It held for a wonderfully long time, really until Annabelle's stream began to die. Marcus had already stopped, leaving Melody to finish off, giving a last little wiggle to shake the drops from her pussy lips into Sophie's already bedraggled hair.

My excitement had been rising steadily as I watched and it was more than I could do to keep my fingers off my pussy. The girls took me back indoors, leaving Marcus to wash Sophie down, and presumably to fuck her. Both Annabelle and Melody were still bare below their waists and I was desperately eager to get what I'd been promised.

'Kneel,' Annabelle ordered as we reached the kitchen.

I went down, looking up as they settled themselves into chairs, side my side.

'You may lick Melody.'

There was no hesitation. I buried my face in the warm, musky flesh of Mel's pussy, lapping up the taste of her pee and wriggling my tongue in among the soft, fleshy folds. She took hold of my hair, guiding me gently down as she slid her body forward on the chair. I knew what she wanted and went with the pressure, burrowing my tongue in between her firm, meaty bottom cheeks to the little tight hole between them. I began to lick it, trying to get my tongue up the hole, and she moaned, tightening her grip in my hair.

'That's right,' she sighed, 'lick my arsehole, lick right inside. Make me come like that, use your nose.'

I pushed in, rubbing my nose on her clit. It was awkward, but it didn't matter. She was in charge and my sole joy came from giving her pleasure, from being made to do such a wonderfully servile, debased, wanton thing, to lick another girl's bottom; to think it a privilege too.

My tongue was right in, her bumhole opening to the pressure, wet and juicy with my saliva. She was pushing out, as if she was going to do something in my mouth, tightening again, loosening, and going into spasm as she came in my face, crying my name out loud, twisting her hand in my hair, forcing my face into her flesh until I could no longer breath, using my face to frig off against until at last she began to relax.

'Oh lovely,' she sighed. 'There really is nobody like you when it comes to licking my arsehole, Penny, there really isn't.'

Annabelle said nothing, but she was waiting, sat splay-legged on her chair. Her top was up, her bra too, two beautiful round boobs cupped in her hands. She had been playing with herself as she watched me lick Melody and her nipples were rock hard.

I crawled up between her legs, close, and hugged her, nuzzling my face in between her breasts. She let me do it and, with a sense of overwhelming love and gratitude building in my head, I began to suckle her, feeding from one breast, then the other until she finally pressed gently against my forehead. I began to kiss her, working slowly down, from between her breasts to her tummy, wiggling my tongue into her belly button, and lower, to the neatly trimmed triangle of her pubic hair.

My treat was coming, the special thing I'd been yearning for so long, to kiss my mistress's pussy. I pulled up, puckered my lips, looked once into her eyes and did it, pressing my face to her sex and planting a single, firm kiss on the warm, soft flesh. I was in heaven and, as I began to lick, she touched my hair, stroking gently, soothing me as my tongue burrowed between her lips to find her clit.

'That is beautiful,' she sighed, 'so beautiful. Lick me, Penny, yes like that, oh yes.'

I had found her clit, flicking the little bud with the very tip of my tongue, just lightly, intending to take plenty of time over her pussy while I brought myself off under my fingers.

'So beautiful,' she said, 'yes, there. Now lower, inside. Yes, deep. Now lower still, kiss my bum, Penny, kiss it.'

She pulled her legs up suddenly, spreading herself wide in my face. The pose left her bumhole stretched taut, stuck right out, the ring glistening with sweat and pussy juice. Once more I puckered up, already rubbing at the warm, puffy flesh of my own sex, waited one last second and kissed her hole, once, twice and then my tongue was up it and I was rubbing my face into her bottom as her legs closed tight around my head.

'You're right, Mel,' she sighed, 'this is where she belongs, with her tongue up a bumhole. Stick it in, you dirty little slut, right up, lick me out . . . Oh God, I never realised it would be so good. Can there be anything so nice as a tongue up a girlfriend's bottom? Oh thank you, Melody, thank you so much . . .'

She trailed off with a long moan, wiggling her bum into my face. I'd heard her words, and for all my dizzy ecstasy it came to me that I was the first, her slut but also her teacher. I never saw Melody get off her chair, but I felt her behind me as her fingers went up into my pussy. A thumb found my bottom, already wet, and popped into the little hole. She gripped me, holding me firmly between bumhole and pussy.

'That's the secret, Penny,' Annabelle sighed, 'make your girlfriend your owner, really your owner. Then nothing need be bad, not ever. Now do my clitty, you filthy little tart, just make me come!'

Her thighs were tight around my head, my face jammed to her sex. I got to her clit, licking urgently, hers to command, to do anything she wanted. I was close to orgasm, Melody's fingers jiggling in my holes, my clit bumping under my fingers. I touched Annabelle, my thumb in her pussy, a finger up her bumhole, licking harder, and she was coming, crushing me into her sex with her thighs, squeezing at her own breasts, slapping them, her back arching, her scream of pleasure ringing out, and so was I, everything blending into perfect, burning ecstasy, together, Slave, Mistress and Mentor.

We went to the tattooist first thing in the morning. Everyone was quiet, not really knowing what to say. I felt strange, unnatural, and being dressed seemed surreal, something bizarre, completely unnecessary for me.

Sophie did the shaving in the kitchen, with everybody watching. It was like a ritual, a formal ceremony, even religious, the preparation of a girl's pussy for her slave mark. Even seeing the baby powder patted on to the bare, pink skin when it was done seemed to have meaning.

We drove to Bletchley in the Range Rover, Marcus at the wheel, Melody beside him, Annabelle, Sophie and me in the back. We had our arms around each other, for the sake of comfort, but nobody said a word.

As we drove, I was thinking that I should have known all along. After all, I'm the experienced one. Turning fantasy into reality can take a lot of courage, a lot of strength, and never more than when a modern girl wants to explore her feelings of submission.

In Bletchley everything seemed to pass in a haze. We met Anderson and Bart at the Plough. The contract was signed and the wine exchanged. After a fair bit of vodka and orange for Dutch courage, we walked to the tattooist and it was done, as simple as that.

It did look cute, really cute, executed in flowing script, deep red, and decorated with blue and yellow flowers, leaves too, set out ever so neatly across her bare pussy mound: 'Slave Annabelle, Property of Melody Rathwell.'

## NEXUS BACKLIST

This information is correct at time of printing. For up-to-date information, please visit our website at www.nexus-books.co.uk

All books are priced at £5.99 unless another price is given.

**Nexus books with a contemporary setting**

| | | |
|---|---|---|
| ACCIDENTS WILL HAPPEN | Lucy Golden ISBN 0 352 33596 3 | ☐ |
| ANGEL | Lindsay Gordon ISBN 0 352 33590 4 | ☐ |
| THE BLACK MASQUE | Lisette Ashton ISBN 0 352 33372 3 | ☐ |
| THE BLACK WIDOW | Lisette Ashton ISBN 0 352 33338 3 | ☐ |
| THE BOND | Lindsay Gordon ISBN 0 352 33480 0 | ☐ |
| BROUGHT TO HEEL | Arabella Knight ISBN 0 352 33508 4 | ☐ |
| CANDY IN CAPTIVITY | Arabella Knight ISBN 0 352 33495 9 | ☐ |
| CAPTIVES OF THE PRIVATE HOUSE | Esme Ombreux ISBN 0 352 33619 6 | ☐ |
| DANCE OF SUBMISSION | Lisette Ashton ISBN 0 352 33450 9 | ☐ |
| DARK DELIGHTS | Maria del Rey ISBN 0 352 33276 X | ☐ |
| DARK DESIRES | Maria del Rey ISBN 0 352 33072 4 | ☐ |
| DISCIPLES OF SHAME | Stephanie Calvin ISBN 0 352 33343 X | ☐ |
| DISCIPLINE OF THE PRIVATE HOUSE | Esme Ombreux ISBN 0 352 33459 2 | ☐ |

**Nexus Classics**

A new imprint dedicated to putting the finest works of erotic fiction back in print.

- - - - - ✂ - - - - - - - - - - - - - - - - - - - - - -

Please send me the books I have ticked above.

Name .................................................................

Address .................................................................

.................................................................

.................................................................

.................................. Post code .................

Send to: **Cash Sales, Nexus Books, Thames Wharf Studios, Rainville Road, London W6 9HA**

US customers: for prices and details of how to order books for delivery by mail, call 1-800-805-1083.

Please enclose a cheque or postal order, made payable to **Nexus Books Ltd**, to the value of the books you have ordered plus postage and packing costs as follows:
    UK and BFPO – £1.00 for the first book, 50p for each subsequent book.
    Overseas (including Republic of Ireland) – £2.00 for the first book, £1.00 for each subsequent book.

If you would prefer to pay by VISA, ACCESS/MASTER-CARD, AMEX, DINERS CLUB or SWITCH, please write your card number and expiry date here:

.................................................................

Please allow up to 28 days for delivery.

**Signature** .................................................................

- - - - - ✂ - - - - - - - - - - - - - - - - - - - - - -